Numbers Never Lie

Shelley K. Wall

CRIMSON
ROMANCE
Avon, Massachusetts

This edition published by
Crimson Romance
an imprint of F+W Media, Inc.
10151 Carver Road, Suite 200
Blue Ash, Ohio 45242

www.crimsonromance.com

ISBN 10: 1-4405-5163-4
ISBN 13: 978-1-4405-5163-5
eISBN 10: 1-4405-5143-X
eISBN 13: 978-1-4405-5143-7

Dedication

TO MY HUSBAND, STAN, FOR SUPPORTING ALL MY DREAMS AND DESIRES
THROUGHOUT OUR YEARS TOGETHER.

AND TO MY CHILDREN, TYLER, KYLE, AND GRACE—THE WORLD IS YOURS IF
YOU MAKE IT SO (AND IF YOU EAT YOUR VEGETABLES AND EXERCISE).

Acknowledgments

My sincerest thanks to my friends, Cindy Davis and Carol Bland, for their fantastic advice and support. My appreciation to Jennifer Lawler, for taking a chance on an unknown author, and inspiring me to work harder.

My love and adoration to my parents, Bob and Agnes Kurtz, who have taught me what hard work, respect, kindness, and loyalty really means—and more importantly what it can achieve.

Prologue

Lenny heard the door open and Sophie Henderson talking to someone. A rather husky male voice replied. The hairs on the back of Lenny's neck prickled and he sucked in his breath. Sophie was supposed to be out all evening with that big guy he'd seen her talking to. What was she doing here? He glanced at the papers on the counter in the kitchen. He needed to get them but they were impossible to reach from across the room. He had the others from her desk but if he didn't get all the copies, it wouldn't matter. No time to grab them now. Most importantly, he couldn't be seen. He looked around for somewhere to hide, or a way out of the apartment—a window or something. Nothing came to his immediate attention. He rushed down the hall, checking each of the rooms for an escape or, at least, camouflage. The spare bedroom was impeccable—apparently unused. So maybe it would work until they left. He ducked into the room and burrowed into the closet, slinking down onto the floor in the corner. He pulled the clothes in front of him.

The pile of papers in Sophie's office proved enough to know she had suspicions. The numbers didn't lie . . . they never did. He'd lived with numbers like this all his life; they'd been his friends through hard times. They'd been his enemy, too. They'd even been his bargaining chip a few times. He was a slave to the numbers and it was imperative to watch them carefully now if he and his associates intended to get out of this one cleanly. Manipulating them was easy—a cakewalk. He'd done it several times. Lately, though, the frequent need to make adjustments was frustrating.

But Sophie posed a problem and he needed to curtail her digging fast before it became harder to deal with. At the present moment, she was almost at the point of discovery, but hiding it better than the guy before. That would make it easier for them to deal with. Regardless, if something wasn't done about this right away, she'd figure it all out and he'd be done. Done with his career. With his family. With life. And the others would pretend they knew nothing about it, silently sitting on their little stockpiles.

He intended to retire next year—but planned to siphon off another two or three hundred thousand first. Then the nest egg would be sufficiently big enough for him to live on for the remaining years. They weren't really hurting anyone by doing this—the money just sat there. The fact that they never seemed to notice or care that the reports were sometimes off showed him that this amounted to "peanuts" for them. They were a government contractor and as long as they kept spending it, the government kept giving them more.

Besides, if the company hired an accounting department that didn't know how to balance the books and find missing dollars, then they pretty much deserved to lose money. Isn't that what a competent staff does?

But unfortunately for Lenny, Sophie seemed a lot smarter than the rest of them, and if he didn't deal with her, she'd ruin it all. Her footsteps clip-clopped down the hallway, getting louder as they advanced. He shrunk deeper into the closet, pulling the musty sleeve of a jacket over his face. He even tucked his shoes under the box on the floor in front of him. The steps plodded past to the back bedroom, the clatter of shoes falling on tile filled the silence. Then the sound of a shower running reached him for a second before a door closed. She was in the bathroom. Did he hear singing?

In a way, there was a thrill to her involvement that enticed him. All this time, only two people had even noticed. And one of them was dead. It was, well, more than a little easy to hide, and therefore, boring. Not so boring now, though. He would need to be more careful in the future. First, he needed to get out of this damn apartment.

Chapter One

A streak of lightning shot into the transformer on the corner, sending fireworks everywhere. "Shit!" Trev cursed, and ducked his head further under his car hood. He had opened it as a prop so that he could attempt to get a better view of Sophie Henderson leaving her building, but now he debated the logic in standing next to all this metal under the circumstances.

Getting soaked to the skin by a rainstorm didn't bother him. The brisk breeze sliced through his jacket and chilled his head, hands, and arms now that he was drenched. He grasped the edges of his stocking hat and tugged it down further over his ears. Drips of water from the car hood trickled along the back of his neck. His ears reverberated with residual crackling from the lightning strike. *No sense in doing this at all, I can't see a damn thing . . . and even though the engine wasn't a problem before, it'll be soaking wet now, so it may not start.*

"Oh shit!" his own words played back through his earphones. "You're supposed to watch her, you dumbass, not talk to her!"

"What the hell are . . . ?" The last thing he needed was his partner, Nate, to get sarcastic right now. He wasn't in the mood. He didn't get the last words out before a wet, cold hand rested lightly on his forearm.

"Are you okay?" Sophie hovered next to him with that oversized red umbrella sheltering her, him, and practically the entire hood of his car. He'd never seen her up close but he knew the umbrella well. He'd watched it going in and out of the building across the street more than a few times lately.

"Yeah. Yeah, just having a little car trouble." Trev looked down at the hand on his arm and smiled without raising his head. Tipping his head further caused rain to run down his face and drip off his chin in a constant stream. He ignored her. *Think*, he told himself. He needed to figure out how to handle this, and quick. He'd blown his cover. Now she'd seen his face and he wouldn't be able to tag along anymore.

"Get the hell out of there, you idiot." Nate's disgusted blast burned in his ear. Trev had had enough of his sideline coaching. It was pouring. How the hell could a person see someone coming across the street in this downpour, especially with the lightning flash blinding him? He'd hated lightning ever since childhood. He played soccer in junior high and lightning struck the goal while they practiced once. It sent their goalie to the hospital with severe burns and knocked him and half the rest of the team off their feet. His ears rang for at least a day afterward.

"You need to get out of the rain, mister. You almost got electrocuted right there. That transformer is still throwing sparks." Sophie pointed at the fizzling shards of light spewing overhead. She stood so close under the umbrella; he could smell her perfume—something spicy, kind of like burning wood. Her wet hand chilled his arm, yet the feminine fingers were long, slender, and void of polish or jewelry. She pulled her hand back to the umbrella.

"I know. I just need to get this damn thing fixed and then I'll be on my way." Without looking up, Trev considered his options. Should he just close the hood as if the car was now repaired, and get in and drive off? Or maybe pretend he intended to go call a tow truck somewhere? No, that would be stupid—the cell phone in his pocket offered a better option.

"Look, this car can wait. You're going to get killed either by lightning or a passing car. With all this rain, you're almost invisible." She was getting soaked as well and it was obvious she was nervous being out there.

"I'm not the one holding the lightning rod in my hand, ma'am, and standing in the street next to the car."

She ignored his smartass remark, checking for traffic. As her glance strayed down the street, Trev's eyes flickered sideways at her, taking in the details. He noticed how the rain curled her hair into tight ringlets. In his line of work, one was trained to identify the shape of the eyes in suspects. Almond. Round. Narrow. Hers emanated round, shaped more like a macadamia nut than an almond. Face Shape: Heart? Oval? Oval. Build? Yeah. She was built. At thirty-two, his hormones shouldn't react so quickly but they did, as if he were still sixteen.

"I'll make a deal with you. Let's go in that coffee shop over there on the corner." She motioned to the lights down the street, practically indistinguishable in the rain. As she moved, he got another whiff of her perfume. "I'll buy you a coffee. We can both dry off and you can call a tow truck."

"Thanks, but I'll be okay . . . you go ahead." The assignment to follow at a distance and not make contact shattered. Most of his assignments were planned well in advance, each step carefully calculated. Improvising sometimes occurred out of necessity, but he obsessed on following orders and this wasn't part of the plan. He was supposed to stay unseen so he could observe the suspects and their interactions. Perhaps the time for improvisation had arrived.

Nate's voice rattled away in his ear, "Abort, man! Abort! Get out of there! Has she seen your face? Are you completely blown or what?"

Trev yanked the earplugs out of his ears.

"Doesn't the water ruin those things?"

"What?"

"Your iPod or iPhone. Whatever you're listening to. Doesn't the rain fry them?"

If that was what it really was, maybe so. This one did a lot more than just music, however, and was built to withstand the most severe weather conditions.

"I hadn't really thought about it. I guess I'll find out, won't I?" No eye contact. He managed to avoid facing her directly. His knit stocking hat, though wet, still covered his head and ears. Continuing to assess the engine for no reason, he weighed the possibility that she might be able to pick him out of a crowd if she saw him again.

"Mister, I'm trying to be a Good Samaritan here, but you're not making this easy. I don't really want to see on the news tomorrow that some guy with a broken down car got ran over by a semi truck in the rain right after I walked away. *But* . . . I don't really want to be on the news, either. So, would you *please* walk across the street with me to that coffee shop and get a stupid coffee? Once I leave, you can do whatever you choose. Of course, if you're smart, you'll leave that car where it is until the rain and lightning subside."

Trev considered the offer. If he complied, Sophie Henderson would know his face, build, and pretty much everything she needed to identify him in the future, so his days of following her would be over. Did it matter? Maybe he should just go along with this and learn as much as possible. He had been under strict instructions to follow from a distance until they gleaned more information, but if he just played along that might actually speed up this gig. Funny, she didn't really look like the criminal type, but then, they never do. Another lightning flash crossed the sky above them, followed by the associated loud thunderclap.

"Coffee sounds great right now, I guess." He stood up from under the hood of the car and his head bumped the red fabric of the umbrella, sending drips running down his cheek. He dropped the hood down and turned toward the amber glow of the lights that came from the distant coffee shop.

"Thank you. You just saved my life." Sophie said. She smiled and turned also, holding the umbrella above his head, her arm extended almost completely in order to get above his full length "We'll see about that. No one in their right mind would be driving in this mess. Besides, I thought you intended to save *my* life." He reached for the umbrella handle. "Here, let me hold that."

She shot a glance sideways at him and released the handle. He noticed that keeping up with him required her to almost run alongside his lengthy stride. He contemplated slowing down, he wanted them out of this mess as soon as possible.

"Thanks." She smiled as he opened the door to let her pass. The aroma of brewed coffee hit them instantly, along with the warmth of the heated room. He closed the umbrella, shook it, and entered behind her, propping the umbrella against the wall just inside the door so it wouldn't drip all over the floor.

"You're welcome." His parents had forced him to open doors for women, children, the elderly, and pretty much anyone else as a child. He did it mechanically this time, thoughts on his job. And right now this woman represented his job. He'd screwed up and gotten too close.

Inside, Trev pulled off his hat and shook it over the floor mat. Water shot everywhere and while it was probably his last vestibule of transparency, the purpose for wearing it evaporated. It would look ridiculous now.

Sophie turned to him, smiling a huge toothy smile. "So, what'll it be?"

Wow. He forced his eyes to remain steady. From a distance, she was noticeable but not really someone that would make you stop and stare. Up close, wow, he stopped and stared.

"Oh, um . . . " He smiled at the clerk behind the counter. Stacy didn't say anything and he appreciated that. Probably not wise for her to make it known he frequented this shop so much. Stacy was cute and he'd flirted with her a lot while he sat watching the building, pretending to read the paper. He thought about asking her out once but decided against it. "Medium latte, plain, please."

He drank enough beverages in this shop to buy stock in it. He'd languished over two cups of coffee just this morning. The latte was his favorite but he didn't drink too many because the milk didn't always set well on an empty stomach. While he liked the coffee in this place, the food sucked—all that fancy muffin and croissant crap. He preferred cereal or eggs and bacon.

"I'll have the same." She echoed his order from behind.

Trev glanced around the room, noticing the people. He'd always been the observant type, a trait that adapted well to his investigative work. He never missed a detail, or at least not very often. Outside the window, Nate walked by and shot him an angry glance before moving on.

Sophie followed behind Trev and couldn't see anything, so he just flashed him a smartass smile. The lady in the corner with two kids never looked up. She busily scolded the kids to stay off the furniture and sit still until Daddy showed up. Two men with laptops sat at tables by the back wall. One clasped a cell phone in one hand, talking animatedly with the other side of his conversation; his free hand moved and waved as if it helped to explain what he said. That epitomized stupidity since the person he was talking to couldn't see his overzealous hand gestures. Maybe he just did it to look important to everyone in the coffee shop.

Trev sat at a small round table at the street side window so he could see his car. If someone happened to come along, the likelihood that they'd see the car in this downpour was slim. If it got hit, he would get his ass chewed out tomorrow. He silently prayed no one would come along.

"Aren't you going to call a tow?" She came up beside him and set her cup on the table across from him.

"I thought I might just wait a little and see if the rain slows enough for me to get back out there." He tipped his cup at her and added, "Thanks for the warm-up juice."

"Thanks for letting me convince you to get out of the rain." She slipped her wet jacket off her shoulders and hung it over the back of the chair before sitting on the tall stool. "So, you must be one of those guys that does all his car work himself, huh?"

"What?"

"You know. The car hood's up, you don't want to call a tow. Are you a closet mechanic?" Sophie hesitated, then added, "Or maybe you're not a closet one but a real one?"

"Nope to both questions—but it's late and I don't think anyone's going to come out in this weather. So I thought I'd take a look myself." Trev hoped the rain would dry up soon so she'd leave and he could wait an acceptable amount of time before leaving himself. He found it increasingly uncomfortable to sit with her and not stare. He usually avoided the awkwardness of idle conversation with women— or anyone really. He shifted his eyes around the room briefly, then glanced in the direction of his car, and finally back to her.

"Okay." She smiled over her cup and looked out the window. "So you're not a mechanic. What *do* you do? And my name's Sophie by the way."

"Nothing all that exciting. I'm a consultant." Calling himself a consultant proved an easy tactic to use in most cases. People consult in almost everything. Use that one and a lot of people just go "ahhh" and leave it alone. Besides, if you said anything more specific, you risked a lot of questions that just got annoying.

"Consulting in what?"

He barely contained a sigh. *Well, so much for that approach. Here come the questions. Come on rain, give me a break and stop.*

"Oh, technology. I'm an IT consultant." *No more questions. Please.*

"Really? I'm in technology, too. I work down the street at Benton & Stanley."

He already knew that. "No kidding? What do you do there?" The best tactic would be to get her talking about herself so that she didn't ply him with any more questions.

"I manage the financial applications staff, but I'm also pretty good on the network side, so very often I get pulled into other areas. Technology is one of those things that if you're good at it, you want to do a little bit of everything."

"Yes, that's certainly true. How long have you been there?" He knew the answer to that, too, but asked anyway.

"Six years."

Interesting. Why would she lie about that?

"That is *if* you count the three years I consulted for them before they hired me." She gave him a smile, then looked out the window again at the tendrils of water rushing down the glass.

Oh, okay, I'll check on that part.

"How do you like it there? Do they treat you pretty good?"

"Sure, sure. Pretty much like any big company. Great benefits and lots of incentive programs to encourage productivity."

"That must be great. Are you working on any good projects right now?"

He wondered if she'd mention anything about it, the reason he tracked her, even in a roundabout way.

"Not really. Financial applications are pretty boring. Not a lot of excitement there." She waved a hand as if to dismiss the topic. "But enough about me. It looks like the rain is letting up a little and I need to get going. So, I enjoyed meeting you." She held out a hand. It occurred to him that he hadn't given her his name at about the same time that she waited for it.

"Trevor." That was the name they wanted him to use on this one. Fortunately, it was pretty close to his real name and easy to work with. "Trevor Adams. And thank you for saving me from the lightning." He winked and watched her pick up the mammoth red umbrella and head out the door before inserting the headphones into his ears and softly saying, "She's on the run now, guys. I'd better stay here so she doesn't think I'm stalking her. I guess someone else will need to pick up my spot on this one."

"You're a jackass." Good old Nate. Leave it to him to state the obvious.

Trev picked up a paper from the stack on the table and started to glance through it. "Hey!" He jolted at the sound of the familiar voice.

Damn, he wished she'd quit doing that. More importantly, why didn't he ever see her coming?

"Yeah?" He lowered the paper. A smile came to his lips on noticing the lip gloss applied to her mouth and the newly smoothed curls.

"Send me your information and if we ever need anyone for any projects down the road, I'll give you a call." She handed him a business card, adding, "Sophie *Henderson*, by the way." She shot one last comment over her shoulder before pushing out the door. "Drive safely!"

Trev silently applauded himself. He knew her name, her birthday. Shit, he even had her dress size, but she had no way of knowing that. Under normal circumstances, he would ask her name and maybe even get a number, he didn't think to do so. An error on his part, but it served its purpose. Maybe she offered the card because she *wanted* him to know who she was. If he evaluated it logically, there might be an opportunity to keep going with this. Yeah, the more he thought about it the more he imagined it might be fun. Nate sounded tired and muttered into his ear, "Let's debrief on this tomorrow morning over at the office . . . say around nine? We're obviously going to have to make some changes."

"No problem. See you then."

"Trev?" *It's a good thing Trev can be a nickname for my real name as well as my cover or things would be pretty confusing,* he thought.

"What?"

"Don't fuck this up. We've been working on this too long."

"Kiss my ass." If the guy weren't his best friend in the world, he'd probably hate him right now. He just didn't know when to shut up.

*

Sophie hurried away from the coffee shop, her big umbrella offering protection from the rain. A slight chill coursed through her. Oh, how stupid! She'd left her jacket on the back of the chair! Oh well, there was no way she'd go back in there again—she already felt foolish for giving him her business card. Going back a *third* time would simply further the awkwardness. She didn't really like that jacket, anyway. Sure, it had sentimental value but pride overshadowed sentiment at the moment. The well-intentioned gift was one she certainly wouldn't have bought herself. It didn't look all that great on her—it was time for something different. She hugged herself tightly under the umbrella and headed to the parking lot where her car sat alone waiting for her to rescue it from this gut-splattering downpour.

"Interesting," she said to herself two hours later as she sat at the kitchen barstool in her apartment looking at the reports she'd tucked into her satchel before leaving the office. "These numbers don't make sense." She sipped from a steaming hot cup of tea as she peered at the papers in front of her on the counter.

Sophie noticed the differences between the data in the old financial system and the reports out of the new one yesterday but thought she'd made a mistake in running the reports. They weren't yet ready to pilot the new software and the official migration was still a ways off, but she'd attempted a data conversion on her own two nights ago just to see how it would run. She should have waited for the vendor to be there and work with her. Sophie's hardheaded reputation about technical things was well earned; she always wanted to try as much as possible on her own so she fully understood it and prepared for any problems. According to the documented plan from the vendor, the conversion process went easy, but the reports she ran to reconcile it to their old system didn't match at all.

She printed copies of all the financial reports from each system so she could go over them and see what she'd done wrong. She probably just didn't select the report correctly.

She set the sheaf of papers down in order, side by side, old next to new, and highlighted the discrepancies so she could find a common denominator. At eleven o'clock, she gave up and went to bed. She would call the vendor tomorrow and ask if he could take a look.

*

Two days later, Sophie was standing in line at the deli near her office when her cell phone jolted her back to reality. Her thoughts had been diverted to work, as usual, and how she'd forgotten to call Jim Doyle, the account representative from Futurenet Finance, about the report discrepancies. Maybe it didn't matter since he'd be here next week anyway.

The display on her phone indicated the call forwarded from her desk phone to her cell. "Sophie Henderson," came her standard greeting.

"Ms. Henderson, this is Trevor Adams." When she paused for a moment trying to place the name, he continued, "You brought me in out of the rain the other evening."

"Oh, yes . . . yes. Sorry, my mind was on work and I wasn't paying attention." She smiled into the phone.

"You left your jacket on the chair at the coffee shop and I thought I'd drop it by for you if that's okay."

"Oh." She really wished he hadn't noticed it. She already decided to write the jacket off and get something else. She laughed a little nervously. "Man, you know, I just can't seem to get rid of that ugly thing. My friend bought it for me last year. I keep leaving it lying around, and it just keeps finding its way back to me."

The silence expanded between them as if her comment caught him off guard. Surely he possessed a sense of humor somewhere? He laughed an easy, untethered chuckle before responding. "Well, I could toss it in the trash if you like and we can just pretend I didn't call."

"No, no. My friend would probably never believe my excuses and then she'd be insulted that I don't wear it anymore. Since I don't have a lot of friends, I don't really want to tick her off." Honestly though, she warmed at the sound of his voice. She wasn't sure why—he seemed a little strange. He was more serious than she liked. Sort of a moody, somber—or perhaps angry?—kind of guy. But then, first impressions weren't necessarily accurate, especially with the torrential downpour they'd endured.

"I'm not at the office right now so if you want to drop it by and you're in the neighborhood, just leave it at the reception desk and I'll get it when I return."

"Actually, I'm at lunch down the street from your office, which is why I thought I'd check. I'm leaving in a bit and should be able to get by there on my way back."

"Oh, that's great! I'm at Joster's Deli, which is—"

"Yep, I know the place. I eat there quite a bit myself. Even better. I can be there in ten to fifteen minutes, if that's not too late."

"Okay, I'd intended to take my lunch back to my desk but I'll just wait here."

"Great. See you in a bit."

*

Trevor hung up the phone and turned to Nate. "Okay, I guess we see where this goes, but I still think we're looking in the wrong direction with her."

"Probably so, but we won't know until we try. If it's not her, then it must be someone close to her. See if you can get a reader on her cell phone while you're there." Trevor wasn't sure how he'd possibly get that done. Installing a reader required replacing the battery with one of theirs. Theirs were made specifically for tracing not just calls, but also text messages. The reader stored it, then transmitted the data file to their server when the communication ended. Getting hold of her cell phone long enough to put in a battery, restart it, and return it without her knowing would be interesting.

Unlike on the day of Trevor and Sophie's first meeting, the sun today was blindingly bright and there were barely any clouds in the sky. Not that it mattered—it was unlikely one would really see the sky a lot from downtown Houston anyway.

It took a while for Trevor's eyes to adjust inside the deli, so he stepped away from the door to keep from blocking the path while the dark room came into focus. The food here was pretty good. The atmosphere stimulated the draw, though. Very fast-paced, lots of noise. It always smelled like bread and grilled onions. He wasn't much on the noise, but loved the aroma. Casually, he surveyed his surroundings. Yep, there she was in a booth near the wall. He didn't smile when she saw him with the jacket in his hand. He just acknowledged her wave by lifting his head a little in her direction, then he worked his way through the crowded tables.

"How's the car?" Sophie asked.

"Fine. Fine. Good as new."

"Did you call a tow?"

He looked around for a chair. Due to the lunch hour rush, seating space was limited. He observed the exceptionally small gap in the booth next to her, thanks to a really huge guy at the next table, and hesitated. He didn't see any chairs.

"Nope, it ended up being nothing at all. How's your day going so far?" He squeezed into the small space, pressing against the big guy in the booth a bit more than was comfortable.

"Sorry. It's a little tight," he apologized.

"No problem. There really wasn't anything else available when I came in or I would have grabbed a table."

"Works for me but you probably are getting squished." This felt awkward, his hip pressed hard against hers, bone against bone, and if he looked up, he would be right in her face, within inches. He didn't look up. She seemed a little uncomfortable, too, as she stared at her half eaten sandwich.

"Are you hungry?" she asked.

"No, I just ate, and besides I kind of need to get going." The words came out sharper than he intended. This was *not* going to work—they were way too close to maintain a decent conversation. Her hip and rib cage burned into his. He couldn't put his arm down—the only place it could go would be around the back of the booth behind her and, well, that couldn't happen. If he turned his head, his nose would be in her hair. Did her hair smell like the perfume he'd noticed the other day? Like her jacket did. It looked soft.

What the hell shoved *that* thought into his head? Trevor cleared his throat and looked around the room. There was nowhere else to move to right now. The bony hip felt good though, he admitted.

"Oh." Sophie's eyes shifted to his hand wrapped around the coat. She reached across him, her chest grazing his arm, and took the jacket from him. "Well, thanks for returning this."

He adjusted himself to get more comfortable in the seat. "You know," he hesitated, "I thought about throwing it in the street and letting a couple of cars run over it before bringing it back. Maybe even a truck or two. Then you'd have a good reason not to wear it." He grinned and looked sideways at her.

The big, macadamia nut eyes crinkled up a little and she choked out a giggle. "There's a nice thought. What stopped you?"

"I didn't want to cause a wreck."

The giggle blossomed now and the teeth came out, full and white, in a laugh. "Well, that was probably smart. I'd hate to see you explain that to your insurance company."

"Yep, that would probably be pretty hard to explain. Well, I need to get going. Nice talking to you again." He worked his way out of the tin can between her and the big guy and stood up, turning and extending his hand to shake hers.

Sophie set the sandwich down and took his hand, holding it briefly and tugging it up and down once. "You, too. Hey, just curious. Did your iPod dry out okay?"

He held up the earphones in his pocket in response and backed away from the table, smiling at her. "Of course, these things are indestructible." He plugged the earphones in his ears, turned and left the deli, but not before he registered the look on her face—disappointment?

"Smooth, real smooth," Nate snickered in his ear. "Now what are you going to do?"

No clue, man. Trev thought it but didn't say it. "I've got it covered," he responded.

It occurred to him that he'd never really surveilled someone like Sophie. Most of the women he'd watched were career criminals and he'd only done so because they associated with someone else he'd tagged. In fact, he didn't think he'd ever tagged a woman initially . . . but thanks to Sophie's Good Samaritan act the other day, he moved to front and center on this one. The meeting with his team solidified it. They harassed him for getting too close, but in the end, everyone agreed it might make it easier for him to get more information.

Nate had made a wisecrack that Trev was the worst person to charm information from someone like Sophie, and suggested that he should take over. Trev responded with something about Nate's interest not being associated with the job and that he'd better put his brain back in the driver's seat.

All joking aside, Trev felt a sudden sense of dread. He was probably out of his league. Maybe she hid the career criminal part of her personality and he was just too stupid to know it by looking at her. She sure didn't look the part, though. Nor did she act it. And he had always been pretty good at spotting the signs. Shit, he really had to pay attention on this one or he'd screw it up. The bureau didn't accept too many mistakes. It was time to go back to the office and do some additional research. Based on the meeting the other morning, they were expecting things to move faster. He wanted to see if he could get more details. Her lunch hour wasn't sufficient for that. He also knew that a barrage of questions too fast would likely scare a suspect. So much so that they might disappear or avoid contact. He didn't want to give her the "stalker" feeling. He'd leave her alone for three or four days while he gathered more information. That should be an acceptable amount of time to wait before he casually "bumped" into her somewhere. Right now, she was their lead suspect. Even though it didn't make sense.

Back in his office, Trev dropped the file with Sophie's details on the desk. He had gotten it from a box that contained files on most of the employees that had potential to be involved. The FBI task force was currently only following her and the head of the accounting department at Benton & Stanley, as they seemed to have the highest level of access. So far, none of the others had been given much attention. He decided to go over the file again, to see if he'd missed anything.

Sophie Henderson was the daughter of Brianna Henderson, a black woman from Chicago. Brianna met Sophie's father in college. He was white, and while the interracial thing didn't matter to them, their differences in aspirations were significant. According to Sophie's neighbor, her parents split up when Sophie was a toddler. Her mother didn't like the city life very much and ended up going back to her hometown after the breakup. Sophie and her mother lived in a small town outside Chicago. Her mother spoke very little of Sophie's father but the neighbor said he was now some big shot in New York. Trev shrugged. Sure. He knew the statistics—72 percent of children in urban black communities are raised by single mothers. This was the norm. Sophie's family proved no exception.

According to the file, Brianna was diagnosed with Stage IV breast cancer three years ago, and died nine months later, leaving Sophie alone.

Sophie graduated with a bachelors in computer science and then went on to get a masters in information technology. Her mother was extremely proud of her and everyone in town knew of Sophie's success. The details went on; nothing stood out. "Blah, blah, blah," Trevor muttered under his breath. Faceless, unemotional facts. Wasn't it interesting how someone's life could be reduced to a non-personal itemized group of details that could describe any number of people? The file listed the stores she frequented to buy clothes, groceries, even music. It had a short list of her routine schedule, the days of the week listed at the top and the places she went on those days. There wasn't anything new.

He ran his thumb over the photographs of her. One taken as she left her office, another as she entered her apartment building.

Her skin was bronzed and silky with no visible blemishes. She was tall and reasonably thin, maybe a bit too much so for his interest. Her macadamia nut eyes were a very intriguing dark brown with gold and silver specks that showed when she was in the sunlight . . . or when they crinkled as she smiled, he remembered. Her shoulder-length hair had a natural tendency to curl into cascades of waves that she appeared to fight by styling it in a smooth, loose knot at the base of her neck and tucking a clip or comb into it. She dressed professionally but understated. She liked dangly earrings but never appeared to wear any other jewelry than that. This last part wasn't in the report, just things he'd noticed.

Two loud raps on the door broke Trev's concentration. Nate entered without waiting for an invitation. "Got a minute?"

"Sure, what's up?"

"I need to make sure you know in case something happens—my Dad's sick. I may have to leave abruptly."

"No problem. You should go. Did you tell Cook?" Cook was their department head.

"The rest of the family is there and I'd just be in the way. He needs a pacemaker. Heart's stopping once in a while. He's had a couple of near misses and went in to get it checked out. The doctor told my family it's not a big deal and he should go home pretty fast after. I'll tell Cook if I go."

"Who cares if you're in the way—that's not important. You need to go."

"I'm thinking about it. I'll let you know. To be honest, I'm not very good with that kind of thing." Nate concentrated on the street below the window as he spoke. He didn't turn around but the tension hung between them.

"I'm sorry, man. I hope it works out okay," Trev said. "I like your Dad." He'd only met the man a few times but he liked him. No wonder Nate had been a little on edge. He watched Nate turn and leave the office without even glancing back.

Nate had overseen the research on this project and it appeared to be done. If he needed to go, it was probably a good time for it.

After Nate left, Trev dug through some of the other files to see what kind of people Sophie was surrounded by on a daily basis, and whether that had any bearing on the situation. He pulled all Nate's files into his office and spent the remainder of the day reviewing them one by one. Nate had sent it all to him electronically but he'd asked Cheryl to print it out so that he could read it without having to sit in front of the monitor all day. As a data security expert, he should be comfortable with that, but sometimes his back and neck just didn't agree. So, Cheryl would print out the data, organize it in files to read, and then when the analysis was done, they'd shred everything. This wasn't unusual. Apparently several of the other techs operated the same way.

By the time he left to go back to his apartment, he had gone through about two-thirds of them. So far, nothing really stood out as interesting about anyone, not even her. Her only marking factor was that she had a higher level of security to all the systems and therefore had easy access to possibly alter or tamper with the systems in order to hide something.

Chapter Two

Friday just before noon, Trev leaned against the brick wall next to the coffee shop where Sophie dragged him the night he met her, and watched the sidewalk. There was an outside seating area with large green umbrellas opened over tables just past where he stood. The speakers on the wall above the seating area were blaring the song "Suzie Q" by Creedance Clearwater Revival. He kept an empty coffee cup dangling from his hand and the stir stick for the coffee in his mouth. He had a nervous habit of chewing the sticks when killing time. The earphones were planted in his ears but he intended to drop them upon her arrival. As it turned out, he didn't even need to invent a way to run into her. She'd called this morning and asked if he could meet her during the lunch hour.

"Hey Trev, every time I hear this song it reminds me of New Orleans," Nate stated in his ear. "They played it all the time at that little sandwich shop where I spent all that time during the insurance fraud investigation after Hurricane Katrina. Remember that one?"

Trev nodded without answering. The mangled stir-stick dropped out of his mouth. Trev stared down the street, his eyes fixed on a target, unwavering.

"Hey, are you there?"

Trev shook his head, pulled the earplugs out of his ears and dropped them into his pocket.

Sophie Henderson was walking toward him, her strides moving in sync with the sound of the music, hips swaying rhythmically back and forth. She moved like a cat. He wasn't sure if that would be the pet variety or the large predatory kind, but she definitely had that smooth, slinky step. Her hair had started to fall out of the knot she'd put it into that morning and small tendrils were whipping into her face as she moved. She wore a sky blue blouse with a black belted skirt and heels. Her stride was a little long, which made the movement of her hips even more exaggerated. The streetlight changed at the block before the coffee shop and she stopped, waiting for the traffic to clear. Once it passed, she sped toward him like she timed her steps to go with the song over his head.

Without thought, Trev swallowed deeply and muttered. "Damn."

Trev forced his gaze from her and looked around the area to see what else was going on. Quite a few people moved by, but no familiar faces, and nothing to catch his attention. This area of Houston remained pretty busy during lunch hour and right after work, but during the other parts of the day, it was manageable. Nothing like New York, Chicago, or some of the other cities up north. This was why he preferred working the southwest region of the states. The cities were more spread out and while the populations were still pretty big, getting around was easier, and you could still get a little "breathing room" somewhere—you just had to find it. Plus, even the winter rain and wind proved bearable—although the summer heat got a little tough sometimes.

Quite a few people headed out to lunch, passing him as he waited. No one stood around and, unlike him, no one seemed focused on Sophie's movements.

He bent and picked up the stick from the ground, then pitched it and the coffee cup into the trashcan next to the door while she crossed the street toward him.

"Hello there." She smiled as she came up to him, holding out her hand.

Trev nodded, his eyes narrowed as he looked at her face. He took her hand and shook it briefly, noticing she wasn't wearing a jacket even though it was still a little windy.

"Decided to ditch the jacket after all?" He raised a dark eyebrow. One look at her bronzed legs told him that she wasn't wearing stockings either. Surely, she was freezing. Even in Texas, the temperature stayed pretty cool in late February.

"No, but I was running late and already downstairs in a meeting so I didn't go back up to my office. I probably should have—it's a little chilly out. Thanks for meeting me."

She hugged herself a little to warm up. Curiously, he noted that Sophie wanted to meet "during" lunch, not "for" lunch. She didn't really say why, but he assumed it was work related. If it were, though, why didn't she just ask him to come by her office?

So, maybe it wasn't work. He liked that thought. Anything that gave him time to learn about her was good. She mentioned meeting here because it was easy to get to. He wasn't interested in going inside though, not this time. He didn't feel like running into Stacy at the counter. Besides, what guy really wanted a croissant or muffin for lunch? Or a sandwich loaded with bean sprouts, avocados, and no meat? That's all the coffee shop served.

"Are you hungry?" he asked.

The past few weeks of watching her, investigating the other staff, and reading all the files told him all he needed to know about her basic habits. She was a workaholic and hardly ever ate lunch so he wasn't sure if she just wanted a coffee or something more substantial. As if on cue, his stomach made a muffled, churning noise.

"A little," she responded. Thankfully, she ignored his stomach noises.

"Let's go down the street. There's really no decent food in this place." He motioned for her to walk ahead, then saw her shiver as the wind came around the corner of the building. He thought to give her his jacket but he hadn't worn one either, so he shifted her to his other side to block the wind. He thought about putting his arm around her, then internally kicked himself for the thought. *Too forward, man—don't do it.* The song on the speakers faded as they moved away and Trevor mused that he'd never think of New Orleans again when he heard that tune. A new image of a black skirt, bronzed legs, and black high-heeled shoes with straps across the ankles would be forever burned into his brain.

Trevor glanced at the couple passing them on the sidewalk, then looked across the street at the group deep in discussion at the light. "So, are you from Houston originally?" He wasn't much on small talk but orders were orders. His required him to get acquainted with her and spend as much time as he could building trust, so they could find out what was going on. Since he already knew the background answers, asking the questions would give him a feel for her honesty. Although, if she really acted as part of this scheme, honesty would certainly not be one of her most favorable character traits.

"No, I grew up in a small town in Illinois. Very nice place but pretty low key."

"Low key is good sometimes. It keeps a person out of trouble."

She gave him a sideways glance. "I wasn't much of a troublemaker. Too many goals and big plans to waste it causing trouble." Her voice was heavily laced with annoyance. "Besides, in a small town, everyone knows what you do and tells your mom if you do anything the least bit out of line. No one wanted to mess with my mom, not even me, so I made sure I stayed on track."

"She sounds like a pretty tough lady."

"Persistent is more how I'd describe her—very persistent about her expectations. While she loved the small town for herself, she wanted more for me." Sophie looked wistfully down the street as they walked. "She wanted me to be more like my father."

"What was he like?"

"Brilliant. Very business savvy. He could turn water into money. He loved the glamour and hustle of the city life."

"What about as a father?" Trevor asked.

"I don't know . . . he was gone before I was old enough to spend much time with him. We got together a year ago but the whole thing was so awkward because we didn't really know anything about each other. We tried and he seemed kind of sad about it." She raised her shoulders and sucked in a breath. "How did we go from talking about where I'm from to what kind of dad I had?"

Even though he didn't enjoy the talking part all that much, he had a knack for listening—always did have. He found it kind of interesting, the discovery process. While he often said very little, he could learn a lot about people by letting them do the talking and somehow that encouraged them to be candid with him.

"I don't know. I guess I'm just a good listener. Sorry if you didn't want to talk about that." He realized they stood in front of the Mexican restaurant that he'd eaten at a few times. "How's this for lunch?"

"Good for me." She smiled, crinkling those macadamia nut eyes.

Once they were seated with menus and drinks, Trev's curiosity got the best of him. They'd had enough idle conversation so it would be appropriate to ask. "So, what is it you wanted to talk to me about?"

"Well, first tell me about your consulting work. What's your specialty? There are so many different types of IT consultants nowadays. I have something that may need someone but I'm not sure you'd be interested."

He expected this would come at some point and he had an answer prepared. "I'm a security analyst. I do security audits, forensics, data analysis for security purposes and advise on better ways to secure a company's data and network." He spat it out easily because to some extent it contained a large degree of truth. He had gone through the FBI's most rigorous data analysis training and forensics program. While he mainly worked on the front line, observing and interfacing with their targets, his expertise in security, and specifically forensics, was strong—very strong. That, in addition to the year-long psychiatric analysis training, a requirement for his field, made him capable of studying suspects and data in a fraud investigation better than almost anyone else in his division . . . or at least he thought so.

He watched her face to see her reaction to his information.

"Wow, I didn't expect that!" She seemed surprised. But not afraid, he noted. "I expected you to say that you're a server guy or maybe a network person. A security consultant is a little more intense than I expected."

He could almost see her mind mulling over his words. He wasn't sure if she was pleased or apprehensive. She certainly didn't look completely scared . . . probably a good sign. Man, she was beautiful. A guy would have to be dead not to notice. He wondered how many men she'd been involved with. The notes were a little sketchy on that part. Not relevant, he chided himself. Still, he wanted to know.

Their table sat rather low to the ground; her long legs didn't seem to fit under it any better than his. He moved his legs to the side as soon as he sat but she had tucked hers under the table in an uncomfortable, sideways sprawl. It didn't last long though, and now she moved her legs to the side and crossed them in the aisle next to her chair. On her slim ankle, above the strap of the shoe, a small silver bangle caught the light from outside the window and sparkled a little. A silver sunburst dangled from the chain. For some reason that seemed totally out of character for the outfit she wore, more like something she would wear with a sundress or shorts on the weekend rather than at work.

When his eyes returned to her face, his skin warmed up quickly when he noticed that she'd seen him staring at her legs, her ankles, and the bangle. She didn't say anything though, thankfully. An unreadable expression crossed her eyes as she held his gaze for a short while.

"Yeah, I guess I'm a little more intense than most people would expect." He smiled a lopsided grin, trying to make light of his work, and take the attention off his wandering glance.

"I suppose in that line of work, a customer would want you to maintain a certain edginess or intenseness—or maybe the word is 'awareness'—that's higher than the norm."

She didn't know how accurate that statement really was. Being exceptionally aware of your surroundings, subject, and any and all evidence was pretty critical to successfully resolving a case—that's why he was good at it. As if to prove it to himself, he noted the three waiters staffing the restaurant. Two male, one female. Each of them handled four to five tables. The larger male must be new. It was obvious by the way the other two kept helping him with his tables, filling glasses, etc. The owner's picture graced the wall by the door. His real face resided in the kitchen. Apparently, he was also the head chef today.

A wind chime over the door jingled every time someone entered or exited the door, which made it easy for him to know when the surroundings would change. The chime was in the shape of Texas at the top with small copper tubes hanging off of it at the bottom. He'd surveyed the room earlier and knew each of the twenty-plus tables and had a basic idea of the people at each.

This time when the low jingle sounded, he watched a group leave the third booth down the wall. Immediately following their departure, two people entered. The man and woman looked somewhat familiar. They weren't part of Sophie's team but he had seen them leaving her building before. Oh yeah, he recognized the guy as the CEO and the lady was one of the board members. He made a mental note to check on them when he got back. They didn't appear to see her yet so it could be an unimportant entrance but he didn't necessarily see it as a coincidence, either. Regardless, he made sure to glance that way periodically. As he remembered, the CEO was also a workaholic who primarily spent lunch hours at his desk and weekends at the office. Strange that two supposed workaholics would both go out on the same day to the same place. It was unlikely that they planned it since he and Sophie had arrived by chance.

"Awareness. Yes, that's pretty accurate," he stated flatly as he brought his attention back to his own table and company. *She fidgets,* he noticed. She hadn't done that before. Now, she seemed a little nervous. She played with her napkin and rubbed her hands together. Did their presence bother her? If so, she'd done a good job of pretending not to see them.

"So, are you working on a project right now? Anything interesting?" she asked.

"Yes and no. I'm sort of in between things, which is nice. There are a few loose ends to tie up on some old projects but that should be done pretty soon. I worked a lot of investigations in Louisiana a while ago so it's nice to be back for a while."

"I'll bet it is. What's Louisiana like?"

"It's a mess right now from the hurricanes. Katrina really demolished New Orleans and parts of Mississippi. Those poor people will probably spend years rebuilding. Some of it just needs to be bulldozed over so they can start from scratch."

"What did you do while you were there?"

"Insurance fraud investigations and audits mostly. I also did some security infrastructure installations for companies in the process of rebuilding."

"So, it sounds like you travel a lot?"

"Sometimes."

"You're from here?"

"No."

"But you said it's nice to be back."

He found it interesting that she noticed his use of words. "I live here now, but I'm not from here . . . originally."

"Oh." She watched him as if waiting for more, but didn't ask.

"I'm originally from Oklahoma. I grew up on a ranch there. My parents are still there. I went to college in Norman like most kids from my area. I got interested in security when I saw some of my college buddies trying to hack the network to gain access to test scores, and all that stuff. I decided to be on the other side of the fence—it seemed—safer." It was easy for him to make up this part. A mixture of truth and fiction, just enough. Same story, different locations.

"So, you're kind of a cowboy type then?" she stated coyly. Her slight hand reached for a chip, dunked it in salsa, then raised the chip to her lips.

"No, definitely not. More of a 'Southwestern geek,' if there is such a thing. I haven't worn a pair of cowboy boots in five or six years. Not since I left my horse on the ranch in Oklahoma." He grinned, teasing her a little. In truth, he hated wearing boots. It was too hot most of the time for that. He'd only put them on if the work required it.

She laughed. "But you *do* own a horse, right?" She gave him a smartass sarcastic smile as their food arrived.

"Well, my family has a whole slew of them, actually."

"Strange."

"Why?"

"You live in the city. You work in information technology. You don't seem that . . . "

"Country?"

"Well, I meant to say that type—the ranch type, but then in a way it makes sense because you seem awfully uncomfortable here."

"Me? Uncomfortable? Nope."

He wasn't uncomfortable in the city but sitting here looking at her certainly proved a little intimidating. She was gorgeous. He'd dated a lot of girls over the years, even lived with one for a while, but he didn't remember one that made him unable to think straight. Not even Linda, the biggest mistake of his life. They ate silently for a while. The pair that came in earlier caught her attention but didn't speak. They just waved and smiled. Sophie did the same back.

"Friends of yours?" Trevor inquired as he looked over at them.

"No. Our bosses. The main ones."

"And you know them?"

"Not really. I've been in meetings where I've made presentations to them. Other than that, I couldn't tell you much about them."

"So, you've drilled me with questions and know my story. Are you ready to tell me why I'm here?" He took a bite of his enchilada.

She pointed at the food on his plate or actually at the almost empty plate. "You really like that, don't you?"

He'd practically inhaled the whole plate of food and she'd only picked at hers.

"Yeah, of course!" He flashed her another smile, wondering if she was stalling. "These are the best enchiladas I've ever tasted. They're awesome. Here, you want to try some?" He pushed his plate toward her.

She looked at the remaining enchilada hesitantly. He waved his fork to encourage her. "Go ahead. You're gonna like it." The hesitation was short. Her hand moved toward his plate.

"Okay, I'll try it, but only because you're practically forcing me." Her fork sliced into the end of the enchilada. She brought it to her lips, grinning at him. As she chewed, she nodded and wagged her fork. "Yep, yep. That's good. Really good."

"Told you."

"Yes, so . . . " She swallowed. " You kind of owe me for saving you from near death the other night, right?"

"Not really. I don't think I was ever in any *real* danger."

"You're still saying that?" She looked up at him with a questioning look that he knew she intended as more challenging than anything else.

"I'm sitting here all in one piece, aren't I?" His gray eyes glinted at her. He was getting cocky.

"Well, you owe me whether you want to admit it or not. So, I want to ask you a favor in return." She hesitated. "I found something last week that I don't understand. I hoped you were a database person and could explain it, but actually your type of experience may be just as good or better. I'm not sure." Okay, at this point he knew the meeting was about business. He looked around the room to take note of changes and shrugged off a twinge of disappointment.

"Don't make it sound like I'm your fallback plan, now."

"No, that's not what I meant, but there're really only two explanations for what I found. Either the data's purposely wrong or someone entered it wrong accidentally."

"I'm afraid you lost me, Ms. Henderson."

"Sophie, please."

"Maybe I should call you Henry, you know, short for Henderson?" He watched in amusement as she reached over with her fork and took another bite of his enchilada. She ignored him poking fun at her name. For some reason, giving her a unique nickname personalized their meeting. Guys did that. Nicknamed their friends, their dogs, their cars, their . . .

"I can't really explain it. I have to show you. Let's just say that some of the finance staff are 'less than capable' in certain situations and if it's an explainable mistake then I need to know that and get it corrected. If it's more than that—well, that's something I don't really know how to deal with yet."

Trev raised his eyebrows a little but said nothing. He watched her face as she became noticeably more uncomfortable.

"I brought the information home the other night. I ran some reports for a migration and everything was, well . . . off. And not just a little. I couldn't figure it out. I need someone better than me to look at it."

"Why don't you just ask someone at work?" It seemed the common sense thing to do but to be honest, he was pretty sure he knew what she referred to. She wasn't the first person to see it. The other person had reported it and started the ball rolling on this assignment for him.

"I thought about that but then I thought maybe I should just keep it to myself for a little bit. If I bring it to anyone's attention and it's just a mistake, they'll think me a suspicious flake. If it's not a mistake, then more investigation needs to be done and the less that it becomes common knowledge the better."

"So, you're trying to hide it? Whatever it is."

"No! That's not what I meant." She shook her head in exasperation. "You just need to see it."

"At your apartment?" He rubbed his chin, or at least the hair on his chin, and showed that wicked glint again.

"No!" Her voice got a little higher pitched. "God, no." She let out a nervous giggle. "This is starting to sound like some sort of crazy pickup line, isn't it?" She looked out the window and smoothed her hair back from her forehead.

He watched, unsmiling, eyebrows pitched. If he didn't already suspect what might be in those reports, yes, he'd think she was hitting on him. There was little he could say so he thought it best to just leave it alone.

She started again. "I can bring them to you somewhere this weekend, or next week if you want."

He kept the brows arched and kicked his head back a little.

"It's not like that! Really!" Her voice raised a couple notches.

He looked at the door, then answered. "It'll have to be this weekend. I'm traveling Monday through Thursday of next week." He wanted to see what she had. "I'll warn you though, just looking at some reports won't tell me very much without the data behind them."

"Well, let's start with the reports. If you think it's needed, I can probably get the data."

"Sounds good. Are you finished with my enchilada? I think you missed a bite." He taunted her as he surveyed the cleaned plate. She'd eaten the rest, even what was left of the beans. Oddly, her plate remained barely touched. It should have bothered him that she'd helped herself to his food, but it didn't.

"Oh, yeah. Sorry." She held the fork to her lips and licked the remaining sauce.

"Let's get back then, or you're going to be late." He reluctantly waved for the ticket and they left. For a brief moment, the thought of getting her to take a long lunch or afternoon off entered his mind. Then reality hit and he admitted she'd never go for it. Her mind was already back at work.

*

Sophie walked behind him to the door and for the first time, noticed how extremely tall Trevor was. Even in heels, she didn't tower over him. That was new for Sophie. She stood 5'10" and with heels could easily go over the 6' mark. As a teen, she hated being so tall and never wore heels. Now, she didn't care. In fact, sometimes it worked to her advantage. Trevor must have been at least 6'5" or maybe more. He held his shoulders very square at all times. It made him look even taller—ex-military perhaps? He moved smoothly and easily.

He stopped at the door and waited for some others to go through. He held it for them with one hand up high, then looked at her and smiled as she walked through. His hair was kind of a chestnut brown color cut very short all around. It would look a little too severe without the facial hair, but the beard and mustache softened the look significantly and made him appear friendly. They were trimmed excessively short and lined the jaw, showing the angular line of his face. Interestingly enough, he groomed it to perfection. Not a hair out of place anywhere. She wondered if he was one of those neat freak guys that couldn't stand to have his house messy and sent his jeans to the dry cleaners to get that perfect line starched in them. The only people she'd ever met that perfect looking were either suffering from extreme psychiatric issues, or military.

"Trevor, have you ever served in the military?" she asked as she passed under his arm into the brisk air. He looked perplexed.

"Why do you ask that? Is that a job qualification check?"

"No, but you carry yourself like someone that has. Kind of stiff."

"Oh, I guess it's a habit." She noticed his hesitation to answer. He motioned for them to walk quickly to catch the light at the corner in front of them. "Yes, I served in the army for a while. It paid for my college education." He didn't add anything more. Obviously, he wasn't interested in discussing it further. He moved ahead of her, apparently determined to get across before the light changed and the cars started moving.

"Interesting." She said it under her breath but he caught it.

"What?" He glanced back.

"Most men I've met that were military would never grow facial hair. While yours is trimmed to perfection," she felt her face flush, "it doesn't seem the standard military issue haircut." What a stupid thing to mention, she chastised herself.

"Ah, but I'm not in the army now and haven't been for a few years." He reached up and rubbed the thin line of hair on his chin. "So, I guess I can admit to having a little rebellious nature to me. I grew this as soon as I was discharged and have kept it ever since. I tried it thicker but it itched too much."

"Not all that rebellious." She teased. "Otherwise you wouldn't trim it so neatly."

"Most women think I'm rebellious enough," he stated without looking at her.

Chapter Three

In April of 2008, an anonymous tip came to the Feds. The source advised there was evidence of significant fraud going on at Benton & Stanley. In the process of reporting the fraud, the person involved stated that he was concerned for his safety and the safety of his family. At first, they thought it was a crank call, one of those conspiracy-crazy lunatics that thought big government was out to get them. The guy's voice was breathless and stilted, and he sounded to be under the influence of something. Upon further questioning, the hotline operator was able to determine that the person did in fact work at the company and had credible information. However, during the call, the person was cut off unexpectedly and did not call back.

In May, another call came, this time from a woman. She stated that her husband had discovered some fraudulent activities going on at his office and he had become increasingly suspicious that their family was in danger. His behavior had grown erratic and he was despondent at home and afraid to go to work most days. Once again during the call, they lost connectivity, but not before she was able to give his first name, which they did a check on and were able to trace back to the IT department head. An investigator called their home and set up a time to meet with him to discuss the suspected criminal activities.

That was when Trevor and Nate started on the project. They were asked to track Mr. Bob Greenwood and see if his suspicions were, in fact, valid. On May 20, 2008 (last year) they were supposed to begin trailing Bob. They didn't participate face to face in the interrogation with him but they listened to it and absorbed the details. Bobby had been the IT director for three years. During the second year, he recommended an upgrade or replacement to the financial system. Many of its capabilities were extremely outdated and he wanted to get them to a more secure and reliable platform. By upgrading, they'd be able to incorporate many of the latest secure online banking features as well as automated payments for the AP system and electronic funds transfers for vendors and customers. All of that would decrease their labor and supply costs significantly.

"Most companies were already this far along, taking full advantage of EFT processes," he said during the interview. "We were still behind and it didn't make sense at the time. If we instituted the online system, the entire process would be electronic. No more handwritten or typed purchase orders. They would be keyed and submitted to the vendor electronically, which the vendor would authenticate. No more keyed-entry of invoices. No more laborious check runs that have to be sorted and mailed." He paused for a breath. "And most importantly, less openings for fraud. The purchase order, invoice, and payment all had to match and once the payment was approved, then the funds were transferred through a method that applies a security key to the transaction. The other side has to have a matching security key, which is randomly generated periodically to assure it's secured. They run on a timer. Every so many minutes, a new key is generated on each side. As long as they're compatible, the transaction can be completed, but it also requires a person on each end to enter a protected password to authorize the transmittal of funds. So, there's no anonymity involved. Every transaction requires certain levels of access and is backed up by an approval process." Bob stepped away from the window and narrowed his eyes as he watched the agent take notes. "It would cut the labor costs of data entry in half and increase the security tri-fold. It was a no-brainer, I thought."

He went on to explain that he was surprised that he met with resistance initially from the executive staff and board members. They stated it was due to the initial expense involved. The auditor was asked to review the process for loopholes. Bob stated that after the auditor review and a meeting where he spelled out in detail to the board committee the savings that they could receive as a result of the change, it became easier to sell the project. Eventually, the board voted and approved the upgrade.

As Bob explained the rest to their investigator, he became increasingly agitated and nervous, watching the windows and jumping if he heard some unusual noise. "The first indication that something wasn't right came about three weeks after the project was approved. I asked one of the staff to run a series of reports for me to pass on to the vendor for review before we started working on the migration."

"What type of reports?" Agent Vincent was the interviewer sitting in their home asking the questions. She had been on the team for about five years and was really good at getting the details.

"You know, financial statements, trial balance, income statement, aged receivables, that sort of thing. The only difference was that I asked him to run it for *all* companies, not just the main one. Once I delved into them, I saw that there were huge differences in what was on the reports and what had been reported during the financial reviews to the board. I thought the reports had been run incorrectly."

"How could they be run incorrectly?"

"Pretty easily, actually. There are all sorts of parameters a person can choose when running them that can skew the results . . . different dates, leaving out accounts, and so on."

"What happened when you ran the reports again?" Vincent prompted.

"They came back the same, but oddly the night I ran them, I stayed late and no one else was there. When I'm there by myself at night, I usually close my office door. I could hear someone moving around outside that night and it made me nervous. Then, as I was running the reports, my office phone rang showing a caller from inside the office— an unknown extension. I let it ring because the place was empty, and I didn't want to get sidetracked with something else. If it was a normal work call, they'd leave a message and I'd handle it the next day."

"Did they leave a message?"

"No, but they called back twice before the power went out."

"The power went out while you were there?"

"Yeah, I thought it odd, too . . . but only on my floor. I looked out the window and could see the upper floors still had light based on their reflection in the building across the street."

"So, did it come back on?"

"I didn't stay to find out . . . I kept hearing the noises. It was a little spooky in the dark, so I left."

"Did you finish running the reports?"

"No, they were still running before the power went out, printing away on my printer. When the power went out, the printing stopped. I just got up and left. I pretty much ran out of the building like a real chicken." Bob laughed as he said it, probably remembering how foolish he looked hustling out of there, peering over his shoulder every few minutes. He leaned toward Agent Vincent, putting his hands on his knees and speaking slowly, "The reports were gone from my desk when I got to the office the next morning. Every scrap of paper off the printer, and the ones that were finished and sitting next to it. Someone had taken them."

"Are you sure a cleaning crew didn't throw them away?"

"I'm sure—they never touch anyone's desk."

"Did you run them again?"

"Yes. And they came out totally different, matching exactly to what the board reports showed. I would have thought I'd made a mistake if I didn't have the matching set at home from my staff member's initial run."

"Okay, so the reports were off." Agent Vincent still hadn't really grasped the relevancy or importance yet. "Why is that a big deal?"

"Because the reports I originally ran showed somewhere in the neighborhood of four-point-two million dollars missing."

Vincent registered the comment silently and sat for a couple of minutes, probably to let it sink in. "Wow. That's a lot of cash.

Are you sure?"

"Dead sure." His eyes stared coldly at Vincent, unflinching. Bob was not a quack. He knew what he was talking about and wasn't about to have someone think he was prone to wild imaginings.

"But how could someone hide so much money? That's huge. It doesn't seem possible."

"By funneling it through a dummy company into other accounts. The company grosses somewhere in the neighborhood of fourteen-point-two billion a year. In the overall scheme of their budget, that's not a large number. For you and me, it's huge, but not for them."

"Do you have any idea who is involved and how they're doing it?"

"No, I hadn't gotten that far. After the night I tried to run the reports, I started getting prank calls at home. When I answered, most times the caller hung up. Sometimes, he would just sit there and we knew he was there but he said nothing. Then one day, he spoke . . . to my wife. He told her 'tell your husband to mind his own business.'"

"What did you do?"

"I called you guys."

"Had you tried to report the fraud internally?"

"Yes, they have a fraud hotline you can call. I tried it. Nothing happened."

"Nothing at all?"

"To my knowledge, no, but they could have investigated it and just dropped it . . . or maybe chalked it up to the ramblings of a disgruntled employee. They seem to do that a lot when a complaint is made."

"Well, that *is* often the case."

"I suppose. I don't know. That's still not a good reason to drop it, is it? Even if it is a disgruntled employee, shouldn't they document the call and investigate? I would think that more of a reason, rather than less. Employees want to believe their company to be ethical and trustworthy. If they think otherwise and complain, maybe there's valid reason."

"Okay, Bob." Agent Vincent was clearly ready to wrap this up and leave. "Is there anything else we need to know? Anything else unusual that you remember?"

"No . . . not really."

"Not really? Or you don't want to say?"

"I think I'm being followed . . . or maybe listened to."

"Why do you say that?"

"I'm not sure, but there are a lot of signs."

"Okay." Vincent didn't appear to believe that part but she didn't say so. She wrote on the pad of paper she had in her lap, then rose to her feet. "I'm going to go back and write all this up. We'll give you a call tomorrow morning and talk through what we want to do next. You'll be home?"

It was a Friday evening and he didn't have plans. "Yes, I'll be here."

"Good. Talk to you then."

Chapter Four

Nate would always be the best friend Trev ever had. They entered the Academy at the same time. They did the majority of their training together and often became partnered together on assignments. In the first few years, they worked with a lot of the older guys and learned a great deal. They'd become pretty good friends despite their differences. Nate, a native Californian, was kind of a surfer type. His parents were both multilingual and spoke Spanish as their primary language. Trev, also bilingual, appreciated that they could often switch between languages when they wanted to talk freely.

Five years ago, Trev met Linda Catlin at a bar. She was there with a group of friends for a girls' night out. Linda emanated an engineered beauty, grace, and glamour, and she had set her eyes on Trevor. He was between assignments and ended up spending the full week of his vacation with her. By the end of the week, on a whim, he asked her to move in with him. Another whim ended up in a proposal. Nate tried to stop him but Trev wouldn't listen. "Trev," he pleaded, "take a little more time, man. What do you really know about her?"

"I know enough."

"Do you? Really? I don't think so. There's something not right about her. I can't put a finger on it but she scares me a little."

"Scares you? You're an FBI agent, how the hell can a hundred and thirty pound woman scare you?"

"Not like that. I think she's going to be trouble for you. I'm sorry, I guess I shouldn't say that, should I?"

"No, and it's none of your business anyway."

Trev lived with Linda for a year. It was a pretty good year. She tolerated his constant travel and sometimes distant personality, or at least she seemed so. Two weeks after they celebrated their first year together, he came home from a trip to D.C. to find her gone. She'd left a note on the kitchen counter.

I'm sorry Trev, but I can't do this anymore. I hate being alone all the time. I met someone a couple of months ago while you were in New Orleans and well, he's pretty great. He's also here . . . all the time. Again, I'm sorry.

Take care,

Linda

The key to the apartment lay on top of the note. All her things were gone. She ran out of his life as quickly as she came into it. Oddly, she didn't leave the ring he'd given her. She said she pawned it. What a cold and cowardly person. She didn't even have the courage to tell him to his face. He should have been devastated but he wasn't. He missed her, but in truth, he didn't like being told what to do. Probably what he missed the most was their physical relationship. Having someone to hold onto at night comforted him after the rougher jobs, especially someone as pretty as she was. Other than that, they had very little in common and he quickly realized that living with her stifled him, or at least he told himself that as often as possible. He wished he'd listened to Nate in the beginning and not wasted a year of his life trying to please her.

After she left, Nate came around every couple of days or so, to check on him. What a good friend. Trev, being the loner that he was, handled it just fine . . . and eventually told Nate, as politely as he could, to back off. The guy was driving him nuts being around all the time.

Today, Nate's words showed his steadfast friendship.

"Trev?" Nate watched Trev walk back toward their pseudo office near Sophie's building.

"Yeah?" The earphones were back in his ears.

"You haven't worn a smile on your face in years—not since Linda left."

Trev sobered up. "I'm not smiling now, either."

"Looked like it to me, dude."

"Shut up. You're kind of a pain in the ass, you know. I think I'm going to quit wearing these earphones."

Nate snickered. "She's got legs a mile long. Looks good in a skirt, don't you think?"

"I didn't notice."

"Yeah, right. I saw you not noticing, remember? It's good to have you back."

"I'm done listening to you." Trev pulled the earphones from his ears and walked into their building. So what if he noticed her? It was kind of hard not to. It didn't matter, anyway. She was a job, just a job. He opened his cell phone and dialed Sophie's number.

It rang four times before she picked up. "Sophie Henderson," she blurted in a bland and professional voice.

"Hey, Henry. Trevor here." Trev liked the new nickname he'd given Sophie though she didn't seem to approve. All the more reason to use it.

"Did I forget something again?"

"No, that's not why I called. Why don't I meet you Friday evening after work and you can bring the reports? If you take them to work with you, we can just meet near your office. Will that work?"

"I can't." She'd hesitated before answering. "I already have plans Friday night."

"Oh, big date?" Why did he ask that? It was definitely none of his business.

"No, not really. A group of us . . . we're taking a friend of mine out for his birthday after work."

"That's good. Not a problem." He couldn't think of anything else to say. "Well, I'd better go. Give me a call and let me know how you want to handle it."

"Hey. We'll be done around eight or so. Why don't you meet me there and I can give them to you then and show you what

I'm talking about?"

"Where?"

"Midtown. Tell me your email address and I'll send directions."

"I live near there so that should work out perfect. I have your business card. I'll send you an email and you can just respond back."

"Sounds good."

"See you then." He hung up without waiting for an answer. When he got to his computer, he shot her a quick email and she responded back with the address. Perfect, he thought. He'll get a chance to see the information that she wanted to share. This will move the investigation along nicely.

Trev found passing time comfortable. On an assignment, he could sit for hours observing everything. The time passed so slowly it often felt like the world was moving without him. He was used to it and learned to be patient. It took incredible strength to drop his youthful impatience for the job. The waiting formulated scenarios regarding what actions to take and what actions might occur as a result. He spent several hours over the next days thinking about what might occur Friday. If the documents proved as expected, he'd still need the data but it would be important to know how much she shared with the others. It also might be good to watch her interactions with the coworkers. Do they get along well or is she more isolated or reserved from them? Which ones had she struck up friendships with . . . and did they possibly fit the profile for this?

His thoughts wandered a little as he looked back through all the profiles of her staff. She had a lot of men working on her team. Many of them young—her age or close—and also single. He wondered if any relationships had developed between them. There wasn't enough information about them, the staff. Why did his investigative team only look at the two managers? The staff probably had as much or more access, and needed to be reviewed more thoroughly. He intended to get the researchers working on that on Monday.

Friday night came way too slow. He'd spent a little time watching her and that ended up being pretty frustrating, just watching. He found himself wanting to hear her voice again.

Sophie Henderson was like a firecracker wrapped up in cellophane. On Friday, he watched her standing at a table near the window, flashing that huge smile and laughing. She was vivacious. Everyone that saw her took a second look, wanting to see that smile again. He sat at the back of the bar with his back to them, looking through the mirror over the bar.

He sipped his drink and watched with interest, observing each member of the small group around her. Three women of varying ages stood across from Sophie all talking at once. He had read about two of them. Sophie's best friend Callie showed up almost a year and a half earlier, he remembered. She'd relocated from New York. He had nothing on the other girl but her name, Christy James. Both worked for Sophie, but Callie became not only the best friend but also the right arm, so to speak.

Jake Wellborn, the tall blond guy next to her, was one of her team. His highlighted hair was spiked on top in that fake-ruffled way. A hole in his ear informed it had been pierced at one time. Maybe he didn't wear the earring at work? His clothes, starched and pressed to perfection, portrayed an affinity for neatness. He was a programmer and according to the files, flagrantly gay. Trev could see it; the clothes and hair pretty much gave it away. No straight guy dressed like that. Jake was a decent guy though, no record. Good grades in school, all through college and graduate school. Smart. Really Smart. Born the only child of a family in East Texas, he distanced himself from his parents since leaving home. Not uncommon for someone who'd gone through what he probably had over the years.

Another young man returned from the bar with a couple of drinks. He squeezed between Jake and Sophie and handed her one of the glasses. She smiled and Trev saw her mouth the words "thank you" at him. That was Thomas Brand. He knew the face but not a lot of details other than he was a systems analyst with only a year at the company. His history was sparse in the agency's files, and judging by his attention to Sophie, that probably needed to be checked out.

Thomas and Jake stood the same height, but where Jake defined fastidiousness in his appearance, Thomas was just the opposite. Wrinkled shirt. Wrinkled pants. Wrinkled jacket over the shirt. He obviously lived alone, did his own laundry, and didn't care. His brown hair hadn't been cut in a while so it looked wrinkled, too. A sizeable growth of facial hair either meant it grew really fast or he'd forgotten to shave. For some reason though, he carried it pretty well—a little slovenly but it worked for him. Trev watched him hand the glass to Sophie and decided to find out more about Thomas. He also needed to go back and check the levels of access each of these people had to the accounting system.

"Hey, Henry." Sophie jumped when he spoke into her ear from her right side. She turned quickly into him, smiling and bumping her drink against his chest. Instinctively, she put a hand against his shirt to wipe away the drips then drew it back quickly and looked down. She tried to step back away from him but found herself jammed up against the table.

"Hello, Trevor. I see you found me."

"You're not hard to find." His eyes looked around the room then settled back on her face, smiling with a slight tip of the lips.

"Yeah, I'm a little tall with these heels on so I tower over everyone most of the time. I guess I kind of stick out." Apparently, she was a little uncomfortable with her height. He slowly let his eyes take in her shoes, legs, skirt, blouse, hair, and eyes.

"That wasn't really what I meant," he responded.

She looked at him curiously and opened her mouth like she intended to speak but said nothing.

"Sophie, who's your gorgeous friend?" Callie asked from across the table as she leaned over to smile up at him.

Sophie snapped her attention back to the table. Her face warmed a little as she responded. "Everyone, this is Trevor Adams, a friend."

Trev continued to watch her face, wondering why she'd introduced him that way. He liked it; it implied a relationship of some sort that would certainly raise questions. Is that what she wanted . . . questions? He turned to the table and shook each of the girls' hands as they gave their names. It turned out the third girl, the one he didn't recognize, was new, a friend of one of the others. He also shook the guys' hands, noticing that Thomas's expression clouded over instantly when Sophie introduced him. Thomas protectively put an arm on Sophie's shoulder and asked Trevor, "So, how do you know my Sophie?"

"I'm not your Sophie," she countered as she shrugged his arm from her shoulder.

"She saved me from an electrocution a while back so I bought her lunch."

This guy's got a thing for her, Trev thought, *but she seems a little resistant to it. The guy's kind of an ass so no wonder.* Trev flashed a charming grin at him and spoke softly to Sophie, "Should I wait? Or come back later?"

"No. No. Please stay and talk with us. That is, if you can spare the time. I promise no one will bite you." She lowered her eyebrows and shot Thomas a warning look as she put a hand on Trevor's forearm, pulling him closer to the table. The others moved around to make room. He towered over her with one shoulder behind her and the other edged toward the table.

Callie winked at Sophie and laughed. "I'm not promising I won't bite you, handsome," she flirted.

"Callie!" Sophie protested.

"Sorry, Soph, but in case you haven't paid any attention . . . your friend here is definitely not hard on the eyes." Callie's eyes wandered up and down Trev as she smiled and fluttered her lashes at him.

"I agree totally." Jake lifted his glass in a salute to Trev, making

Trev look around the room in discomfort. He calculated an appropriate response and thought of none. He wasn't good in crowds and certainly not the flirty type. He had no patience with idle chitchat, but she'd invited him so he'd tough it out.

"Seriously," Callie's friend persisted. "How did you meet Sophie, Mr. Adams? And where are you from?"

Trev's shoulder stiffened against her. He wondered if Sophie could sense how much he wanted out of this conversation. Then she spoke. "Trevor is a security guy and he's here to protect me from my stalker." He glanced at the back of her hair, startled by her comment. Unable to see her expression, he contemplated whether the statement was serious.

"Really?" Callie exclaimed. "Is that guy still bothering you? What did the police find out?"

"Not a thing. I haven't heard anything from them since I reported it."

"Stalker?" The two other guys said in unison as Trev observed her facial expressions. He wasn't sure what was going on but he intended to find out.

"Yeah," Callie retorted. "Sophie met a guy here a couple months ago. He followed her out to her car and tried to grab her. She beat him off with that giant red umbrella of hers and managed to get away. He showed up again but just watched her."

Trev's eyes narrowed and shot to Sophie's face. He leaned down and whispered into her ear so the others wouldn't hear him. "Is this true?"

"Well, partially, yes," she admitted, returning his whisper, her breath tingling against his ear. "He hasn't shown up everywhere but I've seen him again."

"Do you know him?"

"No."

"I need to know more about this."

Trev grabbed Sophie's arm and pulled her away from her friends to a newly cleaned booth. The waitress took one last swipe with a cloth as they approached. Thomas started to follow but Trev saw Callie catch his arm and say, "Leave the lovebirds alone, T."

Thomas growled something back at her, downed his drink, and headed to the bar. Trev pushed Sophie into the freshly wiped seat of the booth and slid in across from her. He was instantly disappointed she was no longer pressed against his chest and chastised himself for even thinking that. She glanced longingly back at the table they'd just left, where her friends remained talking. "You can go back in a minute." He sensed her desire to get away from him. "Tell me about this stalker person."

"That has nothing to do with what I need your help on. It's an isolated incident. Besides, there's nothing to know, really. I came here with everyone after work several weeks ago and stayed late visiting with Callie and Thomas. This guy came up and started talking to me. He wanted to buy me a drink. I said no thank you because I was leaving. He asked if I needed a ride. I said no to that, too. He disappeared so I assumed he got the message. Later when I left, Callie and Thomas went out with me but they parked on the other side of the building so we said goodbye and split. When I got to the car, he popped out of nowhere."

"And?" Trev waited for her to go on.

"He said something like, 'Listen, you rich bitch, you're going with me whether you like it or not,' and he grabbed at me. It had been raining and I had my umbrella so I brought it up and whacked him across the face with it."

Trev smiled inwardly as he remembered that gigantic umbrella and wondered how badly she pummeled the guy. A small snicker escaped.

"What!" she blurted. "You don't think I can take care of myself?"

"No. I just, well, I've seen that umbrella and I wondered what kind of damage you did to the poor guy."

"Poor guy, my ass. Look at my wrist, it's still bruised." She held up her arm for him to see the brown and yellow marks that were faded. He slid a finger across the discolored skin.

"Christ, it must have been completely black and blue then!" He surveyed it, then added, "You reported it right?"

"Yes, or at least I tried to, but I don't know who he is. I never got a name. So, there wasn't really much they could do. You can't really file a complaint against an unknown guy who grabbed you in the parking lot."

"Hmmm." Trev digested the information. He couldn't really determine whether it was just a random incident or associated with the other things. "When did you last see him?"

"He showed up here again the following Friday, but he just stood at the bar watching."

"What did you do?"

"I told the bartender about it and while I talked to him, the guy left. I half expected him to be waiting outside but he wasn't. He just left. Thomas offered to take me home just to be safe. Insisted on it, in fact."

"Good old Thomas. When we leave I want you to show me where you parked that night." He was matter of fact and didn't listen for a protest. "Do you still want to go back to your friends?"

"Not really, but it would be rude not to. If you need to get the reports and go, I can get them for you now."

"I'm not in a hurry. Besides, this is getting pretty interesting. Come on, let's go celebrate your buddy's birthday. By the way, he's really got a thing for you." He waited for her to rise out of the booth.

"Ancient history," she answered.

"So, you were *with him?*"

"Yes. No! Not like that. Not *with him* really. Like I said, ancient history."

"Don't be so sure about that." She might've seen it that way, but Thomas still thought otherwise. Trev followed her back to the table and stood behind her or next to her the remainder of the evening while he listened to the chatter and participated as infrequently as possible.

Thomas seethed as he watched Trev. Like one lion might watch another, both stalking the same prey. Trev pretended not to care. He found it humorous and Sophie seemed oblivious. He smiled at Thomas as if in complete control of the situation. At one point, Trev even touched his hand on the small of her back just to piss him off. Unfortunately, he hadn't expected her skin to feel so blazing hot and as soon as he did it, he dropped his hand back to his side. But not so soon that it wasn't noticed.

Thomas's eyes narrowed as he lifted his drink to his mouth. Sophie felt it, too, and shot a glance at Trev before returning to her conversation with her friends. She didn't smile, but she didn't slap him either, which intrigued him. God, he was enjoying this.

Sophie looked at her watch and leaned down to pick up her bag on the floor under the table. "Well, I need to get going, guys. I'm afraid I'm done for the day and there's something I need to take care of." She went around the table hugging everyone and stopped at Thomas.

"Thanks for coming, Soph." He hugged her.

"Happy Birthday, Thomas. I hope it was a great day for you." She pecked him on the cheek and gasped a short "ugh" as he grabbed her tighter and kissed her cheek, too.

"It was. Thanks so much for doing all this for me." He let her go and she started for the door, waving to everyone.

Trev wasn't really sure what to do. Should he follow her? Should he stay here a little bit then go?

"Are you coming, Trev?" She smiled, holding out a hand to beckon him. He thought the others would likely imagine a different type of invitation in her words. He sauntered after her, feeling like the cat that ate the canary. He didn't look back but he knew the daggers in Thomas's eyes would surely cut him in two if he turned around. It was just stupid competitive male pride, wanting everyone to think he attracted this gorgeous lady in front of him, but still he savored the feeling while it lasted.

"Why did you do that?" he asked pointedly when they moved

outside. He slid his hands into his pockets as he followed after her.

"Do what?"

"Let them think I was with you."

"I didn't know I did."

"Don't play games with me, lady. That's exactly what you did, and you know it."

"But you were, weren't you? With me. Not for reasons that they know about, but you were still there because I invited you, right?"

"Yes, but you let them think it was something else."

"No I didn't. I just didn't make them think it wasn't."

"Back to my question. Why did you do it?" He pulled his hands out of his pockets and rested them on his hips. He stopped and waited for an answer in the middle of the parking lot, not following her. When she saw he wasn't moving, she turned back.

"Because I want them all to leave me alone for a while, okay?" She sounded exasperated. "Callie is always trying to set me up with guys. I can't tell you how many jerks I've gone out with just to make her happy. It's irritating as hell . . . and Thomas is a hoverer—don't you see it? Always around, pressuring me to do this or that. I don't need everyone trying to run my life. To fix me or fix me up. I like the way I am. I don't want to be in a relationship right now, and if they think I already am, then maybe they'll just leave me alone."

"Oh, well . . . " He digested what she'd said, then broke into a slow grin. "Glad to be of service, then." Trevor scratched at his chin for a second. "Just curious. How far am I supposed to take this so your friends are convinced?" He teased her a little, but it was frustrating. Did she really think he was that harmless? That she could use him to run off the others?

"What do you mean?"

"Well, are we done now? Or am I supposed to show up again?" He frowned as he considered the implications of what happened.

"Don't you think it's wrong to use someone to make others stop trying to run your love life?"

He looked down at her. Even with those beautiful legs in heels, she still stood a good four or five inches shorter than he was. Her eyes blazed, full of fire right now. He'd hit a nerve.

"I'm not using you," she spat.

"Yes, you are." He matched her anger in his retort as he put his nose within an inch of hers and glared back at her. "And I walked right into it without a clue. Maybe you could have warned me, huh?"

As they stood there, facing each other down, the birthday party group burst out of the door behind them. They laughed as they stepped into the parking lot, arm in arm.

"Okay, missy. Game on. You wanted a show, you got it!" he muttered under his breath.

Trev put his hand behind Sophie's neck and pulled her to him, kissing her hard and quick, or at least he intended it to be quick but it wasn't. His mouth pressed against hers, forcefully burning into her own. Surprise hit him hard as he felt the need to search every section of her mouth, exploring and enjoying the moistness of her lips. The scent of her skin up close intoxicated him. He trailed his other hand up her side, resting it briefly against her rib cage then grasped her tightly as the kiss ended. "That should do the trick," he whispered against her mouth. Reluctantly he released her, turned, and started walking toward her car. She stood still and watched him move away.

Then he did exactly what she had done to him inside. He turned with a smile and said, "Are you coming, Soph?" Her mouth opened and she stared at him, her breathing short. Behind her, Callie let out a loud wolf whistle. Sophie's eyes burned into him. He was amazed at how much bigger they got when she was angry. He walked toward her car and stopped. His hands shook and his lips burned. He waited for her to follow.

"I have a question for you, Mr. Trevor Adams." Her voice was low and husky as she approached. She waved her car keys, and added, "Did you think that was funny? And . . . " She hesitated as she noticed their location. "How did you know this was my car?"

Trev surveyed the royal blue charger she pointed to, then glanced around the parking lot. He ignored the first question. He grabbed the keys she waved in his face and dangled the silver Dodge emblem on them in front of her. "I guessed. It's the only Dodge in the parking lot except for that truck at the back." He pointed at an old truck with the grill half-missing, and one fender a different color than the other. It looked like it wouldn't move. "You don't seem the type to drive something like that so this made sense."

"That's pretty observant of you." She reached for her keys.

He lifted them out of her reach. "Nope. Sorry. You don't need to be driving right now. There's a gas station two blocks over that's open all night. They have coffee and food, and a little room to sit. Let's go there and you can show me those reports you talked about." He glanced around, noticing that her friends were all gone. The streetlights splashed silver streaks across her hair and cheeks and she looked even more beautiful standing there challenging him.

"I don't really feel like it, Trevor. I just want to go home." She sighed and let her shoulders drop.

"Then I'll drive you."

"No!" She flashed another angry look at him.

"Why not?"

"Because I don't even know you. I'm not getting in a car with you."

"It's *your* car," he reminded her.

"Yes, but. Oh, okay, let's go get the coffee." She started walking toward the street corner to cross.

"What about the reports? Do you still want me to look at them? Or would you rather we just drop it now?"

"You have the keys. They're in the back on the floor."

Chapter Five

Gas stations in downtown Houston can attract all sorts of interesting people at late hours, basically the kind of people one should stay away from. For the general public, it's not a safe place to be after dark. The gas station was lit up like a circus, making it easy to manage.

In the far corner, two people argued . . . apparently a lovers' spat. They tried to keep their voices down but not very successfully. After a minute, the girl stormed out and the guy followed. At one of the tables in the small dining area, a guy, the only other person left in the place, had his head down. He looked to be sleeping—or passed out. The gas pumps outside had no customers. The attendant, a very thin man with dark, receding hair watched them warily from behind a Plexiglas window over the counter.

Trev purchased two large coffees and moved to a table as far away from the sleeping guy as possible so that he could keep an eye on him. Sophie followed.

Trev looked at the reports and listened as Sophie explained what she found and why it didn't seem to make sense. Nothing surprised him. Except her. She wasn't at all the person he thought. The bureau thought.

"I see what you mean. It sure doesn't look right to me either, but I can't really tell anything without looking at the database and seeing the transactions in data form. Can you get me a copy?"

"I don't know." Her voice was tired and drained. "Maybe this isn't necessary. I'm sure it's just a mistake. Let's just forget about it, okay? I don't want to waste your time anymore."

He glanced nervously out the window as a white Toyota pulled up to one of the gas pumps. The loud thumping of the music in the car reverberated such that he could feel it in his bones. He dropped one hand into his lap. His firearm fit snugly in his ankle holster. If he had to, he wanted to be ready. He bent his leg back under him. It frustrated him not to carry the firearm as he normally would. A young Hispanic man stepped out and started pumping gas. Trev watched him as he spoke to Sophie. "Are you sure? You seemed pretty concerned about it before." He switched his eyes to her face so that he could observe her expression. She wanted to be rid of him.

"That was before . . . " She mumbled. Her eyes fixated on his mouth. If it weren't for the guy outside, he'd find it fun, perhaps.

He continued to watch her intently and waited for her to finish her sentence. Her face changed to a rosy red and she looked away from him, gazing out the window to the street. From the corner of his eye, he noticed the young man slide back into his car and leave. He'd only pumped a few dollars of gas. Probably just enough to get him home for the night. It reminded him of high school and his first car. He'd done that at least a hundred times. Pumped just enough to get home, burning up his last few dollars. Trev relaxed and pulled both hands up to the tabletop.

Sophie let out a weary sigh. "You know, I'm pretty tired. Let's just call it a night for now, please?" She got up from her seat, gathered up the papers, and walked out.

Trev rushed out to step in beside her. He held her keys out to her. She reached for them without looking at him. He slipped his hands into his pockets and they walked the two blocks to her car silently. A brown Chevy Malibu whizzed by with two people in it, rushing to make the light as it turned yellow, then red. Once it passed, the streets remained empty as they strode back toward her car. She walked like it was a foot race. That was probably a good thing for this time of night. Best to get off the road as fast as possible.

"Sophie." He broke the silence when they reached the parking lot where her car sat alone. "You're upset and it's late, but you need to keep this in perspective. Forget all the other things tonight that led up to now. They don't matter. What you found in those reports could be pretty serious." He kept his voice low, but sincere.

"No, it's probably just a mistake." She dismissed him with the wave of a hand.

"It's not a mistake. At least, I really don't think so. If what I think is true, you could be in trouble. Don't take it lightly. Get me the data." No asking this time. If she didn't get it to him, he'd find another way. It wouldn't be the first time.

"Okay. Okay." Her voice was exasperated as she unlocked her car. She didn't look at him when she stepped in. "I can get it to you when you get back from your trip next week. I'm beginning to wonder why I got you involved in this to begin with."

"If there's one thing I've learned in my profession, it's to stick with your instincts. Too late for regrets now. I'll be back in town Thursday afternoon. I'll pick you up at five outside your building, unless you still have a problem getting in a car with me?" He tried to smile.

Sophie ignored his attempt at humor. "I'll see you Thursday." She left.

He wanted the data now before anything else went wrong, but it would wait. He watched her drive away and turned to walk toward his apartment. He didn't want to hear Nate or the others ranting about the kiss right now, so he didn't bother to check in, but he appreciated the car trailing after her from a distance. After what she told him and what he knew happened to Bob, if she wasn't part of it, then danger trailed her. From everything he'd seen so far, she wasn't involved.

Chapter Six

The jacket draped over the back of the chair unleashed a gentle smile from Sophie as she brushed her fingers across it. Yes, it wasn't the most flattering color or style—she preferred bold and classy, whereas this jacket was more rumpled and comfortable. However, the sentiment behind it embodied her transformation over the past couple of years since her mother passed.

She reminisced about the bright red coat worn throughout her mother's illness. It had been unseasonably cold in Chicago and that jacket became a staple of every visit to the hospital as the cancer progressed. At the time, she considered it not just utilitarian, but a symbol of bravery and resiliency. Afterward, it became painful to look at. She remembered the discussion with Callie vividly a few months post-funeral. A new staff member, Callie and Sophie had yet to find a comfort with each other. Sophie needed to talk though, and Callie just happened to be present at that moment.

"I can't even open my closet without seeing the red coat I wore to the hospital every day. It's a constant reminder of how different she became from the strong, dynamic woman that raised me. I doubt I'll ever wear that beautiful coat again."

"Then we need to do a wardrobe intervention!" Callie exclaimed as they stood in the hallway at work. "I'll be at your house tonight at seven and we'll take care of that coat. It's time for you to get a new start." She wasn't referring to the coat but that was a good beginning.

Callie showed up at her house that night right on time. They took the red coat to the shelter and donated it, then went on a shopping trip for a replacement. The goal was to get something so completely different that it would be the beginning of Sophie's new start . . . her solo start. Unfortunately, by the time they arrived at the stores, closing time loomed less than an hour away and the choices were slim. Thus, after a short while searching for something in the few remaining open shops, Sophie gave up . . . but not Callie.

When Callie had something set in her mind, she didn't stop until she achieved the goal. That's what Sophie liked about her. And admittedly, they were very similar in most situations. As Sophie sat in the food court at the mall, sipping a tea, Callie presented her with a bag from one of the shops. Inside rested the brownish tan coat that eventually became Sophie's staple. They celebrated by going out for coffee and dessert. The coat wasn't pretty. It wasn't flattering, and definitely the most god-awful color Sophie had ever seen. But, for some reason, it delivered a perfect transition from the bold red garment. Most importantly, Callie gave her a chance to go out and enjoy herself; to stop thinking about the fact that her only living relative would no longer be a part of her life. They made a pact that they would take a night out at least every other week just to keep each other sane. Sophie was never so thankful to find such a friend. It amazed her that they had become so close in such a short time.

Trevor's thoughtfulness in returning the jacket was commendable. The sentiment around the jacket far outweighed the appearance. It was symbolic, now, and Sophie admitted herself a sucker for symbolic gestures.

Of course, he didn't know what the jacket represented, but still he wanted to return it, and she appreciated the gesture. Her hand went to her mouth, remembering her last encounter with him. He could have just put an arm around her or held her hand. That would have been sufficient. But he kissed her. Boy, did he kiss her. Just thinking about it made her nerves turn to Jell-O.

Her mother would have thought him boring, too straight-laced and stiff. Brianna Henderson abhorred anything stiff or straight-laced. She typified the word rebel. After all, she had raised Sophie on her own, despite the many potential alternatives that came her way. Sophie admired that she'd never given so much as a thought to the men that came around. Brianna was beautiful and smart, a tenured history professor at the university—something that came with hardship. She was also the first and only black female professor for the first five years of her career at the school. She maintained that position by knowing which battles to fight as well as which ones to walk away from. She was a champion for change, but in a way that didn't come off as abrasive or challenging. What Sophie didn't know until right after her mother died was the source of that strength. It resided, in part, due to Sophie's father's influence.

Sophie had always thought her father left them during her toddler stage. That's all she knew and Brianna hadn't corrected her. When Sophie met her dad again after the illness took most of the vibrancy from her mother's eyes, anger bubbled under every word and gesture between them. If they hadn't been in the hospital room with her mother at the time, Sophie probably would not have given him a minute.

"Honey, do you remember when we went to New York to live with your Uncle James?" Brianna prompted in a weak raspy voice, with this strange man's hand holding her mother's.

"Not really, I was only four or five at the time. I remember us being in a great big apartment and a big, white, four-poster bed in my room with a pink ruffle around the top. I remember Uncle James being a very kind man and taking me to the park on the weekends. That's about all I remember."

"Well, I wasn't completely honest with you about that, or a few other things. I'm sorry I didn't tell you sooner, honey. This is Uncle James. This man, right here. Only, he's not your uncle. He's your father. Sophie, I'd like you to meet Randolph James Henderson." Brianna gestured her free hand at the man in the room with her.

"Randolph James Henderson, the New York real estate mogul? My father?" Sophie was completely dazed as she looked from one face to the other. Now, she placed the face—from the newspapers and television that featured him every few months. He looked different in person. Still tall, but more gray-haired and haggard. His face permanently tanned, but drawn and wrinkled. As she looked at him, she knew it was true. Anyone that looked at them side by side would see the resemblance. "Why are you here, now? After all this time?"

He shook his head. "Your mother insisted I stay away. When you were little, I went to New York when I got the job working for the mayor's office. I worked there for a little over a year before your mother was able to get away from the university and come to New York with you."

Sophie stared at him, furious. No matter what the story, it couldn't excuse the years she and her mother had struggled. She had come to terms with his absence and now was proud of her mother's ability to cope, as well as her own, but then he was a worthless deadbeat that ran out on them. Wait, he was still a worthless deadbeat, he just wasn't poor, she thought.

Brianna stepped in to help him. "Your dad didn't leave us, honey. I left him. I hated New York. The city life, the constant parties. I hated people staring at us all the time." Her voice became weaker and her breathing a little less regular. "When your dad first started, we struggled financially, but he always had the golden touch. He could turn water into money." She smiled at him and stroked his cheek gently.

"So, you gave up?" Sophie asked. She didn't say it but in her mind she added, *Like you're giving up now.*

"No." The gray-haired man's voice strong and reprimanding, as if to warn her not to go where she tread. "When I made our first few big acquisitions of real estate there, our names and pictures started to become prevalent in the local papers, mostly the 'small town kids do good' type of articles. Some people didn't like us together—they didn't say it but we knew. Some people just can't get past the color of a person's skin enough to know what's underneath. When the first threat came against you, we ignored it as an isolated incident. After the fourth, your mother packed you up and took you home. She was not about to have you live in an environment of intolerance or have to shadow you every minute to keep you safe."

Brianna squeezed his hand. "That wasn't the only reason."

"I know, but you shouldn't have even thought about that. Time would have resolved that issue," he responded.

"Your dad was in the limelight then, a good candidate for political office. He invested smartly and made a name for himself. My presence remained a detriment. That would have been tolerable for just the two of us, but not for a child at that time even in New York."

"That's ridiculous. I can't believe after all that you've taught me that you would have backed down from that," Sophie spouted.

"Perhaps it was silly looking back now. At the time, it seemed the right thing to do for you and for James." So, she called him James not Randolph or Randy? Of course, Randolph is too pompous and Randy is too juvenile. James fit.

"When your mother went home, she managed to get her old job back at the university. I went down four times to try to convince her to return with me but she refused. That was not the life she wanted for you." *So you just gave up, too.* They could build empires and great careers, but they couldn't build a life together?

"I'm sorry, Sophie." Her mother looked at her sadly.

"Why would you let me think Dad didn't want me?" Sophie looked at her mother, trying to suppress the hurt and anger. She turned to him. "And why would you just give up? You never came back again. Never talked to me! Nothing." She couldn't talk about it anymore. She got up and left the room. Left the hospital. That was Sophie's last conversation with her mother before Brianna, her last task in life complete, left this world.

As Sophie remembered strained meetings with her father after the funeral, she struggled to control the emotions. He tried hard to spend time with her, but years of absence made it almost impossible to catch up. They were complete strangers. Sophie found herself unable to understand or forgive the silent years of her childhood.

Sophie didn't talk about her dad to anyone. She wasn't embarrassed by him, but she made a place in this world on her own and she wanted it to stay that way. In a way, she guessed that was probably a trait she'd inherited from him. She didn't want to be defined by her rich father, even though on numerous occasions, he asked her to come to New York to attend events with him and his new wife.

Sophie sighed as she picked up the jacket from the back of the chair and returned it to the closet near the entrance to her apartment. Everything that she had believed about her life three years ago evolved completely differently. She turned out the lights and retreated to her bedroom.

Chapter Seven

From the street, the FBI Branch Office at 1 Justice Drive in Houston looked like any other office building in the area—a sleek, shimmering structure with beautiful glassed windows, rising from the street.

The box of files that Trev carried containing the information on Benton & Stanley's staff came from this office. Generic information, a one pass effort to glean the basics related to his case. He marked several of the files for review and intended to work with Cheryl Harper, one of the key analysts, to delve deeper into the lives of some of the individuals.

The next four days at the office would consist of staff meetings where he would update his supervisor on the status of his cases, the primary one focused on Benton & Stanley. After the update, he'd spend the remainder of the week with Cheryl and other staff researching the files he'd brought with him. Trev dreaded parts of it. He knew he'd get some flack on his interactions with Sophie. While he had trailed her and the others almost full-time lately, his focus up until a couple of months ago centered on multiple smaller cases. The incident with Bob brought this case to the forefront; all other efforts were subsequently sidelined so this one could be moved along at a faster pace.

Fraud against the government was always a matter for federal investigation, but once it became life-threatening to citizens, the criticality in solving the case escalated and more resources were involved. Trev and his team excelled in the details. That was the beauty of technology—there was always a trail. Even for those who think they've cleaned it, tiny little pieces of telltale data like tracks in snow remained, and his team knew how to look for it.

Sophie's file was in the box, too, but he intended to focus more on the others this time around. His background in technology and psychological profiling were normally pretty accurate. She didn't fit—or maybe he just didn't want her to fit.

First on the agenda—his update meeting with his supervisor.

"Okay, where do you want to start?" Cook asked matter-of-factly. Cook's first name was Stephanos but he hated it. No one dared to use the name. He'd supposedly even once threatened to fire someone for doing so. Rumor or not, Trev never took a chance on it. Cook heard the updates so many times he had a pseudo-routine for his staff. They presented the updates in whatever form they chose. Then he prodded for details or if concerns arose. He recorded the discussions and then had his assistant compile it into an agency overall report. Confidential items were marked as such and compiled separately. All paper reports ran through the shredder when they left the meeting, and the data handed to his assistant was encrypted as required.

Cook adjusted the collar of his shirt and picked up a pen, keeping it hovered over the notepad in front of him. Trev normally documented his cases electronically and provided a paper copy for the meetings, knowing it wouldn't leave the room. The electronic copy was transmitted to their secured server in a folder for each case. The team and Cook were the only ones with access to view the information.

"Let me just give you status updates on the cases that are either closed or in the final phases." Trev began.

"The Katrina and Rita work?"

"Yes."

"Is it necessary? There's not much new is there? Aren't they all in litigation right now?"

"Yes, for the most part. Nate and I were summoned to testify on two of them in a couple months. Other than that, no changes."

"Good. Let's don't waste time on those then. Let me know how it goes in court. What about the Benton & Stanley case? Anything new with the girl?" Cook asked.

"I got too close."

"I heard." Cook watched him.

He explained details of the night of the storm.

Cook narrowed his eyes and listened. "Sounds like excuses to me. Nate didn't warn you?"

"I guess his vision was also impaired by the rain. He tried to help. Anyway, it turned out fine. Good, actually. I met with her a couple of times since. She showed me the reports that Greenwood mentioned. He was right. Someone is skimming money—and it's not pocket change. From what little I saw, we're talking big money. Millions, two or three at least."

Cook wrote a couple of notes on the white pad in front of him, then sat back and continued listening.

"I met a few of her friends. I want Cheryl to dig a little deeper on them, as well as her administrative assistant, and a couple of people in the finance department," Nate said while Cook wrote more notes on the pad.

"Not a problem. Give her the names, the details. She'll get it. Or just pass it all to Nate to handle." Cook shook his head. "No, not Nate. Forgot. He's visiting his family over the next couple of days. He'll be back before you meet her again, though. You heard?" He referred to Nate's dad.

"Yeah, that's a shame. I don't know his Dad that well. Met him a couple of times. Good guy." Trev rolled his pen back and forth between his fingers. "I hope it all works out."

"Me, too," Cook agreed. "Be prepared. He might be off-focus for a little while."

"Understood. So, if you know he'll be back in time for my next meet, then you know Sophie—"

"Sophie?" Cook's eyebrows lifted. "You're already using first names?"

"Yeah." Trev ignored the remark, which was half-hearted at best. "I meet her again Thursday evening. She's getting me a backup of the database. As soon as it's in my hands, I'll get it to the data forensics guys." He scooted back in his chair and looked out the window. Trev knew what to expect and braced himself for the questions and the warnings. How long were they going to side-step? Cook already knew about the kiss. You can't hide anything when followed.

"So, you didn't just get too close in the rain," Cook said. He didn't look up, just wrote a few more notes on his tablet. This was his way of asking.

"Yeah. But it turned out okay. Didn't it?"

"You tell me." He leaned over the table now, his hands clasped together on top of the pad he wrote in. The man was a master of saying everything with just an expression. Right now, he simply frowned.

"For all she knows, I'm just a colleague, and it was a method of showing I had her back. I guess in a way, it served to build trust." If Cook's eyebrows weren't already up, he'd have sworn they rose even more. Then he looked down at the pad in front of him, exhaling a sigh of disbelief.

"Is that right? And you want to take that further." It wasn't a question. Trev knew he'd screwed up. He didn't need a reminder, but this felt like a sitting with a shrink. Cook didn't move for a minute or two, then added, "Be careful. You're getting pretty close to crossing the line."

"I know. It's under control."

"Really? Is it? I've seen her," Cook reminded him.

Trev's temper flared, "If you have something to say or you want me off the case, then do it. Otherwise, let's drop this right now. I told you it's under control. I get what you're trying to say, but there's one thing you need to remember." He leaned forward over the table and jammed his forefinger on the polished surface. "Just from the short amount of time I've spent with her, we obtained more information than we were able to get the past few weeks. If I keep this going, we should be able to close this out in no time. And, I know you don't believe it, but she's *not* the perp. I've done this long enough to know." He shoved his chair back and stood up to walk toward the window and look down on the street. "Besides, you know others have done much, much worse in the past. I'm a fucking saint compared to, well, most of these guys."

"Others—maybe. Not you, and that doesn't make it right. Don't take it somewhere you can't get back from." Cook surveyed his pen thoughtfully before continuing. "Anyhow, I'm not making changes right now. Just keep going. But you need to back off a little if you know what I mean."

"You don't have to tell me that, but what am I supposed to do if she doesn't back off? She doesn't know who I am. If I stop it cold, then what happens?" Trev turned, slipped his hands in his pockets and challenged Cook.

"Good point." Cook tapped his pen on the table surface a few times, thinking. "Just play it out, I guess. But be careful."

"Can we get back to the case itself? Judging by what I've seen so far, they'll probably go after her just like they did Greenwood."

"Then I guess it's good she trusts you, right?" Cook tapped the pen again and rubbed his neck with his other hand. "Sit down. I'm getting a crick in my neck looking at you." He gestured with the pencil to the chair that Trev lunged out of earlier. "Tell me about her friends."

Trev pulled out four manila folders and slid them across the table to Cook. "The top one's her assistant, Anna Kinnier. Then Callie Madison, the best friend. She's also one of Sophie's analysts. Next is Jake Wellborn, a beginning programmer. And Thomas Brand. Thomas is also a programmer but I think there's a relationship there—or maybe there was at one time. I've put what I know in the notes on each file." He motioned for Cook to open Anna's file and started talking again. "I don't have much on any of these guys and the files are lame, at best."

Cook frowned. "Why's that?"

"Everyone concentrated on Sophie and the accounting

department head, I guess." Knowing what he knew about Nate now, he wondered if Nate hadn't followed up on these yet simply because his thoughts focused on his Dad. "I had planned to get with Cheryl after this and start working on them."

"Good. Then don't let me keep you. And I want an update before you leave on Thursday. Tell me what you find on these guys." Cook pushed the manila folders back to Trev and motioned at the door, then he flipped his cell phone open. "Cook here," he blurted into the phone as he waved and turned his back.

Trev walked down the hall to Cheryl's office. He didn't knock, just walked in and stood over her desk.

"Good morning, Trev." Cheryl's eyes looked up over the reading glasses that perched dangerously low on the end of her nose. "How's the investigation going?"

Cheryl's ability to dig out seemingly unimportant but helpful details had helped many an employee bring closure to their cases during her many years with the agency. She had the unfortunate curse of looking older than her forty-three years, especially with the addition of the reading glasses. In her twenties and thirties, she admitted to wearing them to appear smarter so she'd be taken more seriously on the job. She refused to allow her abilities diminished by her small stature and feminine looks. Her ability to look older than her years was a great asset then as it gave her a look of experience and credibility. What she lacked in experience, she over-exuded in intelligence and perseverance. Now, though, the glasses proved a necessity and less important as a tool to support her many years of proven excellence on the job.

"It could be better, which is why I'm in the office the next few days. There're a few people I'll need your help on. I'm fairly certain one of the lead targets we've been tailing has little or nothing to do with the investigation. Plus, I want to pull a few things on each and every staff member in the accounting and IT departments. No one really sticks out right now, but I'm pretty sure that if we get the bank records, as well as personal property information on some of them, we'll see some alarms. I also want job history, home addresses for the last ten years, and purchase history, if you can get it."

"No problem." Cheryl gave him a professional smile. "Bank record requests and purchase history usually take two to three days for that large a group but it shouldn't be a problem. What else?"

"Here's a list of the names. The files are minimal on these and it's not enough to really work with. Start with the top one there. If I could get that as soon as possible, it would help tremendously." Trev decided to take a different approach than he'd been instructed. He wanted to concentrate first on the staff around Sophie and the accounting manager. "Here's what I'm looking for on each person." Trev handed the list of names and details to Cheryl.

By four p.m., Trev had addresses, phone numbers, family details, past employers, and past addresses on Anna and Jake. Thomas and Callie required more time. Cheryl unearthed criminal background checks and credit information. She had relationship status, aliases, family members, and details of all available criminal and civil cases. Trev sat at the conference room table and spread the information out in organized piles. Most of the information came in electronic form and he'd do further analysis with the data itself, but this was a start. Once he'd seen enough, he pulled his cell phone from his pocket and dialed Nate.

"Hey, man, are you busy?"

"I'm always busy. What do you need?"

"I need someone to tag another person for a few days. Just a few days, shouldn't require much. I want to know everyone she talks to, everywhere she goes, where she lives if it doesn't match what we already have, what she does on her off time, etc. Get as many pictures as possible. Then I want to do the same with another person. Can you do it or is there anyone else available? They're both women. Her assistant and a friend."

"Is this related to the current case?"

"I think so, but it may not be anything. I just have a hunch."

"Okay. Send me the address and I'll get someone on it. You know I'm going to see my dad, right?"

"Oh, yeah. Sorry. Can you get someone on it before you leave? And just update me if something's found?"

"Sure, no problem."

"Sorry to bother you, man," Trev said.

"No bother. I'll be back Thursday morning. I'll check in with you as soon as I hear something."

"Great! Thanks!" Trev hung up and sent the address for Sophie's assistant Anna Kinnier via text to Nate. He leaned back in his chair and sat there looking at the file in front of him. He wondered if Benton & Stanley had done background checks on their staff recently. Two of Sophie's friends—ones he'd met—had records. One a simple possession charge, the other aggravated assault. The assault charge on Thomas set off warning bells, even though it eventually dropped off his record. The possession charge from six years earlier was on her best friend—and it wasn't just a marijuana charge, either. People with that history sometimes carried residual problems. He wondered if she remained clean, if she'd stayed out of trouble and away from her past associates.

Trev sat in a car in the parking garage when Thomas Brand and Sophie came from the building. They talked as they strolled to their cars, then she moved past him. Trev had made sure to choose a dark corner where his presence couldn't be seen. Sophie's car exited the garage and drove away, but Trev wasn't concerned about that. He planned to tag Thomas tonight. The background file on him had shown a criminal record as well as an alias. That, along with the assault charge, was enough to suggest good old Thomas concealed a past he wanted hidden. At least he wanted to conceal it from Benton & Stanley.

Trev spent the next two days following Thomas. By Wednesday night, he decided nothing about Thomas indicated involvement.

The guy had a pretty colorful past for sure, but his interest in Sophie was apparently just that. Thomas had been in a lot of trouble up until he turned twenty, spent some time in jail for the theft of a four-wheeler that he totaled while joyriding with friends. He then cleaned up his act and started going to college at night while working days for a roofing company. A New Jersey transplant, he left there when he graduated. He moved to Houston with a new degree in computer science and a new name. The new name didn't make sense. Trev figured he'd ask Cheryl to check that.

Thomas frequented a health club on Smith Street, where he sometimes spent a couple of hours or more working out at night. Trev watched from outside as much as he could, but never really saw Thomas talk to anyone other than the staff. According to the file, the assault charge occurred at the health club. One of the staff eagerly provided the details. It was filed by a girlfriend he'd dumped. Apparently, she wasn't very happy about being jilted and attacked him in the parking lot. He tried to hold her off and in the process knocked her down. Later, when he threatened to file charges also, hers were dropped.

The sound of his cell phone jolted Trev back to reality as he sat outside the health club Wednesday night. He chewed on the stir stick from the coffee he'd purchased at the drive-thru earlier, remembering a skirt, heels, and the song "Suzie Q." Not like him to drift off like that. He frowned.

"Yeah?" he muttered into the phone without dropping the stick in his mouth.

"The first chick was apparently boring as hell, man." Nate didn't say hello or how's it going, he just stepped straight to the facts. "She has two kids. She gets them right after work and goes home. She lives with her mom—or her mom lives with her, I don't know which it is. I can find out if you want. Other than that, there's nothing. She gets very few calls and isn't seeing anyone."

That pretty much matched with the information Cheryl derived.

"Okay, well I thought it might be good to check her out. She's Henry's—I mean Sophie Henderson's assistant, so she might have access to all her email, passwords, etc." He mentally crossed one name off the list. "What about the other girl?"

"That's a little more interesting." Nate baited Trev a little, making him wait for the details. "Callie's residence didn't match with the records. She's in an apartment that she's only had for the past four months. Prior to that she lived down in Stafford."

"Why does that matter? People move all the time."

"The address she lives at now is two blocks from Sophie," Nate added flatly. "Before Stafford she lived in New York and worked for a large real estate company in their IT department."

"Really? She doesn't sound like a New Yorker."

"She's not. She graduated from Stephen F. Austin in ninety-nine and took an internship in New York. Apparently she hated it and moved back to Texas the following year."

"Okay, so she moved close to her friend and decided to get away from the cold. What else?" Trev didn't see any relevance yet on her, either. He began to think he'd wasted everyone's time on these other people.

"There's a boyfriend, too. A really creepy guy—dark hair, dark mood, and around almost every night. Gone by morning."

"No kidding? She acted like she was single and looking when I met her the other night."

"From what I'm told, this is not the kind of guy you bring home to Mom or introduce to your friends."

"Hmmm. Maybe he's not really a boyfriend."

"Probably not, more like a boy toy if you ask me. Some girls really like the bad boys. Hell, most girls like the bad boys." Nate's voice remained monotone.

"Yeah, and speaking from a guy's perspective, we're all bad boys, given the chance. You know you'd give your right arm to be someone's boy toy." Trev laughed at the possibility.

"Hell, yeah. Who wouldn't?" An appreciative chuckle came through the phone.

"Okay. Well, thanks man. Oh, hey. How's your dad doing?"

"So far, so good. He hasn't had any more fainting spells but he's taking it easy. They've scheduled surgery for next week. Putting in a pacemaker. I'm still coming back tomorrow, though. It's really weird being here. Like everyone's just watching every step he takes, waiting for him to fall or something. We're all driving him nuts. My sisters are crying all the time. I've got to get out of here."

"I don't blame you. I'm not very good at that kind of thing either, but it's good that you went."

"Yeah, I know. I'm glad I came, too."

They hung up. Trev found it interesting, and vaguely odd that Callie entertained a life Sophie didn't know about. They seemed to be best friends. Normally your best friend is the first one you talk to about that kind of fling. They might find it exciting to talk about this bad boy, sex-capade thing, wouldn't they? Maybe not.

Thursday, Trev waited outside the front door of the Benton & Stanley building, perched against one of the concrete abstract art pieces that graced the front of the building. He considered it might be disrespectful to lean against something they likely paid several thousand dollars to put in, but to him it was just a chunk of ugly concrete. Apparently the birds agreed with the analogy. The top of it was completely covered in bird crap. At least three birds roosted on it at that moment, about five feet above. A sign in front of it talked about the artist and what the piece represented. *Amazing that people actually get paid for this stuff.*

Sophie found him looking up at the birds to make sure he didn't become a target when she approached.

"Hey there," she said with a hint of a smile. Apparently, she was over her angry mood from the other night.

"Hey yourself. Ready to go?" he responded lightly.

"I thought I'd just give you the data and then you can be on your way, if that's okay." She started to reach into her purse.

"No." Trev grabbed her arm and glanced around the area looking for familiar faces, of which he saw two. An older, gray-haired gentleman on her staff, along with her assistant. Both seemed to be rushing off to lunch, headed in different directions. "Let's get out of here. I have some questions for you." He pulled her into step beside him and walked with her toward his car, parked down the street.

"Why can't you ask me here?"

"Too many people around. I think it would be better to be somewhere where no one sees you handing me data from your office, don't you?"

"Oh, okay. Although I don't know that anyone would notice."

"Probably not. Better safe than sorry."

"You make it sound so clandestine." She giggled. "Like we're spies and I'm passing you secret information."

Trev grinned to lighten the mood a little. No need to alarm her unnecessarily. "Do I? Sorry," he said sheepishly.

"Where are we going?" Sophie asked later as they drove down the street headed south, out of the city.

"I don't really know. I didn't make a plan." Trev thought about taking her to dinner, or maybe a movie, but that would be kind of "date-ish" and as much as he'd enjoy it, it wouldn't fit what she expected of him. This merely presented a chance for her to give him the data so he could start digging into the transactions. Still, he was hungry.

"Then why don't I just give you this," she pulled a USB drive out of her bag and placed it on the car's console, "and you can take me home." He clenched his jaw at her apparent rush to get away from him.

"I could do that." He said it very slowly then looked at her sideways. "Do you have plans this evening that you're in a hurry to get to?"

"What?" she seemed startled. "No, not really. I just didn't want to take up any more of your time." Her stare made him uncomfortable. She kept looking at his mouth. His thoughts shot back to the kiss he'd forced on her in the parking lot last week.

"If I was worried about that, I wouldn't be here." Trev pulled the car into a small parking lot and killed the engine.

"Oh, well . . . "

He turned to face her. "Listen, you're uncomfortable because I kissed you, right?"

"Well. Yeah, of course."

"Just forget it. Consider it over with. It was just to help you out of a bind, okay?" He watched her face, noticing that her cheeks seemed to have a little more color and her lips, full and shiny with lip-gloss. She looked fantastic. He wanted to smash his lips against hers again and lick the lip gloss off. Forget it? Yeah right. Easier to say than do.

"I didn't really need your help. I can take care of my own problems," she said.

"Then why did you put me in the position of playing the part of a non-existent boyfriend?" He arched a brow at her, unsmiling.

Sophie shrugged and turned to look out the front window. "I don't know. You were there, and you were just so . . . "

"So, what? So safe?" His interest was piqued.

"No. So . . . so . . . sexy! Okay?" She blurted it out. "There. Is that what your ego wanted to hear?"

Trev was startled at first. Then his lips twisted into a grin. "That's not really what I expected to hear, but I guess I like it."

"Shut up. I'm sure you've heard that before."

"No. I've been called a lot of things, but that's never been one of them." He observed her obvious discomfort. He would catch hell about this when he talked to Nate again. The guy was probably laughing his ass off just listening. He pressed the button to turn off the listening device. They'd just have to let him wing it from here. "So, did it measure up?"

"Measure up? What do you mean?"

"The kiss. Did it meet expectations?" He quirked an eyebrow, enjoying the fact that she squirmed a little under his scrutiny.

"Stop it, Trev. You're messing with me." She twisted a curl between her fingers and looked out over the dashboard, averting her eyes.

"That's not an answer, Henry. You sidestepped the question." He pulled the curl from her hand and looked at it briefly before shifting his eyes to hers. "Did the kiss fulfill your goal to ward off your friends?"

"Oh." Her fingers were fumbling against each other now as she averted her eyes from his. "Yes, I suppose so—as fake kisses go."

"There was nothing fake about it, Henry, but go ahead and tell yourself that if you want to." He watched her fidgeting with curiosity, his eyes glancing slowly across her face and down to her lips. "I'm hungry." He wanted to change the subject. This repertoire was interesting but uncomfortable. He wasn't one to discuss this type of thing, never had been. He usually bought the girl a drink or two, maybe dinner. If luck smiled on him, he got to spend a few hours in bed with her and then he left. Sophie wasn't the type for that. The only woman he ever stayed with, well, that didn't turn out so great. Trev pulled the keys from the ignition and opened the door to get out of the car. "Come on, let's eat."

He left her sitting in the car and came around to open the door, not looking at her as she stepped out. She wasn't making it easy, though.

"What's the plan now?" she challenged him.

"No plan. I'm hungry. I'm going in here to eat. If you don't want to come, then you can leave or wait in the car," Trev explained. As much as he liked looking at her, he wasn't interested in any more tap dancing around whatever they had going on.

"Wow, you're a real charmer."

"I wasn't trying to be," he answered smartly.

"That's a relief, because you were failing miserably."

Trev held the door for Sophie to enter the restaurant in front of him. The strong smell of garlic and oregano hit them. He stood in the entry, his chest almost touching her back, and he got the hint of that spicy perfume again for a second. He leaned down to speak softly in her ear as he stood behind her at the door, "I liked your first description of me better, anyway."

Sophie's big eyes darted a quick look up at him just as a small chubby man hustled up to them and clasped Trevor's hand. "So good to see you, my friend, and wonderful to finally meet your beautiful lady. Come right this way. I have a great table for you." The man motioned for them to follow.

Sophie fell in behind the man, turning to look at Trevor with her eyes arched. "He knows you?" she mouthed at him. Trevor nodded and followed, watching the curls bounce loosely on her shoulders.

Dinner was exceptional, as he knew it would be. An hour later, they left the restaurant having consumed a bottle of wine, two wonderful dinners, and a shared dessert, which Sophie reluctantly ate because Trevor insisted.

"That was fabulous!" she admitted eagerly, her macadamia nut size eyes glowing.

"Glad you liked it. That's one of my favorite restaurants. I eat there every Thursday unless work interferes."

"Don't you get tired of it?"

"No, they pretty much pamper me because I'm there so much. And I bring a lot of people with me."

Sophie wore an unreadable expression as she asked, "A lot of girlfriends?"

He laughed. "No. Didn't you notice that they thought you were 'my beautiful lady' when we arrived? I've been here with a lot of clients and coworkers, but not women."

"I thought he probably said that to every girl you brought in there," she remarked.

"I wish I had that kind of luck," Trev responded as he opened the car door and held it for her. The wind was blowing gently. Another waft of the spicy perfume hit him as he eased the door closed and he caught himself, before letting out a groan.

With Sophie's directions, they arrived at her apartment in less than fifteen minutes. "Just let me out here." Sophie motioned to a fifteen-minute parking spot in front of the main entrance to the apartment complex.

"I'd rather walk you up if you don't mind." He didn't just drop a woman at the door no matter who she was.

"It's really not necessary."

He frowned. It irritated him that she resisted such a little thing that was really safer for her in the long run. "Too bad." He pulled into a short-term parking spot and got out of the car. By the time he had circled the car to open her door, she was already out and walking toward the entrance.

"You're a little scary with that old-fashioned stuff," she mentioned lightly.

"I wouldn't exactly call good manners old fashioned. I was brought up this way and it's just become second nature. I don't notice I'm doing it most of the time but I doubt I'd stop anyway. It's respectful."

Trev glanced around the apartment complex, taking in her environment as they advanced up the stairs and approached the door to her apartment. Everything was pretty quiet.

"Thanks for the dinner and the company." Sophie put her key in the door and turned it.

"I should thank you actually for saving me from lightning and for trusting me with your security issue." It sounded dumb, he knew, but he was stalling. He watched as she opened the door and slipped partially inside. She turned and stood facing him in the doorway. The curls were escaping from the knot at the base of her neck; they framed her face gently. Trev grasped one of the curly strands in his fingers, rubbing it between his thumb and forefinger, "and if you ever need more help with that other issue, just let me know."

"Very funny," she shot back as she tossed her head to remove her hair from his grasp. "And what exactly would that entail anyway? Kissing me in front of my office for everyone to see? Or maybe feeling me up, too? Pretending to have sex?" He watched her face redden as she looked down at her shoes.

"I'm not much at pretending, but any and all of that sounds good to me." He flashed a devilish smile and leaned in, putting his face and mouth directly in front of her. "Or would you prefer to take care of it yourself?"

Sophie answered with a question of her own. "Why do you do that?"

"What exactly?" he said softly, his lips barely moving.

"Get too close and then start doing that animal magnetism thing," she answered breathlessly.

"I could say the same thing about you. Why do you do it?" The warmth was there, between them, smoldering gently.

"I don't. I'm not."

"Oh, yes you are." It angered him a little that she was so beautiful and that he wasn't immune to it as he should be. He could hear the warning bells going off and Cook telling him to back off again.

"No! I don't do that. I'm not like that."

"The hell you don't," he said. "I mean aren't. Look at you. Shit, your eyes are inviting me in but you're pretending you don't want it."

"Stop talking like that." She put a hand to his chest, pushing him back, but he just moved in closer.

"Then stop looking at me like that," he whispered.

Trev couldn't help himself then. She was gorgeous. He crushed his lips to hers, gently at first but in seconds he was overwhelmed with the need to taste more. He pressed his mouth harder against hers, thrusting his tongue between the fullness of her beautiful rounded lips and rubbing the wetness of her mouth. He wrapped an arm around her waist and pulled her against him, feeling the warmth of her chest and hips sear into his. Somewhere in the back of his brain, common sense told him to back off but the rest of him didn't listen. He wasn't very gentle and didn't intend to be. He wanted a response and was determined to have it. He knew she felt it, too. He wanted her to kiss him back. He put his other hand behind her neck as his lips wandered over her face and nibbled at her ear. He heard her suck in her breath sharply. He returned to her mouth, her lips were plump and open, inviting him in again. He should stop, he told himself again. Stop. Just do it. Back away.

Then Sophie grabbed the sides of his face with both hands and strained his mouth to hers, her tongue feeding on his. Caught off guard, Trev staggered against the doorjamb, steadying himself against the hard lumber as desire surged through him. Sophie moaned a low pitched, sexy sound and he matched it with a guttural groan that escaped without his consent. The kiss deepened and his lips were throbbing from the feel of her tongue against his. *Is this really happening?* he asked himself. She was insatiably sensual as she clung to him. He tried to string some rational thoughts together and remind himself that he was in control. This needed to end. But she had her fingers tangled in his hair and was pulling him in. Her hand moved up the inside of his shirt to his back. *Wait,* he thought. *Who, exactly, is in control, again?*

Trev pulled back, gulping air, forcing distance between them and disengaging himself from her grip. "Yeah," he teased, "not an ounce of animal magnetism in you." His breathing was ragged as he bent down and playfully bit her lip. "Good night, Henry."

Trev removed himself from her doorway and descended the steps to the parking lot. The faster he got away from this apartment complex, the more likely he wouldn't do something really, really foolish. Like sleep with a suspect. Kissing her was stupid enough. What the hell was he thinking? He didn't look back. Too dangerous. He knew he was treading on thin ice and could just imagine what Cook would say next time. He shrugged his shoulders nonchalantly. At the moment he didn't care. She had practically devoured him. Unfortunately, he realized he would let her do it again in a heartbeat. In fact, he wanted her to. Control? Who was he kidding? He had to go and fast.

Chapter Eight

Lenny listened to the mumbling of voices at the door, knowing it was only a matter of time before he was discovered. He needed to act quickly and get out of her apartment, preferably without being seen. Most definitely with the reports she'd brought home. There was no way to explain breaking into his boss' apartment, so he had to get out. Now. He had already made the adjustments to the system to clear the trail and rectify the reports earlier in the day. He just needed to destroy the printed copies she'd run. They were the only copies, and once she ran them again, she'd just think she made a mistake, or at least that's what he expected her to do.

He heard a little more commotion. What do you know! It sounded like she was making out with that consultant guy her friend had been talking about! He grinned a little at the thought of kissing Sophie Henderson. She was definitely a hottie. Everyone at the office thought so. One of the new guys, Thomas Brand, had even tried to make a play. Idiot. Never get personally involved at work. It was a recipe for disaster. She took care of him pretty fast, kicked him to the curb without a thought. Too bad the dumb schmuck didn't recognize what hit him. He still followed her around like a puppy.

He heard a little bit of moaning and some words and then the door shut.

Her footsteps went into the kitchen and a thump echoed as her keys and purse were deposited on the counter. He burrowed back into the closet as far as he could, hoping there was nothing in this room that she'd need. He let out a quiet breath of relief as the footsteps continued into the next room and then the water turned on. The clatter of her shoes hitting the floor confirmed that he had a small window of time to make a move. Apparently, she was going to take a shower. A part of him wanted to see if he could get a peek but that would be too dangerous. Right now, he just needed to get out, get the documents, and get as far away as possible.

He moved the clothes aside and placed a forefinger in the door slot to ease it open. He peered out and saw nothing, heard nothing other than the running water in the other room. A small jangle from the hangers above clanked as he rolled his large frame out of the closet and rose to his feet. A dress had clung to his shoulder and he flipped it away as he looked around the room, then out the window searching for the fastest way out of the apartment. *Damn apartment has only one access . . . and it's the front door.* He grabbed a stack of papers from the room he was in and shoved it inside his jacket, then eased himself toward the kitchen. There was a stack there too; he'd have to get them both. A small creak from the floor stopped him in his tracks. He stood still for a second to see if it had been noticed. Nope. The shower was still running and there was no indication of movement from that direction. He tiptoed into the kitchen and snagged the papers, adding them to the ones in his jacket. He zipped the jacket up and moved toward the door.

Clump, clump, clump, clump. Someone was running up the stairs, taking them two or three at a time. The footsteps pounded closer and closer to the apartment. Then there was pounding on the door! *Shit! Shit!* He searched the room frantically for somewhere to hide, a window to climb out of, another closet but found nothing. More pounding at the door and a voice this time. "Sophie, answer the door!"

He ducked into a crevice formed beside a weird looking cabinet and the wall just before a loud, wood-splintering *crack!* shattered the silence. He didn't dare look out. Better to stay behind the cabinet.

A scream echoed down the hallway. She was yelling at the guy now. Trevor. His name was Trevor. The guy had seen him through the window. *Shit! He knows I'm here!* No time to wait. Gotta get the hell out of here.

He slid the cabinet out again. Good, they were arguing back in the back. Go. *Now.* As he slipped out from behind the cabinet, it swayed, then tilted. He didn't stop to see what happened next. He ran.

He jumped through the opening Trevor had made for him in the door, and pounded toward the stairs as fast as he could. A crash behind him said the cabinet had tipped over. He lunged down the stairs taking them in fours, barely touching down as he jumped from one to the next one. He prayed he didn't lose his balance before he got to the bottom. He was way too old for this acrobatic shit. Thankfully, a couple of years as a volunteer firefighter had trained him to descend stairs like these.

As he touched bottom, he sprinted toward the street, wheeling right as he got to the corner and slipping into the closest backstreet he came upon. He'd have to circle back for his car, but fortunately he'd parked it on the next block, so getting out should be no problem.

He reached into his jacket and felt the papers there. Good. Every one of them still in his possession. He smiled as he drove to the nearest all night printing shop and deposited them in their shredder bin before calling in a report.

Chapter Nine

Outside Sophie's building, there was little activity. A few cars passing, but not slowing down. As Trev strode toward the car, the lights of the passing traffic cast a highlight across a man standing in the shadows on the other side of the street. He looked a little startled, but his face wasn't familiar. Trev reached for the door of his car to get in, but then he followed the man's gaze upward and froze. The man was watching Sophie's window. *There was a man in her apartment!* Specifically, in the guest bedroom—and he was moving around as if he was trying to hide.

Trev flashed back to the shadows on the corner but the man that was watching was gone. Trev raced into the apartment building and bounded up the stairs. He had turned the mic off and left it in the car earlier. That was stupid. He needed backup. He punched the speed dial on his phone. When the voice on the other side responded, he blasted out, "There's someone in Sophie's apartment!"

"What? Who?"

"I don't know. He's in her guest room!"

"Does she know?"

"No. I just left her. I saw him as I was getting into my car."

"Get her out of there! Now! We'll be there in five minutes."

"I can probably get him."

"Don't be stupid. We don't want her in the same shape as Bob. Just get her out."

At the top of the stairs, he pulled the gun from his ankle holster and crouched outside her door. It was quiet inside. That was good. Maybe. Trev pounded on the door. He waited what seemed like forever for a response and pounded again. "Sophie! Answer the door!" No response.

"Fuck it," Trev muttered as he threw his shoulder hard into the door, splintering the doorjamb. Ironically, it had been his support as he had clung passionately to her just minutes earlier. Now, he had just destroyed it. A scream came from the back of the apartment. He advanced quickly down the hallway, firearm raised. He looked into the room that he'd seen through the window but no one was there. The closet door stood open and some clothes lay on the floor in a heap—but no intruder. The hangers swayed back and forth. Whoever was there couldn't be very far. He swung back toward the hall just as Sophie sprinted out, tying a towel around her and dripping.

She screamed again, then stopped when she recognized his face. "What are you doing, Trevor?" Her hair was matted in bedraggled strings of water that trailed down her shoulders and her face.

He stopped running, looked around her bedroom, his firearm still poised and ready. He smelled the steam and soap from her shower.

"What are you doing with a gun in my house?" she blurted.

He darted his eyes back to her face briefly. "There was someone in here. I saw him from the window."

"What! You were looking in my window?"

"Yes. I mean no. I saw a shadow in your guest room. I thought you were in trouble."

"So, you broke down my door and barged in here like the Mod Squad!" Her eyes were huge. She was screaming at him and backing away, squeezing the towel tighter around her.

"Shut the fuck up. There's someone in here! I saw him. Come on." Trevor grabbed her hand and started dragging her. She leaned back, resisting as best she could but he was too strong. Keeping the towel in place severely hampered her ability to resist. Still, she dug her feet into the carpet as she braced her full weight away from him.

"No! You're flailing a gun around. Who the hell *are* you?" She was terrified. "I'm not going anywhere with you! I'm calling the police!"

"Yes! Yes, call the police. Here." He tossed his phone to her. "I've already made the call but go ahead. Then get some clothes and come on! *Now!* I'm telling you there was someone in here. You're not safe."

Trev advanced into her bedroom, opening drawers and grabbing things. He pulled out a T-shirt, panties, and a pair of running pants. He stuffed them down the waist of his pants, looping them through his belt, for lack of a better way to carry them. Then he grabbed Sophie and hoisted her, towel and all, over his shoulder. With his gun still raised and one hand holding her on his back, he started moving back toward the door of the bedroom to leave.

A loud crash reverberated from the living room. Steps thundered out of the apartment and descended the stairs.

"Did you hear that?" Sophie blurted as Trev plopped her back on her feet and started down the hall. By the time he got to the railing of the stairs, all he could see was a dark shadow disappearing down the street. He ran back and yanked his phone from her hand. He hit the speed dial again and raised it to his mouth.

"He's running down Gifford Street behind the apartments, heading west. Are you close yet?"

"Two blocks away."

"See if you can catch him. I'll get her out. I think I saw a tan colored jacket and blue jeans, but that's all. He was under the overhang of the steps and I didn't get a good visual." He looked up to see Sophie staring at him, her mouth gaping. "Hey, Nate?" he added, "There might be two. I saw another guy watching on the street opposite her apartment before I came up. Brown hair, rough looking. About five-ten, muscular. Dark jacket and jeans. The baggy type."

"Who are you?" Sophie yelled.

"I'm the guy who just saved your fucking life." He didn't want to spend a lot of time explaining—not now and definitely not here. He narrowed his eyes, challenging her to argue further.

"Now, let's get you the hell out of here."

"Okay. Okay. But don't you *dare* pick me up like a sack of potatoes again." She was trembling now as she held a hand out in front of her to keep him at bay. The shock of what just might have happened sunk in. "I can walk."

"Good. Then, let's go." Trev grabbed her hand and glanced around the room. He yanked her with him, moving quickly out of the apartment and toward the stairs, his gun still ready in his other hand.

Three minutes later, they were back in his car speeding away from the apartment complex.

"So, you drop the f-bomb and a few other choice words a lot when you're under crisis," she stated flatly a short while later.

"Huh? What?" He looked at her, dumbfounded. Water continued to drip off her hair and down her neck. The towel was loose . . . too loose. His jaw tightened a little and the tension started to drain. Then he laughed. "Do I?".

"You don't know what you said?"

"Yeah, I guess I do get a little out of control. One of my many flaws. A guy's gotta say whatever gets the point across. Sometimes nothing else fits."

"I can think of a few words that might work."

"Don't bother trying to save me, Henry. That's a lost cause. My mouth has been washed out with soap so many times, I should bleed bubbles."

"Remind me never to make you mad." Sophie looked out the window, her hand on the door latch as if ready to escape.

"You already have," he admitted. Mad that she nearly became a statistic.

"Really?" she looked at him, bewildered. "Why?"

"Jesus, Henry." He turned his eyes to hers as he used the familiar pet name he'd given her. He was shaking a little, which was totally out of character. "Get your hand off the damn door latch. If you try to get out while we're moving this fast, you'll end up in the hospital." He paused. "You could have been killed just now, and you were arguing with me. When something like that happens, you don't think, you don't talk, and you definitely don't argue about what to do. You just *move*. You just fucking move as fast as you can."

"That's not really a fair thing to say. I just met you a couple of weeks ago. How am I supposed to know you're not the bad guy? You know—some psycho? You bash in my door, wave a gun at me, and carry me out like a kidnap victim."

She had a point. His knuckles were white as he gripped the steering wheel and raced the car around the corner. Better just to stop talking. He turned three or four more times, circling back on his route before entering the parking garage and stopping the car. There wasn't anywhere else to take her right now, not without notice.

"Stay here," he ordered. She started to open her mouth in protest but his finger flew up in her face. "Don't!" was all he added before he pushed his long legs out of the car and stood, then walked to the back. He opened the trunk, pulled something out, and then came around to her side. The door was yanked open and a jacket thrust open between them, shielding the door. "All right. You can get out now, but hold that damn towel closed, will you?"

"What?" She looked down at the towel gaping open all the way to her hip bone. "Oh!" Grabbing it around her, she stepped out of the car into the jacket. Trev promptly wrapped the jacket around her and zipped the front of it all the way to her chin.

"That ought to work until we can get you inside." He put his arm around her and started walking her toward the door to the elevator. His eyes darted around the garage and watched the street. Her hands were caught inside the jacket, holding the towel together as he bustled her forward. A couple stepped out of the elevator and looked at them curiously but didn't say a word. Trev nodded at them, then pushed her into the elevator. He punched the button for his floor, swiping his access key. He was glad for the security in this building. No one could enter without an access card plus the key to their own apartment. This would help to make sure that even if someone was able to follow them to the garage, they couldn't easily follow them up.

"Where are we?" Sophie's voice was tired.

"My place." He gave her a warning look that told her to keep her mouth shut. He wasn't in the mood for any snide comments.

"Oh. Okay," she uttered softly. Then the tears started flowing. Trev plopped her down on the couch, locked the door, set the alarm, and disappeared to the kitchen. He couldn't deal with tears.

Chapter Ten

"Here, drink this." Trev handed Sophie a glass of Scotch and soda, without the soda. He was amped and she was terrified. If he tried the traditional "hold 'em and hug 'em" way of comforting, he was liable to rip that towel right off her. He was more than a little scared of Sophie Henderson. She was understandably unnerved by their escape, but he needed information right now, not tears.

Sophie took a huge drink and immediately gasped and coughed. "That's not water!"

"Oh. Guess I should have told you that." He grinned apologetically. "Scotch—it'll calm your nerves."

"My nerves are just fine." Sparks flew from her eyes and it occurred to him that maybe he should have put it in a plastic glass. She was so upset right now she might throw it at him. "Do you want to tell me what's going on?"

"I was going to ask you the same question." He watched her, unsmiling. "Do you have any idea who that guy was? An old boyfriend maybe?"

Sophie handed the glass back to him with most of the liquid still in it.

He pushed it back at her. "Drink," he ordered.

"And if I don't want it?"

He shook his head in exasperation. "Just do it, okay? I'm not very good with the tears and stuff—it'll help with the shock, so I'd appreciate it if you'd just humor me." He leaned against the wall next to the front door, his hands behind his back, anchored heavily by his body. He felt the clothes he'd tucked in his belt loop for lack of a better place to put them and yanked them out.

He needed for her to be covered up so he could concentrate on asking questions. "You want to go put these on?"

He tossed them on the couch from across the room, not budging toward her. Sophie had downed the drink in three solid swallows. She twisted her face up as it went down her throat, likely burning all the way. *Great,* he thought, *now she's either going to puke or pass out before I can talk to her. That was probably a dumb idea. Should have poured a smaller glass.*

She looked at the three small pieces of clothes and then at Trev. "Of everything in my room, this is all you could get?"

"What's wrong with it? Underwear, shirt, and pants. What else do you need?" His voice gave away his frustration.

Sophie's faced softened a little and he thought he noticed a look of amusement pass over her. She shrugged. "I guess you'll find out, won't you? Where do I change?" She stood up, her long legs stretching beautifully from underneath his jacket. The warmth of the Scotch was settling in apparently because she teetered slightly.

Trev motioned to a door off the kitchen. "Bathroom. Don't plan on going anywhere else because I'll be standing right here when you come out."

"Got it, boss, but I'll need you to release me from this straight jacket." She smirked. He moved toward her, unzipped the jacket, and watched as she stepped into the bathroom. She exited a few minutes later, standing with one arm across her chest, clutching her upper arm. She had smoothed her hair back and twisted it together somehow. Her breasts were jammed into the T-shirt, bra-less, leaving nothing at all to imagine. Several inches of belly showed between the shirt and the pants that set low on her hips. Her waist curved perfectly between the two pieces of cloth and the darkness of her breasts protruded perkily from the tightly stretched cloth even though she tried to cover them.

"Holy shit!" Trev blurted without even thinking as he stared at her. He turned around. "Put the jacket back on!"

"Why? Don't you like what you picked out?" *Is she really toying with me? Must be the Scotch talking.* He shook his head, afraid to speak, then cleared his throat.

"Are you shitting me? If I'd known the shirt didn't fit, I wouldn't have brought it. Let me get you something of mine. I'll be right back." His voice was scratchy.

"Nah." She giggled. "This is fine." She moved toward him, tripping on her own feet, blocking him from going to his bedroom. The Scotch had to be hitting her hard now. Her movements were really exaggerated.

"The hell it is!" He darted past her and picked up the jacket off the floor. When he turned back to wrap it around her, she was right in front of him, pressing against him. "Stop it, Soph," he growled.

"Why? What's wrong with it, Mr. Psycho, Gun-Waving, Cowboy Dude? After all, you picked it out, right? Underwear, shirt, and pants. What else do I need?"

Trev panicked. *Okay, gotta get out of here. She's sloshed and probably a little hyped from the commotion, too.* "Come on, Henry, give me a break. How was I supposed to know the shirt would fit you like that? It was in your drawer." His eyes pleaded with her to back off, his hand was against her waist, touching the heat of her flesh, pushing her back from him. "I'm really trying to hold it together here. Would you knock it off?"

"Why are you trying to 'hold it together'? What's the problem?"

That was just plain brutal, he thought, to look like that in those clothes and not be someone he could even make a play for.

"There wouldn't be a problem under normal circumstances. You look fantastic. Really." He grinned. "In a sexy, slutty sort of way." His voice was strained and broke at the end. "I just wanted to try to keep this on a professional level since right now, I'm sort of working for you, but you're killing me, Soph. I can't look at that! Not if I'm going to keep my hands off." If he got through this and maintained his restraint, he was going to deserve a medal.

"So, what did you call that last kiss? A business meeting? You're a big talker but deep down, you're not really the 'player' you make yourself out to be, are you?"

"Huh?" He used his free hand to drape the jacket around her. Once he had it over her shoulders, he used both hands to pull the bottom together and zip it back up around her. "There we go. Much better. I'm beginning to like this jacket." He smiled with relief as he felt the circulation start to return to his face. "It works great as a restraining device."

"Trevor?" Sophie looked up at him. Tears had formed in her eyes again.

"Yeah? Are you okay?"

"Why would someone break into my apartment?"

"Who knows?" He put his hands on the shoulder of the jacket, glad not to be touching her skin. "He was probably just a burglar and he wasn't expecting you to come home."

"But I did, and," tears were beading up in her eyelids now, "he could have been a rapist or a murderer."

"Hey, now." He put his hand under her chin and tilted it so her eyes were looking into his. She bit her lip to keep it from trembling. That was it for him. She was scared, really scared. All the rest was just an act. He wrapped his arms around her shoulders and hugged her to him, stroking the curls out of her wet eyes. Her face was buried against his chest. "He ran out so it's not likely he was going to hurt you. Besides, you're fine now. Right? Just a little scared. There's nothing to worry about."

"I don't understand all of this." She was swaying a little. "I'm sorry, Trev." The tears were coming now.

"Look, I know I said I don't do well with tears, but it's okay to cry a little. You just went through a pretty traumatic event. It's allowed." He was trying to lean down and look into her big wet eyes but she was just looking away. Then suddenly she lunged over and . . . dammit. She puked all over him.

"Ahhh." He sighed. *So much for just passing out.* He should have never given her the Scotch. Or at least he should have just given her a little, but how was he supposed to know she would chug it down?

"I'm so sorry, Trevor. I didn't mean to do that. Oh God, I'm sorry!" She clutched her mouth and wiped her chin with the sleeve of his jacket. Her face was pale and blotched, her mouth hung open in disbelief, completely humiliated. She looked down at the mess on his shoes and pant legs and her face scrunched up again. The tears came non-stop and she gasped and sputtered as they flowed freely. She tried to use the arm of his jacket to wipe his pants, but he grasped her arms and pulled her up. He held his breath to keep from reacting to the pungent odor.

"It's okay, Henry. It's okay. I shouldn't have given you the Scotch." God, she was adorable. Tears, puke, everything. She was a mess, and really upset that she'd gotten it all over him. She smelled horrendous now. He felt bad for her. She had been through hell tonight and all she was worried about was this.

Trev pulled the jacket back off her, not daring to look at the T-shirt underneath. He got a towel and wiped her face and hands, then carried her back to the bathroom in his bedroom. "Let's get you into the shower," he lowered her to the side of tub. He started the water running, tested it to make sure it wasn't too hot, then switched it to the shower. "There you go," he whispered, then started out of the room.

"Trev?" She looked at him, teary-eyed, and he felt his chest tighten.

"Yeah?"

"Can I change clothes?"

He looked at the puke-spattered pants and shirt. "Of course. I'll find something for you, but it's not going to fit."

"Anything's better than this," she said. As he closed the door to the bathroom, she was already struggling to strip out of the pants and shirt. He wanted to help but that would be more than his self-control would endure right now. He found a shirt and shorts and set them by the door, then he retreated to the living room to clean up.

Thirty minutes later, he went to check on her and found her asleep on his bed wearing his clothes. One foot dangled over the edge of the bed, touching the floor. He smiled at the well-known attempt to stop the bed from spinning. So much for asking questions about the break-in. He hit the speed dial on his phone and got Nate. "Tell me you found him."

"Nope, he was gone. You're going to need to come back over here, though. It looks like he's taken some things and I'm not sure what. We didn't see anyone else, either. Looks like it might just be a burglar."

"Okay. Not tonight man. She's passed out and I doubt she'll be awake enough to look at it till tomorrow. Can you put someone in there to watch it for now?"

"No problem. See you tomorrow." Nate didn't ask where she was and Trev was glad. They'd assume he put her up in a hotel—that would have been the logical thing to do. He wasn't sure why he had chosen not to. Something about that other guy watching made him nervous.

Trev went into the guest room he used for an office. He surveyed the room, sparsely decorated with a few recognitions from past work, along with pictures of his family. Two pictures of him in his uniform as he graduated from the academy. One was with his parents, the other with the rest of his family. Another in his army gear with his prior unit. He took down the pictures and placed them in the appropriate files. He locked everything in the closet and looked around to make sure he hadn't missed anything. He would have to explain himself tomorrow, most likely, but it was better not to get too detailed until they had the rest of the information back from Cheryl.

One last look in on Sophie and then he would grab a blanket and get a little sleep on the couch. She looked beautiful. Clean and content, sprawled across the bed with her hair tumbling everywhere on his pillow. He gently picked her up and slid her legs under the blankets, then pulled them up over her. He sat on the side of the bed for a couple minutes watching her.

Trev's hand played with the edge of the blanket that was draped across her shoulders. He felt her mouth on his again, her tongue working against his, his legs weakening as he leaned against the doorjamb. Then he shook his head and brought himself back to the present. She sure looked nice in his shirt. He had to stop thinking this way. He let out a soft sigh and headed to the couch.

*

At six a.m., Sophie awoke to the smell of something cooking. She washed her face in his bathroom, then snooped through his drawers for toothpaste and maybe an extra toothbrush. She found the toothpaste in the same drawer as a hand revolver, but no toothbrush. She used her finger to brush her teeth as best as she could, then picked up the handgun and carried it to the kitchen.

"How many of these do you have lying around?" She waved the holstered weapon at him as she entered the kitchen, stopping when he snatched it from her hand and placed it on the counter.

"There are a few, but I'll move them if it makes you uncomfortable." Trev had showered already and was wearing a pair of loose fitting scruffy tan shorts and a white undershirt. His short dark hair was wet and shiny, the facial hair still had a couple of water drops beaded up on it. He was barefoot and as he leaned against the kitchen counter, looking at her, she thought it strange that she was staring at his feet. How could a person's feet be sexy? But they were.

"Here, have some coffee." He stood and poured a cup for her. "Do you want anything in it?"

"What? Oh. No, that's fine." She took the cup. Her head was hurting pretty bad and she pressed a hand against her forehead. She watched his movements, searching for some indication that would explain who he really was.

"Take this, too." Without looking at her, he handed her an

aspirin he'd set out on the counter. She took it gladly and gulped it down with a sip of hot coffee.

"Thanks," Sophie responded sheepishly. "I'm sorry about the mess."

"No worries. It's all cleaned up now. Your clothes are in the dryer and should be done pretty soon if you want to put them back on." Did he really think she'd be able to get that outfit back on after it had gone through the dryer? Was he kidding?

"Yeah, right." Sarcasm dripped from her mouth. "The last time I wore that shirt, before last night of course, was eight years ago."

"Really?" Trev laughed. "Why do you still have it?"

Sophie looked down at her hands. "My mom bought it for me. I just felt like keeping it was a way of keeping her."

"I guess that makes sense." He felt bad for her, losing her mother left her with no one to really support her. That must have been awful. "Well, it still fits like a glove." Trevor smiled again, taunting her. "Aren't you glad you still have your girlish figure?"

"Ha! Yeah, right. You really are pushing it, you know."

"Just being honest." He shrugged.

"You're mocking me. I didn't have a girlish figure then—I was built like a boy, all skin and bones. I've put on a little padding in certain areas since then."

He looked at her in his T-shirt and shorts and an unreadable expression clouded his eyes. The shirt was so big it was falling off one shoulder, showing her skin and the tiny mole on the back of her shoulder. He glanced at it, then back to her eyes with no change in expression. The shorts were rolled up several times at the waist to keep them from falling down. Even with rolling them up and tying the string tightly, they still sat a little low on her hips. It didn't matter though because the shirt completely covered them as if it were a dress. She sat down at the counter and lifted one leg up. She pulled it against her on the chair, tucking her foot under the other leg.

"There's nothing boyish about you, Soph," he stated as he set plates on the bar in the kitchen. "I've made breakfast. Have a seat and dig in." The space between the counter and the table was minimal and as he moved past her and slid into the stool next to her, he grazed her thigh with his leg. His leg was warm, the hair on it soft and fine.

They ate in silence. Sophie was keenly aware of the way his arms stretched against the cloth of the T-shirt he wore. She'd only seen him in work clothes up to this point. His arms were evenly tanned and muscular. His hands were big with spidery fingers. He had a nasty scar on the underside of his upper right arm. She wondered how that had happened. It disappeared into the sleeve of his shirt as if to hint there was more to be seen underneath.

Sophie broke the silence. "You're not really an IT consultant, are you?"

"Not exactly, but I do have a lot of expertise in computer forensics and I'm kind of a type of consultant."

"Who do you work for?"

"The government."

"Why are you here?"

"I told you that already. I'm sort of in between assignments right now. I . . . we . . . my team was investigating several cases of fraud in Louisiana up until a couple of months ago." She could see that Trevor was uncomfortable with the questions, but there were too many of them. So many that she wanted—no, that she needed—to know. Why was he here? What was with all the guns? Was there really an intruder or was that a ruse? No, she heard the crash and heard the guy run out of her apartment. That was real. Wasn't it? She had kissed this man standing here. She had wanted him. Hell, she still did, but who was he?

"And you're working on something else now?"

"Yes." Bluntly. "But I can't discuss it with you, not till it's over." The expression on his face frustrated her, but she nodded as if she understood. She hadn't picked up her fork yet. She just sat there with her arms wrapped over her raised leg.

"So, are you married?" she asked.

His eyes darted to her face when she said that. "There's a change of subject. No. Are you?"

She laughed. "You saw where I live; you know the answer to that."

"I could say the same thing to you." He waved his hand at his apartment as he forked a piece of egg, reminding her where they were. "Why are you asking?"

"No reason," she lied. "I guess I just wanted to make sure I hadn't been kissing someone else's man last night."

Trevor's hands stopped suddenly. He became very still. His gaze was focused intently on the plate of eggs in front of him. He chewed his food and swallowed. A thousand pictures flew through her head, all of which included his mouth and hers. Touching. She noticed a twitch in his jaw before he said gruffly, "Aren't you going to eat?"

"I'm making you uncomfortable, aren't I?"

"Yes." He dropped the fork and stood up, but she placed her hand on his arm. He stared down at her, towering above her chair, his jaw clenched as he looked at her hand, then her face.

"Why?"

"Look, you just went through something pretty scary and you're a little stunned, whether you know it or not."

"I guess so. I'm also a little queasy because *someone* was trying to get me drunk . . . quite successfully," she teased.

"That's *not* what I was trying to do." Finally his gaze moved to the window over the kitchen sink, then he continued speaking in an exasperated tone. "I thought it would calm you down. I didn't know you were going to gulp it down like shots. I also didn't know you couldn't handle alcohol. I saw you drinking with your friends and thought . . . " He paused for a minute. She thought he was going to say that he thought she was a heavy drinker because he'd seen her at the bar. Obviously, he wasn't paying as much attention as he thought he was.

"Henry, you need to shut up and eat," he barked as he pushed her plate in front of her and moved around the counter. His facial expression closed. She had made him angry. He snapped at her, "We're going to have to file a complaint and check on your apartment today. Is there anyone you know that you've had a tiff with? Anyone who doesn't like you?"

Sophie sat quietly, sulking from his roughness. She shook her head. "I can't think of anyone." She paused for a moment and gave in to the need to explain herself. "The drinks the other night were ginger ale and grenadine, for the most part. I usually drink one real drink and the rest are just soft drinks. Sometimes I'll drink a few beers."

"Hmmm. I get it. You like being in control. You're not a drinker."

"It's more a distaste for hangovers from my college days. I had too many of them and I just don't want to go there now. At twenty-eight, I'm a little too old for that, don't you think?" she asked. Finally, she got a brief smile out of him. A silent pause hung between them for a few minutes.

"Any ex-boyfriends that might carry a grudge?"

"No." She hesitated. "On the grudge part."

"What does that mean?"

"It means yes, there's an ex-boyfriend or two, but no grudges involved. We parted amicably. Or at least it seemed so."

"I'll need names." A hard rap on the door came and Sophie jumped. Trevor smiled at her. "It's okay. I asked the police officer on your case to see if they could send some clothes over for you. We have to go into the police department to file official reports. I thought it might be hard to do that dressed in my shorts and shirt, or at least it might be uncomfortable."

"I hope they're bringing work clothes. I need to get there soon." She looked at the watch on her arm and frowned. "I'm going to be late."

"You're not going," Trevor stated matter of factly.

"Of course I am."

"Soph, someone was in your apartment last night. Someone

with bad intentions—whatever they were. You shouldn't be thinking about work right now, but about who did it and why." He watched her fidgeting with the bottom of his shirt, twisting it in knots. "Why don't you call and let your boss know you won't be there today. Go ahead and tell him about the break-in if you want to, or just tell him you're sick—that's your choice. But you aren't going to the office today."

"Don't I have a say?"

"No, not really." He grinned at her and she felt herself warming up reluctantly. "I'm not letting you out of my sight until we know what's going on."

"That's really sweet, but I can take care of myself. I've done it for a long time now. It isn't necessary for you to hover over me, not to mention it's a little bit creepy."

Another loud rap on the door came and Trevor stood up hesitantly. "Creepy or not, you are *not* working today and you're stuck with me. Let me get the door. I'll be right back." He jogged to the door in his bare feet, checked the peek hole, disabled his alarm, and stepped outside.

The voices in the hallway rumbled softly, too softly. It was impossible to make them out or know what they were discussing. Sophie rose from her chair and moved toward the door. The voices were almost arguing but in a hushed tone. When Sophie got close enough, she leaned against the door and looked through the peek hole. All she could see was the back of Trevor's shoulders. A voice on the other side of the door said, "Okay. We'll do it your way, but she needs to stay contained until we have the data analysis done. You know as well as I do what could happen."

"I'm telling you," Trevor's voice sounded like he was talking through gritted teeth, "it's not her."

"You're talking with the wrong body part, dude, but they're going to back you for a while just because we don't want a repeat of what happened with Bob. Stay in contact though. If you don't, they're probably going to pull you."

"It's under control. Completely under control," Trevor responded.

The door handle rattled. Sophie raced back to her seat. The voices continued for a second or two, then the door whisked open and Trevor came back in. He locked up and armed the alarm, then started toward her. "Here you go." He handed her a bag. She recognized it as her bag from the top of her closet.

"Who was at the door?" She wondered how much he'd say and if she should be more afraid of him as she lowered the bag to the floor beneath her chair.

"A friend."

"A friend that brought my clothes from my apartment and has been rummaging through my personal things? Is my apartment wide open?"

"No, I called a locksmith last night after you—" he paused "—fell asleep. He said he'd replace the door and the locks. My friend met him there, got your clothes, and brought me your new keys." Trevor held up two keys, dangled them for her to see, and then handed them to her. "It's possible that whoever was in your apartment had a key. There were no signs of forced entry before I knocked the door down. We would have noticed it when we got there. And since you live on the second floor, it's not likely the guy went in through the window. Have you given keys to anyone?"

"No."

"What about a hide-a-key? Is there one lying around somewhere?"

"Of course not, that would be stupid in an apartment complex that size."

"You'd be surprised at how many people do that."

"Stupid people. Not me," she said defiantly, then moved to her feet and grabbed the bag of clothes. "I think I'll go see what's in here to wear that might actually fit."

Trevor stood in front of her, glancing at his T-shirt and her legs showing underneath it. "Don't change on my account," he replied smugly, then added, "Sure you don't want to wear that shirt your mother gave you? Just for sentimental reasons, you know."

"Funny, funny. You'd like that, wouldn't you?" The sarcasm was still there.

"Damn right. I think that image will be burned into my brain forever." He tapped a finger to his hair to punctuate the thought.

"You didn't seem to like it very much last night when you zipped me into the straight jacket." Sophie shot him a reproachable look.

Trevor leaned into her hair, putting his mouth against her ear, and she felt the warmth of his breath ticking the inside of her earlobe. "That was for your own good, woman. You're dangerous."

"Me? *I'm dangerous?* You're joking right? Tell me, Trev." She turned her face to look him seriously in the eyes, her nose within an inch of his. Realizing she was too close for comfort, she leaned back to peer up at him. "Are you one of the good guys—or one of the bad guys?"

His chiseled mouth turned slowly up and his eyes were shining as he responded, "It depends why you're asking. If it's about the break-in at your apartment, I'm one of the good guys. If you're asking me to give you fashion advice on what to wear . . . " His eyes glanced down at her legs. He drawled slowly, "Bad guy. Definitely bad guy." His hand squeezed her forearm. She pulled back from him, feeling like a scared rabbit, not sure whether to stay or run. He dropped his hand from her arm.

Her face was flushed as she slipped past him. She wondered if he was still watching as she padded away to change clothes. Why did she trust him? He was devious in the way he looked at her. He didn't even try to hide his thoughts, but in a crazy, sexy way, she liked the honesty of it. It was scary. But exciting. She wondered what she would do if he followed her at this moment. Was that all part of his plan? To make her want him? And what exactly was his plan anyway? She had no idea.

Chapter Eleven

"Okay, I got the copies and have already sent them to the shredder." Lenny huffed into the phone. He was seriously out of breath from his effort to get to his car without being seen. He adjusted his rear view mirror as he talked with his cell phone cradled between his ear and his shoulder. As he pulled the car into the traffic, he glanced nervously around for pedestrians. No one running after him, no cars following. Good.

"Good." The voice on the other end repeated his thought. "Did you have any problems?"

"Yeah, she came home while I was there."

"What? You're kidding?"

"No, I'm not. She had a guy with her. Some friend that's a security guy. Or at least that's what I heard from Callie." His breathing was stilted as he punctuated the words, stopping for breath periodically.

"What happened?" The voice on the other end was clearly wondering if he'd been spotted and what to do next.

"I hid behind one of her dressers and skipped out when they were in the back. They didn't see me, but," he swallowed and took a deep breath, "they knew I was there. The guy saw me through the window. I don't know if he saw enough to recognize me but he knew I was there."

"Shit! What a mess." Silence continued between them for eons. "Okay, let's don't panic yet. Wait a few days. Let's see what happens."

"I think I need to lie low for a while," Lenny suggested. He wanted out before there wasn't a way to get out.

"No!" Another lengthy silence while thoughts were gathered into a plan. "Go to work as normal. Do your job. You need to see what she does and there's no better way to do that than to be at work. Besides it'll raise more suspicion if you're gone."

He considered that for a minute. As much as he'd like to run, it did make sense. Whatever she did next would likely tell them how bad it was going to be and if they needed to worry. "Okay. I'll go."

"And, Lenny?"

"Yeah?" *Here it comes.*

"Don't call me on this phone again. And don't talk to me at work, either. I don't want to see you. If you need something, drop a note at the house and I'll get back to you."

That was what he expected. They were already starting to hide. They were digging their holes now and would be crawling into them pretty soon, leaving *him* standing out in the open to take the heat. He threw the phone across the car and pressed his foot harder to the gas pedal.

Lenny had finally gotten his lungs back and they no longer burned from the running. His breathing was normal, but his face was still beet red with anger. *Okay,* he thought, *that's the way this is going to go, is it? No, sir. Not this time.* He saw what they had done to Bob and knew that he could easily go the same way if he didn't plan appropriately.

When Bob died, he started making copies. Of the transactions, of the notes, of the emails. He even recorded the conversations. It was all stored in a lockbox at the bank. That was his insurance. His ace of spades. "Don't call you. Don't talk to you," he repeated. "Don't kid yourself. If I'm toast, you're toast."

He grappled for the phone, dialed home and waited for his wife to pick up. "Hey, babe." He spoke cheerfully. "I got to the store by the house and they didn't have any light bulbs left. So I ended up going on to the hardware store over on Buffalo Speedway. I'm on my way back. Is there anything else you want me to pick up?" He had gone out earlier, pretending to be pissed off that the lights over the bathroom sink were burned out. They'd been that way for two weeks and neither of them had bothered to replace them since the ceiling light still worked. It was a good excuse to go out though and gave him coverage to do what he'd needed to do.

"I can't think of anything," she said. "I put your dinner in the microwave. You can heat it up when you get back." She hung up on him. He smiled at her aggravation. He'd pretty much lost his temper over the stupid light bulbs. The light bulbs didn't matter at all; he was simply sick and tired of this entire scenario he was involved in. When they started it, the technology was so primitive it was easy to find ways around it. But recent months had brought all sorts of ways to block, detect, and encode the data. So much so that once the new system was in place, they were done. They had all agreed it wouldn't continue. He was the brains behind it all. They had the clout but he handled the numbers. Still, he needed them to take care of the roadblocks. And lord knew, there had been a few. But this new system was more than a roadblock. It was a dead end. The technology had finally advanced to the point that it would not be possible to continue.

The board stalling to make a decision for a few months helped. It let them up the amounts and get more put away. It also let him concentrate on covering any and all loose ends in the data, getting the transactions straight. His thoughts darted back to her apartment. What a rush trying to get out of there undetected. He thought he would be terrified if something like that ever happened but he wasn't. It was almost like pulling someone out of a burning building or a car crash. "Ah, what fun." He sighed and then laughed.

On a whim, he dialed back the first number and when the voice answered, he said, "Hey, me again."

"I thought I said not to call!"

"Yeah, you did, but I just thought of something. You might want to get the auditor on notice just in case. If she moves, we need to shut it down quickly."

"I already knew that. You don't need to call to tell me."

He liked the exasperation on the other end of signal. He also liked that every word was going to be held for posterity in case they tried to screw him. The line went dead and he laughed.

Chapter Twelve

"Sign right there, ma'am, and you're all done." The friendly officer pointed to the red X he had marked at the bottom of the form in front of Sophie. "Sorry it takes so long to do this but it's important to have all the facts."

She nodded at his cherub-like face, signed the paper, and stood to go. Her back was against Trevor as she tried to move forward a little to put distance between them. He put a hand on her shoulder and smiled. "Thank you, Officer Sheridan. We appreciate your help. If you find anything out—anything at all, here's my card. You can call me at that number."

Trevor leaned forward, putting his chest completely against Sophie's side and handed a business card to the officer sitting at the desk in front of them. He always felt so warm. The guy was a radiator.

The officer's eyes bulged at the card as soon as he looked at it. "Oh! I didn't realize you guys were involved in this." He looked embarrassed and seemed to be recounting the conversation to make sure he'd handled it correctly. "Nice to meet you, Mr—"

"Don't worry about it," Trevor interrupted. "Just let me know if anything comes up. Sophie here is a good friend of mine." He winked at the officer and put his arm around Sophie's waist. He corralled her quickly out of the room and into the hallway.

Once outside, she looked at him, eyebrow raised. "Good grief, it takes forever to get a report filed. I'm glad I wasn't bleeding or passed out."

"Yeah, me too—about the bleeding, that is. I think I would have enjoyed the resuscitation efforts if you had actually passed out."

Sophie landed a hard elbow to his stomach and led the way out of the crowded police station. Trevor clutched his gut, laughed, and followed her.

Their next stop was her apartment. He'd called ahead to let them know when she'd be there. A uniformed police officer was waiting at the door.

With his hand holding the knob, Trevor stopped, turned to Sophie, and spoke. "Let's don't waste a lot of time here. They need you to look around and see if anything's missing. That'll get added to the report. If you need anything more than was in the bag earlier, get it." She guessed his patience was wearing thin, too. He wanted to get going. After all, they'd spent almost the entire past twenty-four hours together. His constant movements at the police station and his shortness with the investigative officer were a dead give-away.

"So, I'm not going to be back in my apartment today?"

"No, not for a couple of days. It's not safe."

"Okay, do you think you could drop me by a hotel when we leave here, then? Or maybe take me to Callie's?"

"Not a problem." Why did he give her that stupid grin? If she didn't know better, she'd think he was making fun of her. He swung the door open and she bristled through, bumping his shoulder in the process. "By the way, you look great this morning," he murmured.

She glanced back and looked at him a little startled. He looked almost glad to see her flush. "Oh, thanks. You look pretty great yourself." She meant it, too.

*

The apartment was in decent shape. The main damage came from Trevor's forced entry. At first glance, nothing seemed missing. Trevor waited in the living room while Sophie toured all of the rooms with the police officer. Her apartment was larger than his and had a nice balcony off of the kitchen/dining area. French doors opened onto it and he checked them to make sure they were locked and had a safety bar. He glanced out the window; visibility from the street showed only part of the room. Sophie obviously liked bright colors and was a fan of abstract art. A single large bright print hung over the sofa. A smaller matching one was on the wall next to a small glass top dining table.

"Hey Trev!" Sophie's voice beckoned from somewhere in the back. "Can you come here for a minute?"

"Sure." He headed down the hall, checking each room. He found her in her guest bedroom/office. "What's up?"

"Other than the cabinet turned over in the kitchen, this is the only room that looks any different." The officer started to explain, "The closet's open and some of the clothes are on the floor. It looks like the burglar was hiding in the closet when she arrived home. He made a run for it when the door was open."

Sophie's face turned ashen. He noticed the look of fear that crept in and settled on her. "There's nothing missing," she told him. "There are plenty of things to take but it looks like they're all here. So, what did he want?"

Trevor didn't want to scare her, but the facts all pointed to something other than a burglar. If he was in her apartment hiding, he was waiting for her to come home. In that case, his motives could have only been a few and none of them were good. He wasn't going to lie. "He wanted you."

"Me? Why?"

"Who knows? Maybe you have an enemy out there. Or maybe it was just a random thing." Trevor surveyed the room once more, noticing a curled piece of paper on the floor. "Wait, did you have a stack of paper there on the corner?" He pointed to the side of her desk.

Sophie's eyes followed his gesture and she nodded. "Yes, the reports. Most of them were on the desk. One of them—the one with all the highlights—was on the counter in the kitchen." She hurried to the kitchen with Trev right behind her. The kitchen counter was empty. They looked at each other quietly.

"So, all that's missing are some papers?" the officer clarified.

"That's what it looks like," Sophie responded.

"Okay, then. I guess there's nothing more for me to see. I've already taken a few pictures of the rooms, so I guess we're done." The officer extended a hand to Sophie. "Thank you, ma'am. You'll get a copy of the report for your insurance in case you want to claim the damage. If you think of anything more that might help, please call us."

"You bet. Thanks for your help," she responded as he exited the apartment. She turned to Trevor and quietly voiced the worry he had seen in her face, "This is bigger than just a burglary, isn't it?"

"It would appear that way. Let's get out of here." Trev took her arm and guided her down to his car. She went quietly, not uttering a word. He noticed the fear in her eyes and the truth was, she probably should be scared. The missing reports meant someone was concerned about them. Trev frowned at the implication that all of this meant danger for Sophie.

Thirty minutes later, they were hurtling west on I-10 in Trev's car. A furrow had appeared between Sophie's eyebrows, and didn't look like it was going away any time soon. Periodically he glanced at her from the corner of his eye. She seemed to be steeling herself for something. He'd half expected the tears again but there was none of that. Her face showed concentration now. And maybe just a hint of fear.

*

Why would anyone break into my apartment to steal those reports? Sophie asked herself. It didn't make sense. If the reports were just set up wrong, there would be no reason, and a burglar wouldn't have even given them a look. No, whoever took them knew she had them and knew what she was doing. They probably thought these were the only copies. Or maybe by taking them that she'd get scared and drop it. Regardless of their motivation for taking them, the act itself had been the final piece of evidence in what she originally thought was the least likely possibility of all—someone definitely had tampered with the data. But why? And what did they think she knew?

Sophie frowned out the window. The skyscape of Houston diminished in the rear view mirror. She had no idea where they were going, but right now, just the fact that it was away—far away—from her apartment and the office, gave her a sense of relief. She wished she had seen the intruder so at least she'd have an idea who to look for. All she knew was this was a man, or at least that was what Trevor thought. He caught a glimpse of the person running away. No details of any significance, nothing. It could be anyone. She was glad he'd been there but didn't understand exactly why he had been.

The buildings eventually became farther and farther apart. Then, after riding silently for almost an hour, the buildings gave way to fields of grass with an occasional herd of cattle or horses. Trevor never let up on the gas.

His jaw was clenched as he stared forward. His one hand on the steering wheel maneuvered the car from lane to lane as needed, the other hand was on the console between them, his fingers tapping to some classic rock music on the stereo. He was tall and lanky. She had thought him thin until he scooped her over his shoulder without even bracing himself. After feeling his shoulder under her, she realized he was solid as a rock. He had a tendency to wear long sleeve shirts with the sleeves rolled up. The shirts fit closely at the waist and shoulders but almost completely covered the hardness of his build.

God, he smelled good. She watched his fingers tapping with interest. There were a spattering of scars across the knuckles but they appeared to have been there for a long time. His skin was tanned, or at least had a natural darkness to it. She had a sudden urge to reach out and touch him, and she did, putting her hand over his and tucking her fingers under his palm. "As much as I am enjoying getting out of the city, it might be nice to know where we're going. Do you think you could reassure me that you're not kidnapping me?" She smiled weakly and noticed Trevor's lips curving up and the glint reaching his eyes. Nice eyes, she thought. They got really smoky dark when he kissed her. Oops, why did she think that!

"But I am kidnapping you." He squeezed her hand and held it tight.

"What?"

"Not really. Don't worry. I just thought you might need to get away for a while. It's obviously not safe at your place or your work. I'm taking you to a friend's ranch. It's not too far and if you're nervous about it, I can always take you back whenever you want."

"How far is not too far?"

"It's about thirty minutes from Fredericksburg." His eyes watched her intently.

"Fredericksburg! That's over two hours away!" She wondered how far would be too far for him in terms of distance.

"Yep. It's far enough for it to be difficult to get to, but not too far to get back in a reasonable amount of time. And quiet enough that we'll hear anyone coming from a mile away."

Sophie's cell phone rang and she jolted. He clenched his fingers around hers, holding them tightly, not letting her answer it. "Whoever it is, don't tell them where we're going, okay?"

"So, you really *are* kidnapping me?"

"No. The fewer people that know where you are, the easier it is to keep you safe." He released her fingers adding, "Now, answer your phone."

"Sophie Henderson." The call was from her office according to the number and it had already gone to voicemail. "Too late.

Whoever it is can leave a message."

"Good," Trevor muttered. His hand was still sitting on the console as if he wanted her to take it again. She slipped her hand under her leg and stared out the window, watching the countryside fly past. *He thinks I'm dangerous. That's a laugh. Look at him, sitting there. He takes up the entire car with his size and his attitude.* He scared the hell out of her, but not necessarily in a life threatening way. It was more of an *I want to get my hands on every inch of you* way. Sophie shook her head to clear the thought from her mind. *Don't think like that. You don't even know this guy.*

She dialed her voicemail to see who called but the electronic voice on the other side spoke back to her: "You have no new messages." Apparently, whoever it was either didn't have anything important to say, or didn't want to leave a message.

"What's wrong?" Trevor asked, noticing her head shaking.

"No message." she muttered. *Now I'm going to obsess over who it was.*

He smiled, flashing that perfect wicked grin at her as if he knew her thoughts.

Chapter Thirteen

Their car rattled over the cattle guard in front of the iron gate around four in the afternoon. The gate had a punch pad to open it and Trev punched in the numbers. A gravel road dropped down and around a steeply curved hill on the other side of the gate. Short, scruffy trees and thick undergrowth enveloped the road on either side. Sophie raised a brow and gave him a questioning look. Her mouth had strained lines around it as if she tensed for action. "This is getting a little more intimidating by the minute, Trev. What's down this road? You're not planning to kill me and bury me down there are you?"

He burst out laughing and pointed ahead. "Down that road about a mile is a ranch house that sits on about seventy acres of land. Most of it looks like this," Trev waved his hand at the brush. "It's rented out as a hunting lodge part of the year and has a lot of exotic deer wandering around."

"Sounds great, but isn't this a little remote?"

"Yep. And *safe*—which is one of the reasons we're here." This time *he* took *her* hand. He wrapped his big fingers around hers and squeezed tightly. "There are no people here, Henry. No one to watch over your shoulder for. Except me, of course. You'll be able to relax for a while, and like I said, you can go back whenever you want to. Once you see the place, I bet you won't want to."

"And you said *I* was dangerous," she muttered. He rubbed his thumb over the back of her hand and set it gently back in her lap.

Trev smiled and eased the car down the hill. They rolled around the corner and the view opened up to a gorgeous expanse of tall grass on the right side of the road with a small stone house in front of them. Behind the house, a small creek rolled along gently, water gurgling its way on down into a wooded area some distance beyond the house. They pulled up to the house, gravel crunching loudly under their tires as they approached. Not a soul in sight and anyone that approached would be heard way before they arrived. Yes, this would be safe.

Trev put the car in park and turned to face Sophie. "Henry, I promise you. I'm not going to hurt you. You'll be fine here." His face was somber and his eyes held hers, darkening with intensity as his words came out. "Trust me, okay?"

"You scare the shit out of me, Trev," she admitted.

"Yeah, well, you scare the shit out of me, too." His eyes continued to focus on hers. "But in a different way. Right now, I think I'm okay with that." He opened the door, stepped out of the car and came around to open hers but she was already out. "Let me just take a look inside to make sure it's not a mess before you see it. Would you mind getting some of the stuff out of the trunk?"

Trev was already in the house when he spoke the last words. The screen door closed behind him. He touched his hand to the small wooden sign above the door that had the words "Prater Ranch" burned into it when he passed underneath. It had been done with a kid's wood burning set. The letters were a little non-uniform and tilted to the right.

"Prater Ranch?" Sophie asked when he returned.

"Yep, that's the name of the people that own this place. Okay, in we go." He gathered everything she had not already gotten and followed her into the house.

The house was deceptive from the outside. It appeared much smaller than it was. Once inside, it opened up to a wide expanse with stone floors and large glass windows that allowed a view of a beautiful courtyard with a firepit and several lawn chairs surrounding it. At the end of the courtyard, rocks stepped down to the river behind it. Three bedrooms down a hallway extended off the back side of the house; each room had French doors opening to the courtyard. The main part of the house was just a very large living room, a game room, and a huge, country-style kitchen that all seemed to flow into each other.

"Wow, this is fantastic!" Sophie couldn't help but appreciate the rustic ironwork, Austin stone, and wood furniture. "It's so comfortable."

"I had hoped you would think that." Trev smiled. "There's a hot tub out there where the yard drops down toward the creek, and a small pool, too. You can sit in the water and watch all kinds of wildlife wandering on the other side."

"Really?" She was in awe. She stepped out onto the courtyard and walked to the end to see. "Oh, my God! This is great! Your friend must love it here. I don't think I'd ever want to leave."

"It belongs to his family. They only use it for hunting and fishing but they work so much, there's not much time."

"What a shame." She looked around. It would be impossible not to relax here. It's so peaceful. A person couldn't help but enjoy it. "I wish I brought a swimsuit," she said softly looking at the water.

"There might be an extra one or two in the second room there. That's the girls' room. You can put your stuff there for now."

Sophie went to the room, dropped her purse and cell on the dresser, glanced around at the bright colors with a smile, and returned to the kitchen where he waited. Trev opened a cabinet and pulled down a glass.

"You want something to drink?" he asked. Strained and awkward was all she could think of at the moment.

"I'm okay." She held up a hand and shook her head. Sophie's cell blared at her from the other room.

"Better get that," Trev said. As she headed down the hall, he added, "Mind if I listen in?"

"Why? It's probably just work questions."

"Could be, but right now, any call could be something we need to check out." He raised his voice to reach her as she stepped into the room. The tone stopped as she approached. She snatched the phone from the dresser, noticed the fact that she had three voicemails, and carried it back to the kitchen where he waited.

"They left a voicemail. Looks like I have a few." She played them back. Two from Callie and one from her assistant. They just wanted to check on her. She gave him a questioning glance. He waved a hand at the cell and nodded.

"Go ahead."

Before she dialed, it jumped into action again, startling them both. With speaker phone active, she answered. Callie again.

"Jesus, you're hard to get a hold of. I assume you're still sick?" Callie blurted as soon as Sophie spoke.

"Yeah, this thing is a tough one. It's really got me down." Sophie warmed at the thought that she was becoming quite the actress. It wasn't usually her style.

"What is it, a flu or something? You want me to come by and stay with you for a while?" Nice of her to offer.

Trev frowned and shook his head. "No! No need. I'm not at home."

"I gathered that. I went by your place last night. Why's someone guarding the door?"

"I didn't know they were. I've been staying with Trevor. I guess the guy I reported the stalker to finally took it seriously." Sophie swore she heard Callie intake a quick breath. A small stretch of silence occurred.

"You're at *his* place? Wow! I had no idea he was a serious thing. Are you sure you're okay? He hasn't kidnapped you or anything?" Trevor almost choked on the water he'd just drank from the tap.

Sophie wasn't sure how to answer that one. He held up a finger and wagged it. "Of course not, he's right here—you're on speaker."

"Hey, Callie," Trevor chimed.

"Oh, hey. Are you taking good care of my girl there?"

"That's what I'm here for. She's just not—responding as eagerly as expected to my bedside manner." He grinned.

"Okay, I'm not *even* going to ask what that means but if you need a better patient, just let me know. Soph, take care of yourself and get back in here. Don't forget we have lunch plans on Friday."

"Let's play it by ear, Cal. I'm about half dead now. If I kick this thing soon, I'll be back in." Sophie was getting frustrated with all the lies she had to weave together. Change the subject. "How's everything going at the office? Any big emergencies?"

"Not a one, but are you still planning to do the migration next week?" That piqued Trevor's interest. He moved closer to the phone.

"Oh, crap. No, I won't be ready. Can you call them and see when we can reschedule it for?"

"No problem."

"Anything else going on? You doing okay?"

"Sure, if you call drowning in debt okay. I need a sugar daddy. Know any likely candidates? Someone with a nice stash of cash that I can live off of for, I don't know, the next twenty years?"

Sophie laughed. "If I did, do you really think I'd introduce him to *you*? I'd hang onto that myself, girl."

Trevor shook his head and turned back to his water glass by the sink. He filled it again and took a drink.

They ended the call and Sophie slipped the phone into her pocket. "See, nothing to worry about. Other than my projects are all falling apart."

"You plan to call back your assistant?"

"No need. I'm sure Callie's probably already at her desk right now, letting her know we spoke and that I'm still out."

"She sounds like a bit of a gossip." He emptied the rest of the water glass and slipped it into the dishwasher.

"No, but there's some kind of competition going on there, between them, as to who knows more about me. I don't get it."

Trevor shrugged. "Women. I'm going to make some phone calls for work. Why don't you make yourself comfortable? If you want to swim, poke around in that room and see if you can find something to wear." He drew his phone out of his pocket and dialed a number. "Have fun," he added before he turned around and walked to the front yard to make his calls.

Sophie went back to the room, searched around a bit, and found a suit she could wear. She decided to lie on the bed for a moment and rest instead. She felt exhausted and the bed was so lusciously soft.

When Sophie woke four hours later, the light was dimming in the window so she knew the sun was sinking into dusk. She stretched and rose to see what Trevor was up to. She found him down by the creek. He was wearing swimming trunks and cutting wood with a hatchet. His shoulders and chest were drenched in sweat. The minute she saw him, she stopped walking. Her breath caught in her throat; her mouth went instantly dry. *I could stare at that for hours.* He was solid muscle, head to toe. The scar on his arm continued across his underarm, ending just below his rib cage and served to only enhance the edginess of the rest of his body. She wondered what the story was behind the scar. More importantly, she wondered what he'd do if she reached out to feel it, to feel him. If a guy could be sumptuous, Trevor definitely fit the bill. As she stood there with her mouth open, watching him move, he looked up and saw her. *Oh crap, there's that grin. Does he know what I was thinking?* He waved.

"Well hello there, sleepy head! I thought I was going to have to come wake you up before long."

"Sorry. What time is it?" She ran her fingers through her hair trying to calm it down but the curls didn't want to cooperate. She couldn't take her eyes off his naked chest. Who would have known all that muscle was under those shirts!

"It's around nine, I think. My watch is inside. Are you ready to go back to Houston?" He gathered up the wood and carried it toward her.

"I, uh . . . it's late." She was still staring.

"Yes, and if we leave now, we can get back by midnight." He

dropped the wood into the firepit in front of her with a loud thunk.

"Where would I stay when I get there if I can't go home?" She hadn't thought to ask Callie about staying with her earlier.

"That's up to you." Trevor put his hands on his hips and looked at the wood, then at her. "But I need to know if I should light this fire or not."

Christ, she thought, *you already did.* Sophie walked toward him, meeting him at the firepit. She stopped in front of him. "Sure. Light it," she whispered. She didn't know what came over her then. Someone else had taken her senses away. She slid her hand up his chest and behind his neck, pulling his face down to meet hers and then she pressed her lips against his mouth. She couldn't believe what she was doing. She never pounced on a guy like this, but it was virtually impossible not to touch him. Especially after the way he had kissed her the other night. This was more than a little out of character for her. She started to pull away.

Without hesitation, his hands flew to her face, both of them cupping the back of her neck, pulling her back to him. His thumbs were rubbing against her earlobes, as he crushed his mouth to hers. He smelled of sweat, cologne, and wood. Sophie's hand dropped to Trevor's chest and then his waist, squeezing his flesh as she pulled him closer. She loved the feel of his skin stretched over the hard muscles. She couldn't help the faint moan that escaped her lips. She heard a low answering groan from inside him and his tongue glided around the inside of her mouth before trailing down her neck. Oh, he was good.

"Trev?" she said softly.

He lifted his head, his breathing was rasped and heavy, and looked in her face to see what she wanted.

"Please don't be a bad guy." Her eyes were on fire as she reached for him.

"Oh, Soph," his lips brushed gently against hers, "I'm not. I swear I'm not. Surely you know that?"

"I believe you." Sophie sighed. She didn't really understand why he'd helped her so much. Why he'd brought her all the way here just to protect her, but right now she didn't care. She wanted his skin against hers. Surely that wouldn't be a big deal. Just that. She wanted to feel the warmth of his chest touching her own. She reached up her arms and lifted her shirt over her head as she watched desire leap into Trevor's eyes when he saw her breasts, covered in small wisps of lace, released from the cloth.

"Aw, Henry. You're *so beautiful!*" His head dropped to kiss her again and she caught her breath when his tongue stroked the inside of her mouth before descending to lick the bareness of her skin on his. Lord, he knew what to do with his mouth and his hands. Just how to touch, and where. All she wanted to do was get closer, to crawl inside those arms. Every inch of him was hard as concrete against her and she wrapped her own arms around him, clutching into his skin to mold him closer. Her legs felt weak and she stumbled a little as his hand pushed her breast up to meet his lips. She quivered as he moved from one side to the other, taking his time caressing.

"Are you cold?" He stopped to look at her, his eyes dark and burning. "Do you want to go inside?"

"Yes. Inside." She wasn't cold. It wasn't possible to be cold when he did that, but she didn't think she could stand up much longer.

His eyes crinkled when he laughed softly, as if he knew what she was thinking. He slipped the shirt back over her head temporarily, then took her hand and pulled her inside the house to the first bedroom he found. She didn't really understand why he wasted the time to get her shirt back on but she wasn't going to argue. As she followed behind him, she watched the ripples in his back as he moved. She placed her free hand on them so that she could feel the motion.

Chapter Fourteen

When Sophie woke in the middle of the night, she knew her life had changed so significantly that she'd never return to what she thought of as normal. There were so many reasons for the change and very little she could do to corral it back in, even if she wanted to—and she wasn't sure she did. Someone had broken into her apartment for a reason, not just a burglary. It had to be more than that. And she was pretty certain it had a lot to do with the problems she'd found in the accounting reports. Whoever it was, they didn't want her to see what she'd seen.

Amazingly, that all seemed secondary to the change that happened last night. As she snuggled against the chest of this intoxicating man, listening to him breathe, she knew she'd never forget how he felt against her in the dark or how he smelled of sweat, soap, and wood at the same time. Trevor was a stranger in so many ways but he was warm, and strong, and passionate, and most importantly—safe. His hands had played over every inch of her during the night. Obviously, he was well practiced at this, because it took him no time at all to turn her into a panting crazy woman.

She had struggled to pull him closer and closer. She'd found herself smelling his skin on his stomach, then tugging the dark hairs on his chin with her teeth. She was embarrassed remembering it all. He had laughed at her hunger to feel and touch and taste, but his laughter let way to a flood of other words, soft words, and gentle words as he caressed her back while she lay on his stomach. Then stronger, more demanding words when her hands and mouth moved down his front. When they eventually came together, he'd taken complete control and his movements were strong, forceful, and demanding. He ceased words altogether and just let out a loud, guttural curse as he called out her name. She barely noticed it because she was panting and lost in her own wave of emotion.

Now, his leg sprawled lazily over her thigh, trapping her to him possessively.

"You awake?" he said softly.

"Mmmm, sort of," she whispered into the pillow. "Not really."

"Come here." He wrapped both arms around her and hauled her against his bare chest. Instant electricity, she thought. "I'm not sleepy," he spoke into her ear. Then he proceeded to show her just how awake he was, how awake he wanted her to be, with his hands and mouth. When he was done and she thought she was going to die, he smiled in the moonlight from the window as she lay against him.

"Are you sleepy now?" she said. "'Cause I'm exhausted."

"In a good way, right?"

"Yeah, a really good way."

"Okay. Get some sleep, babe. We have a lot to do tomorrow." He kissed her hair and squeezed her shoulder with his huge hand. Sophie closed her eyes, thinking how nice it was to have someone call her *babe*. She'd always thought it corny before, but it sounded good now, real good. She tried to sleep, but her four-hour nap had pretty much pegged out her sleep meter. And with everything he'd done, she couldn't really block it out of her mind long enough to think about sleep. She couldn't stay here against him like this without wanting more of him. She extricated herself from his leg and arm and slid quietly out of the bed.

*

Early Saturday morning, Sophie followed Trevor up and then down a pathway nestled among hills. The lane was edged by trees of unknown variety and it meandered in what seemed like a completely unplanned route.

"Where are we going?" she spoke between breaths as they climbed a pretty steep incline. He had a black backpack over one shoulder and a small satchel in his other hand.

"You'll see in a few minutes. We're almost there." He glanced back to make sure she was able to keep up.

Keeping up didn't pose a problem. Controlling her over-active sweat glands was another matter. That was one of the things she hated about herself—even the smallest amount of exercise caused her to be a complete puddle of perspiration. She envied the girls that could still look beautiful while exercising or even at the beach. She wasn't one of them. She ran five miles a day when she could and she looked like she'd been in a rainstorm every time. When they crested the hill, the path headed downward and opened into a large grassy field. At one end, there was a line of rocks piled up like a fence line. The field itself looked like a dumping post for people's old equipment. There was an old lawnmower, a tractor, parts of different cars, and several empty barrels.

"Here we are," Trevor proclaimed with satisfaction.

Sophie looked around. "Where exactly would that be?" She couldn't help but show a little sarcasm and he looked sideways at her with an eyebrow arched.

"This is school for you."

"School?"

"Yeah, today you're going to learn to shoot." He started down the hill without checking to see if she was following. There wasn't anywhere else to go anyway.

"Shoot? I don't need to know how to shoot! I've already told you I don't have a gun."

"Listen." Trevor walked to her, and stood over her with his eyes only inches away. "I heard you, but after what happened the other day, you'd be a lot safer if you at least knew how to protect yourself if something else happens. Everyone should be able to defend themselves if they ever need to, even someone as naïve as you are."

"I'm not naïve!"

"Yes, you are. You live in the fourth largest city in the country. A city that's in the top ten for number of annual murders, and you walk around thinking nothing bad will ever happen." He picked a small twig from her hair. "Chances are it won't, but wouldn't it be smart to at least be prepared just in case?"

"But I . . . "

"Don't argue with me, Henry." He focused on her mouth and she thought for a minute he was going to kiss her. "It's important you at least can defend yourself in a crisis. I'm not asking you to shoot anybody, just learn how to use it so you can take care of yourself if you have to." He turned and descended the hill to the rock wall. When she caught up with him, he had placed the backpack on the wall and was unloading a few handguns along with several boxes of shells. He set the satchel next to the backpack and motioned for her to follow him.

"Here." He handed her one of the handguns and a fistful of bullets. "The button on the side here," he pointed, "is the safety. It's in the on position right now. Keep it there unless you intend to shoot something. If you move it to the off position—there— put it back as soon as you know you're not going to use it. That's probably the one mistake more people make than anything. Safety stays on except while shooting, then it goes immediately back when done shooting. Got it?" He raised an eyebrow at her.

"Got it."

"Here." He placed several shells in her hand. "Watch me load and then load yours."

Sophie observed his movements and mimicked them until both guns were filled.

"See that old lawnmower out there?" He pointed. She nodded. "We're gonna start with that. It's close and should be pretty easy to hit."

"That's close? I can barely see it."

"Watch me." He turned the safety to the off position, raised the gun with his right hand around the handle, thumb on the trigger, and his left hand under the gun to steady it. He planted himself firmly against the wall, aimed, and pulled the trigger. "Now you."

He stood behind her and watched as she copied his actions exactly. "Good. Where were you aiming?"

"The lawnmower."

"Try again." She lifted the gun again, aimed at the mower and pulled the trigger. Nothing happened. Trevor looked puzzled. "Aim about a yard to the right of the mower."

Sophie lifted the gun and aimed at a clump of dirt that emerged from the grass. When she pulled the trigger, a small poof of dust rose from the ground.

Trevor smiled faintly. "Do it again. Same place." Another small dust cloud rose nearby. "Good, now hit the lawn mower again and listen carefully when you pull the trigger."

Sophie held her breath. She did as instructed and heard a very, very faint ping as the bullet hit metal. "I hit it!" she smiled and turned to Trevor. He put the safety back on before she got completely around.

"Yeah, you did. Every time." He grinned. "For someone who doesn't like guns, you're a pretty good shot. Let's try hitting something farther away."

They spent forty-five minutes aiming at the various piles of junk strewn across the field. Trevor reminded her frequently about how to hold the gun, how to anticipate the wind, various safety rules. When they ran out of shells, he returned everything to the backpack.

"One last thing," he said as he pulled the other satchel open and reached inside. "If you ever have to use a gun to defend yourself, shoot here, here, or here." He pointed to both shoulders and legs. "Start with the legs. Hitting someone there will maim them and most likely give you time to get away. But it probably won't kill them." He hesitated. "The only time you should ever shoot at the head, chest, or abdomen is if it's your life or theirs. And you better be sure."

Sophie's eyes widened as she weighed his words. "You're scaring me again."

"I'm not trying to scare you—just prepare you. You'll probably never need to use that, but if you do, don't you think it's good to know what you're doing?"

"I guess so."

"Good. You hungry?" He pulled a couple of bottles of water and two paper bags out of the satchel. He handed a drink and bag to her and moved closer. "It's just sandwiches, but it'll take us a while to get back so I thought it might be good to eat here." He sat against the rock wall, patting the rocks next to him for her to sit also.

"Okay. I'm not really hungry but the drink sounds good."

Despite her words, she bit into one of the sandwiches. He watched her eat, his mouth twitched a little when she finished the last bite.

"What's so funny?" she asked noticing his attempt to keep a straight face.

"For someone who's not hungry, you sure have an appetite."

"Blame it on yourself, buddy, between last night and this morning, you've given me quite a workout." As soon as she said it, she got a little embarrassed.

"In that case, you better eat another sandwich." His eyes sparkled in the sun as he chuckled. "I wouldn't want you to run out of energy later."

She looked away, hiding her own smile. "It's probably time to go." She rose from the wall.

"No." His voice softened. "Not yet." He stuffed their trash into the satchel, pushed her gently back onto the wall, and spread his lanky legs so they held her captive against the rocks. "Kiss me, Sophie," he murmured. And she did. "Are you still scared?"

"Scared as hell," she admitted as he wrapped his hands into her hair and kissed her senseless.

Chapter Fifteen

The afternoon sun was searing into their skin by the time they returned to the ranch house. "I think I'm going to jump in the pool for a minute. I'm burning up." Trev pulled off his shirt and walked toward the back of the house. Sophie felt her stomach flip watching the muscles flex in his shoulders. His skin was damp with sweat and had a slick sheen to it.

He strode back through the living room in his swimming trunks a couple minutes later. She swallowed hard when she saw his bare chest and arms. "Come join me," he said, as if giving an order. He hesitated at the back door and smiled over his shoulder, "That is, if you're not too scared."

"Are you daring me?"

He was already out the door and headed down the courtyard, whistling something as he strode toward the pool.

Trev was under water when she wandered up to the pool in the borrowed bikini. It fit a little loosely but still covered her well enough. His head emerged and he rubbed the streams of water from his face with his hands before opening his eyes. When he saw her standing there, he moved to the edge of the pool in front of her.

"Henry, you are fucking beautiful." He squinted into the sun shining from behind her. He put his hand on her ankle and stroked her calf sending small trickles of water down her leg.

"The suit's a little big." She walked to the pool steps and lowered herself into the water. It was deliciously cool and she slid in quickly. He was in front of her before she went very far. He circled his arms around her and pulled her tight against him. Trevor's mouth covered hers and a tingle pulsed through her stomach; the warmth of his body engulfed her like a blanket. He pushed her back to the edge of the pool. His hand slid under the small piece of cloth covering one breast and he squeezed gently, his mouth trailed down her shoulder and back up her neck.

"The suit's perfect." He muttered against the skin of her neck. "You're perfect."

"Not as perfect as this," she whispered stroking a hand across the muscles in his chest. She trailed her fingers across the scar. "How'd this happen?"

"Sailing."

"Yeah, right. Seriously, how'd you get it? If you don't want to tell me, that's okay."

"I'm not lying. I was sailing. First time out. I'd gone with a friend. Actually, it was part of a job. The wind was pretty strong and caught the sail and it flew from one side of the boat to the other. I didn't know anything about sailing and didn't know what he was saying. It caught me full on and sent me over the side. I ripped my arm trying to hold on for dear life."

"I didn't know you sailed."

He smiled, "Obviously, I don't. Never went on a boat again after that. I had more stitches than Frankenstein."

"That must have hurt."

Her hand slid down his stomach where it stopped, resting her fingers at the top of his trunks. His eyes narrowed a little. He lifted his head back to look at her. She slipped her fingers into the waistband, stroking his abdomen and he groaned loudly before crushing his mouth back to hers.

"That was nothing compared to what you're doing to me. You're gonna kill me, woman, I know it." He breathed against her lips. "I think I'm the one who should be scared." He hugged her tightly and the tingle in her stomach spread through the rest of her body. Her hand slipped further down his abdomen, pressing against him, feeling him respond to her touch. She saw him catch his breath for a second as she stroked him. Then his hand was on her wrist, holding her still. "Not here, babe." He spoke softly and pushed her toward the stairs.

"Why not?" She looked around at the trees. "We're in the middle of nowhere."

"See that little place at the top of the hill over there?" He pointed to a wood and stone structure that looked miles away. "That guy's good friends with the family that owns this place and he's got the biggest telescope I've ever seen in that little window you see at the top. We do this here and the whole town of Tervis, population one hundred and fifty, will know about how the Pr . . . I . . . screwed the gorgeous girl in the pool at the Praters' ranch."

"Oh. Well, I probably won't see any of them anyway, but I get it. I guess it would be kind of embarrassing for you."

"Not for me. I'd be the town hero." He grinned. "You, on the other hand, might be afraid to show your face here again." He pulled her hand up to his lips. "Let's take this inside, okay?"

"Okay." She wondered if he would even want her to show her face here again regardless. They ascended the steps toward the house. He laced his fingers between hers and, with gentle impatience, tugged her past the towel lying on the chair. Sophie smiled and reached behind her back. A little gossip might be good for him. Besides, she'd never see them, anyway. She pulled the strings to the bikini top loose as they started across the courtyard and slid the top over her head. She lifted her hand to her side and let the garment drop from her fingers onto the stone. "I wouldn't want you to go completely without a little hero worship."

Trevor's eyes slanted sideways at her. "Damn," he exhaled. His jaw twitched as he strengthened his grip on her fingers. They continued their pace into the house as he shot a protective scowl over his shoulder at the hills.

*

It was dark again when they lay exhausted on the bed in his room. His heart was pounding fast but steadily under the palm of her hand as her cheek rested on his chest. Trevor was flat on his back with one arm draped over her shoulder. "Trev?" She lifted her head and looked at his face. "Why don't I fix us something to eat?"

"Did the sandwich wear off?" He raised his hand and rubbed his eyes with his thumb and forefinger.

"A long time ago."

"Yeah, me too. Why don't we drive into town and get something?"

"You mean so you can gloat?" She grinned. He responded with a short laugh.

"No, not to Tervis, I was thinking maybe a little farther, into Fredericksburg. Tervis rolls up the sidewalks by eight so nothing's open there." He raised his arms above his head and stretched a long, sexy stretch before adding, "Come on, get up." He rolled her off him and spanked her gently on the behind to get her moving.

An hour and a half later, they were sitting outside under a latticed roof over a large patio, eating pizza and drinking wine. A lone guitarist was singing in the corner of the patio as he strummed along on the guitar. There was a cool breeze blowing just enough that they had to anchor their napkins to keep them from being whisked away.

"This is nice." Sophie sighed.

"Yeah, it is. Really nice," Trevor admitted. He patted her thigh under the table and took another bite of pizza. "So, tell me something." He swallowed. "Do you happen to have another USB copy of the accounting database anywhere?"

"Yeah, sure. I made two copies in case you couldn't read one of them. Why?"

"I left the one you gave me at the office. I kind of thought we could go back tomorrow morning and look at it but I don't have it. Also, again, who has access to the server besides you?"

"The two network admins and one of our DBAs." She looked at him.

"What about client side access to change the data?"

"There are quite a few with that but mostly in the accounting department. In my area, there are only two people. The DBA and a systems analyst that's been doing the financial reports for years."

"I need names. Write them down." He removed the knife that was holding his napkin in place and handed the napkin to her. "You have a pen in your purse?"

"I'm repeating myself, but why are you asking?"

"Soph, I think you already know that, don't you?"

She studied his expression curiously. He squeezed her leg where he had patted it earlier, and smiled. "Whoever wanted those reports knows you know something's wrong. So, if what you did find is important to them, maybe criminal, they'll be back because they know that you know."

Yes, she'd already thought of that. She wasn't sure how to deal with it and truthfully, didn't know exactly what she'd found yet because she hadn't spent enough time with the data to tell.

"We need to know what's in the data before your office opens on Monday so we know whether you can go back or not."

"Of course I can go back! I have to work. How am I supposed to pay my bills?"

"Depending on what's happening, it might not be safe to go back. I know you've thought of that, too."

"Yeah, I have, but it seemed a little melodramatic." She talked quietly.

Trev raised his wine to his mouth and took a slow drink before answering. "Crime usually is."

"I don't even know if there is a crime right now." She handed him the napkin with the names on it.

"No, you don't, but I do this for a living, and I'm pretty sure." He folded the napkin and pushed it down into his pocket. "Let's go home and get some sleep so we can leave early tomorrow, okay?"

Sophie found it interesting that Trevor referred to the hunting cabin at Prater Ranch as home. It lent a familiarity to their time together that seemed a little too "relationship-like." To some extent, it made her uncomfortable, but she still liked the feel of his hand as he reached for hers to guide her reluctantly out of the patio.

"Trev, what am I going to do if it really is that bad? I'll probably lose my job." She spoke the fear she'd felt several days before.

"It'll all work out fine. You're going to be great."

When they got back to the ranch, Trevor remained outside and made some phone calls while Sophie went in and changed to her nightclothes. She slipped between the sheets in the girls' room and closed her eyes. She couldn't sleep, wondering what would come of all the changes in her life. The door quietly opened and Trevor spoke from the doorway, "Henry?"

"Yeah?"

"Are you mad at me?"

"No, why would I be?"

"Are you afraid of me?"

"No, not really."

"Then why are you in here?" He sounded hurt.

"I don't know. I just wasn't sure."

"Wasn't sure of what?"

"That you'd want—" She wasn't really sure he wanted her there and she wasn't going to assume he did. She heard him walk to the bed and toss the cover away from her. Then he lifted her up and carried her back to his room. He slipped her under the covers and slid in next to her, holding her against him.

"If you don't want to be here, you can leave whenever you want to, but if you think I don't want you here, you'd be wrong," he whispered into her hair. "I wish I could stop wanting you here. It would be so much easier for both of us." He was so warm against her back. It made her feel really, really safe—and wanted.

"You feel great, Trev," she murmured as she drifted off to sleep. Really great.

*

The ride back to Houston was quiet. Too quiet. Trevor was focused on driving and didn't seem to want to talk. After an hour of silence, Sophie laid her head back on the seat and closed her eyes.

"You tired, Henry?" *Finally, he speaks.*

"No. Just tired of talking to myself. You haven't said a word since we got in the car," she muttered grumpily. "What's bugging you?"

"Nothing." His lips tightened. "I was just thinking about, well, everything I need to do over the next couple of days."

"And I got in the way of that?"

"No. That's not what I meant. I'm worried about how it's all gonna pan out in the end." She had no idea what he was talking about but it sounded like she should.

He slid his fingers around hers and squeezed. "I didn't mean to ignore you. I was just deep in thought, I guess. What do you want to talk about?"

"Nothing really." She closed her eyes again. Now she was ready for some quiet time.

"Nothing at all?"

"Nope." Her thoughts were screaming *Yes! I want to talk about YOU . . . US. What's going to happen when we get back? Do we act like this never happened? What do I do if we really do find a problem in the data? Why are you here? Now that the weekend is over, are we over, too?*

"Okay, then." He squeezed her hand one more time, then let it go.

Chapter Sixteen

They arrived back in Houston just before noon on Sunday. Trev never told her where they would stop first. He didn't ask where she wanted to go and knew he couldn't take her back to her place yet, not unless he went with her. He doubted she'd ask him to, so he took the only option that seemed easy and plausible—he took her to his apartment. It was the best way to keep her safe, he told himself, and they could use his computer equipment to investigate the data.

She had nodded off but woke when they got into the city and the stop and go driving became more difficult for sleeping. He looked at her on the passenger side with her hair pulled back and the sunlight flickering across her face. That same face had lain on his arm all night, her soft breathing had tickled his flesh. He still felt the warmth of her back against his chest and the thought made him want to go back to the ranch.

Things were probably going to get sticky now. She would hate him when she found out he had been following her for a long time. If he told her now, he'd risk everything they'd done so far on the case. If he didn't, he would most likely lose her when she found out. There wasn't really a choice—he had to do his job.

"Here we are," he stated quietly as they pulled into the parking garage.

"Why don't I call Callie to come get me? That way you won't have to babysit me anymore."

"I'm not babysitting you. We need to work together on this if we're gonna figure out what's happening at your office. I need your help." Then he corrected himself. "You need my help."

Sophie sighed. "I wish we could have stayed there longer. I liked your friend's ranch."

"Yeah, me too." She had voiced his own thoughts. "Wanna go back?" He quirked an eyebrow at her, wishing she'd say *yes.*

"No." She stretched her arms above her head, hitting the roof of the car. "We're here, let's do this."

Was it possible to be disappointed and relieved at the same time? He turned off the car and walked around to her door to open it.

"Let's don't go up just yet." He had a thought. "Let's go down the street and get some lunch. I'm hungry. What about you?" He knew it was probably risky to have her out in the open, but he wanted it to be normal. Like it could have been if they'd met differently. He wanted her to be with him under her own volition, not because he was keeping her safe.

Sophie lifted herself from the car, taking the hand he'd offered. When she rose, she was against him, not really touching him but he felt her. He waited for an answer.

"Sure, sure. Yeah, we skipped breakfast so I'm a little hungry, too."

"Are you a breakfast person?"

She nodded as he turned to walk toward the door of the garage, keeping her hand in his. "Most important meal of the day!" she answered cheerfully.

"That's right. Most important," he agreed. "I'll make breakfast tomorrow." She looked at him when he said it and he wasn't sure if she smiled a little or not.

"Who said I'd be around for breakfast?"

"That's up to you. If you want to go somewhere else, just say the word."

"I really want to go home."

"Okay, well, not that word—anywhere but there or work." He squeezed her hand and they walked to the deli near his apartment. He made sure to keep an eye on every person there—and watched the street, also.

It took a while to get the data restored onto his computer because he didn't have the right version of SQL database software to read it. Once he loaded the right version, they restored the data and started digging through the transactions looking for the detail that she'd seen on the reports stolen from her apartment. Without the reports, they were working mainly off Sophie's memory of the transactions, so backtracking through the various tables of the database was tedious at best. By ten p.m., Trevor had determined that the database had indeed been manually edited to hide the transactions. He also saw that most of the transactions ended up going to a trust fund called Brotherhood of Hope. The address was a post office box so that wouldn't help a lot. He'd have to get a subpoena for the state filings on the business name and the bank records.

Trev went to the bedroom for a little privacy and called Cheryl on her cell, expecting to leave a message. "Hey, Trev! You're a hard man to get in touch with." She was cheerful for this time of night.

"I need your help. I need to subpoena bank records for the Brotherhood of Hope trust fund. I'll email you the address and bank account number."

"No problem. Hey, we got the bank records back on the folks you asked for last week. I tried to call you Friday but I just kept getting voicemail."

"Oh, sorry. I must have missed the ring. Why didn't you leave a message?" He was pretty sure the records were going to be inconclusive so he only listened halfheartedly as he glanced toward his office at Sophie. She was sitting at the desk, tapping a pen up and down, looking bored and beautiful.

"I wanted to talk to you directly and a message might have been a problem for you. Wasn't sure."

"Anything I need to know about?"

"Well, yes there is. Boss wants you to bring the girl in tomorrow morning. Apparently, she has a string of deposits to her bank accounts from anonymous sources that date back quite a while."

Trevor's knuckles turned white as he gripped the phone. His eyes widened as he watched Sophie tapping away. He tried not to sound panicked. "Are you sure it was her account and not one of the others?"

"Trev, come on! Do I ever get people confused? Yes, it was her. Looks like you guys were on the right track. Have her here around nine."

"Got it," he confirmed, his voice hollow. His stomach felt sick. He thought he was going to vomit. *How could I have been wrong?*

"Oh, and Nate's doing the interrogation. They think you're probably a little too involved." The phone went dead as she hung up but he couldn't lower it yet. He just stood there, watching Sophie tap a pen to his desk as if nothing at all was wrong. *Fuck!*

Chapter Seventeen

Another rainstorm brewed outside and Lenny grabbed his jacket and umbrella before leaving for the office. Even though their garage was covered at work, he intended to take a trip to the lockbox during lunch and deposit his latest copies of data and recordings. This was starting to be almost a daily occurrence lately. There were too many loose ends, too many tracks to cover. He had a splitting headache most of the time from trying to keep it all straight.

The traffic was moving pretty well for rush hour and it gave him time to think on the way in. He wasn't satisfied with just lying low. They needed to do more than that. He didn't want things to get to the point where they did something crazy—like they'd done last time. They were only trying to scare Bob. He wasn't supposed to die. Unfortunately, the guy had an overactive imagination and his jittery paranoia caused him to hit an embankment too hard and flip the car. That wasn't supposed to happen. That had been the turning point. When the realization hit as to how far they would go to cover this up, the likelihood of him being able to get out became nonexistent.

Use the numbers, he told himself. It had taken most of the night to set up the script that would make the edits necessary to finish his cleanup work. While doing so, he also added in a small script that would solidify her place in this and take the heat off his team. Just one tiny transaction and she'd be in hot water. Unfortunately, it had to be done at the office. The VPN tunnel to the bank would only work from their office IP address. And it required an authorization to complete.

So he told his wife he had to stay late to convert some data for the boss. He'd go eat something, hang around for a few hours, then go back and run the script.

He dialed the number again and waited for an answer.

"What." Irritation spewed from the speaker of his cell.

"Talk to the auditor about testing the security of the accounting system and validating the transactions. I'm setting it up tonight so it should be ready for an audit. That will get her out of our way."

"I thought I told you not to call me."

Lenny ignored his outburst. This needed to get done, and the sooner the better. For all of them. "Look, you're the only person he'll take the order from."

"You sure that's going to work?"

"Yes. Once I've done the transaction updates. Just get the auditor checking it out asap."

"Okay. I'll meet with him later this week, but once he's done it, we'll have to fire her. She has to be gone before any more deposits are made. People are going to ask questions."

"And you'll do what you always do. You'll publicize the audit results and they'll insinuate that her management of the applications resulted in theft of company property. In this case, it's company funds, which will be even more incriminating. Once the board hears the results, they'll demand that she be fired but by that time it will already be done."

"What if she fights it?"

"Why would she? It will ruin her career if it gets out that she's been involved in something like that. It's in her best interest to be silent."

"She's not the type to be silent. She'll want an investigation."

"Then give her one. Have the audit team check it out. You know they'll back us up. Besides no one is going to argue with the auditor . . . she doesn't stand a chance. It's kind of a shame, really. She was just trying to do the right thing. Do her job."

"I don't like it, Lenny. This is getting messy. We're done after the next round."

"No problem."

"I swear to God, if you call me again, I'll come after you with a tire iron."

"Got it."

"I'm not kid—."

Lenny clicked the cell closed, hanging up before the last word fell. He thought it humorous that the little weasel believed he was capable of touching him. The guy was half his size and probably couldn't even take on Sophie in a fight. Besides, he was older than dirt and hadn't worked out in years.

Random drops of rain hit his windshield with a loud smack as he exited the freeway and turned toward his building. The storm was coming and he was more than prepared.

Chapter Eighteen

Trevor stood watching Nate interrogate Sophie through the glass. He was exhausted from a long sleepless night. He'd feigned a request to investigate something on another job in order to avoid Sophie. When she'd fallen asleep in the chair across from his desk, he had gone to bed, only to have her creep in later and wrap around him. As much as he had wanted it, he hated himself for not recognizing the truth. For not keeping his head straight.

He knew she couldn't see him but still he felt the anger in her eyes as if they were focused solely on him. It's a sickening feeling to make love to someone, believing them to be one thing and then find out they're something else. She had fooled him completely. He believed her. All her actions and all her words had convinced him she had nothing to do with the fraud that was occurring at Benton & Stanley. Yet, when it came right down to it, her bank statement told the truth. The numbers didn't lie. They never did. Sometimes they could be misleading, but in the end, what's in the data can't be disputed. Even if someone doctored a report, it was usually easy to track it through the data and the timestamps associated with each modification. Especially in accounting systems where no entry was ever deleted, it just got archived. Changes were always new entries, not replacements. Easy to track if you knew what to look for.

He had believed every word she said and even now, he couldn't believe he was watching them break her down. He was sick. Sick to his stomach. How could he have been so stupid? He'd never made a mistake like that before, never misread anyone this significantly. He was losing his edge, all because he let himself get sidetracked, let himself be attracted to her.

Still he watched her through the glass as Nate talked and he thought he saw innocence in her eyes. He was imagining it, he knew, but she didn't react like he expected her to. Maybe he was just hoping for a miracle but he wanted to believe her. Probably because he'd let himself get way too involved. He let himself act toward her as if she were just someone he would have met and gotten involved with in a normal way like people do—like couples do—and not someone he was supposed to investigate. Last night, she had tried to wake him and make love. He'd kept his eyes wrenched shut and sprawled on his stomach. It had seemed like hours before she finally accepted that he wasn't going to wake and rolled away. Still, he was seconds from turning into her when she stopped and he hated himself for his weakness. Trev turned from the glass, ran a hand through his hair and sighed. Unable to look away, he turned back.

Interrogations were not Nate's strong suit, he usually preferred to leave that to Trev, as Trevor was normally pretty calm and unruffled no matter what happened. Nate's temper tended to ignite quickly and, once it flared up, he became impatient with the ways suspects tried to negate or avoid their guilt.

As Trev watched through the glass, he remembered how she looked at him when they lay in his bed together. Her eyes had been electric with emotion and passion, so he thought. How could a person be like that with him and pretend the way she had? She had acted as if she knew nothing about what was going on, and he'd believed it all, yet, she was lying the entire time.

The room was like a box—almond colored walls, a door, a window that showed nothing. She obviously knew it was there for them to watch her. She had no indication he was standing on the other side.

Nate thrust his hand out to Sophie. "I'm sorry. I forgot to give you my name, ma'am. I'm Nathan Hernandez. I'm a fraud investigator for the FBI. My team is investigating a report of fraudulent activities at your office."

Sophie watched him warily. She did not accept the hand right off and when Nate grew tired of waiting, he dropped it to his side but continued to make eye contact.

"Mr. Hernandez, why am I here?"

"As I stated, we're investigating fraudulent activities at your place of employment and we have reason to believe you may know something about it." Nate didn't flinch. He rested one hip on the table. "That's why you're here."

"I don't know anything about it," she said with a tint of challenge in her voice. She lifted her chin in defiance.

"Well," Nate lifted up from the table and leaned against the wall behind him, putting his hands in his pockets, "actually, it has a lot to do with you. We have some questions we need to ask."

Sophie kept her chin up and continued to glare at him. "We? Who's 'we'? You and the people on the other side of that window?" She motioned to the smoky glass she had been facing for what seemed like an hour.

She glared at the glass, and the anger in her eyes seemed to be hiding a hint of something else. Trev thought maybe panic. Tension showed around her eyes and it made him uncomfortable to watch—and angry, too, that she had tricked him so adeptly.

"Yes," Nate responded, "that would be accurate. Mainly though, it's just me right now. Agent Prater will likely join us shortly." He moved back to the table, pulling out the chair across from her. He lowered himself into the chair and dropped the folder he'd been holding under his arm on the table between them.

"Wow." Sophie's macadamia nut size eyes widened as she took in the FBI logo on the folder. "This must be pretty serious if you guys are involved."

"Yes, it is. Benton & Stanley is a contractor to the federal and state government. Therefore, fraudulent activity against their business constitutes a crime against the government. And that usually gets us involved." Nate's gaze remained somber to further accentuate the seriousness of the issue.

"That makes sense but I don't see what that has to do with me, or why I was brought into this room." Sophie eyes slanted as Nate opened the folder and pushed the bank statements, turning them so they faced her.

"Please take a look at this document, Ms. Henderson. This shows a series of automated deposits into a bank account in your name." He paused so she could glance down the page. "Can you explain the source and reason for these deposits?" He didn't smile, just watched and waited.

*

Sophie's stomach caved in; she thought she was going to be ill. *They think I did it.* As the intensity of the situation hit her, a series of emotions flashed through her veins. Anger that they would even think this. Terror that the truth would not be easy to prove. Loneliness—she wished she had family with her. Someone on her side. "I don't think there's anything I should talk to you about without an attorney present. I've done nothing wrong but this is scaring the hell out of me."

She bit her lip to stop the trembling. After a few minutes of silence, she continued, "Mr. Hernandez, am I a suspect in something? Do you or your agency believe I am involved in this fraudulent activity you're talking about?"

"At this point, we're just looking for answers, ma'am."

Sophie watched him warily. "I'm a little surprised you don't have the answers to the questions you've just asked me. You're the FBI, right? Surely you have access to the transaction details? I mean, look. You have a copy of my bank statement. Why don't you know the rest?" Her eyes let the anger fully show.

"According to our records, most of the deposits on that statement were made anonymously to your account via an EFT.

We've requested a trace on the transaction numbers and bank codes. We'll likely have the answers tomorrow, but right now, I'm asking *you* to give me a straight answer." Nate's voice was agitated; the impatience had begun. As Sophie gauged the level of frustration in his eyes, she wondered if this guy was one of those chair-throwing types one sees on television. Hopefully not. Still, he looked more than a little agitated with her responses. Two loud taps on the glass came from the other side of the window and interrupted her thoughts.

"Excuse me a moment, Ms. Henderson. I need to step out of the room." He moved toward the door, speaking over his shoulder. "I'd like an answer to that question when I return."

Sophie let her eyes move around the room, darting from the window to the door, then to the papers on the table. She worked hard to fight back any dampness in her eyes. She wouldn't let them see weakness. She'd done nothing wrong. They could accuse all they wanted to, she wouldn't be intimidated by it.

Where was Trevor? He knew she was trying to figure out what was going on. He knew she wasn't involved. He'd left her in the lobby for a few minutes to go to his office. He said he'd be right back but it had taken a long time and she was almost to the point of going looking for him except she wasn't sure where to go. He didn't say which office, not even which floor. And then this lady and man had grabbed her and escorted her into this room.

Sophie lowered her head onto her hands and pressed her mouth against her forearm to stifle the trembling of her lower lip. This was serious, really serious.

The door opened abruptly and Agent Hernandez returned followed by, of all people, Trevor. "Ms. Hernandez, this is my partner, Trevan Prater." Nate gestured to Trev. "I believe you know him."

Sophie's head shot up off the table, her eyes focusing on his. "Trevor?" Her voice pleaded for an explanation . . . *what's going on?* Her eyes narrowed as she watched him squirm.

*

"It's Trevan. Trevan Prater . . . assigned to this investigation." He had to stick to the formalities now, stick to the job. Still, her eyes desperately pleaded him to help her and his stomach felt even sicker.

"Investigation?" she repeated. "So, you were investigating *me* all along? You've been lying to me this whole time?" The lip trembled again and the moisture in the back of her eyes started to spill into her lower eyelids.

"Not completely." He wanted to tell her the parts that were true, that pretty much all of it was real, except his identity. But then, she had lied, too. So, what did it matter?

"Not completely?" Even with tears hanging in her eyes, he could see the flames of anger searing in the background. "Not completely. You pretended to be someone else, right?"

"Yes."

"So, you're not a security consultant, are you?"

"Not in the generic way, but I do specialize in cyber- and computer-related crime." A single tear managed to bubble over the lower lid and roll down her cheek. *Crap, I'm screwed.* He still wanted to believe her, wanted to wipe that tear away. He clenched his jaw and looked down at his hand on the table as he stood over her. He saw his hand shake and he clenched it closed to stop the jittering.

She continued. "And this investigation is why I met you in the first place—why you talked to me, and pretended to be," Sophie's hand motioned from Trevan back to her, "whatever this was."

"It's why I kept talking to you. It's not why I met you. You talked to me first, remember? That wasn't supposed to happen." He didn't look up. He couldn't. Her eyes bored holes into his face right now, but he couldn't look into them. The truth was different than he admitted. It wasn't just about the investigation—as much as he wished it were. Even now, he couldn't believe the facts.

She stood up abruptly but Nate grabbed her shoulder and pushed her back into the chair. She glared at him. "Get your hands off of me, asshole. I don't know what this is about but I have *nothing* to do with it." Her eyes were slivers of wet fire as she leaned toward Trevan. "The transactions you're so concerned about are deposits into an account set up by my father when I was a child. The payments are from a trust fund established on my behalf so he could ease his conscience for being such a lousy dad by giving me money."

"Ms. Henderson." Trevan spoke softly, trying to keep his emotions invisible. He didn't want to be here, didn't want to be doing this, but the evidence seemed overwhelming. And now she tried to cover for it. He had to do his job. "Your father has been out of the picture since you were a small child."

"Yes and no, *Mr. Prater.*" The sarcasm in her voice was almost syrupy as it dripped off her tongue. "Or should I call you *Agent Prater?*" She didn't even try to disguise the hatred she was so clearly feeling for him right now. "My father's name is Randolph James Henderson. The deposits you see there, all but that last one, which appears to go to another account, as I said before, are from a trust fund he established for me when I was three years old."

The shock couldn't really be hidden when the words had sunk in. "Randolph Henderson? The real estate tycoon?" he questioned with disbelief.

"Yes, Trevor. Trevan. I mean, *Agent Prater.*" The words just kept getting harsher and harsher as they tumbled out of her mouth. "Is that so hard to believe? That I would be the daughter of a man like that?" She clenched her hands into fists, then released them repeatedly. "Call him, check it out. Or better yet, just get a copy of my birth certificate. I can't believe you haven't already done that. I realize you can't fathom that a man like that would be married to someone like my mother and that I would actually be his daughter. But it's true."

Sophie squared her shoulders, her bottom lip was still trembling and Trevan had the distinct impression it was taking every ounce of her composure to keep the tears from flooding.

All he could do was watch her.

Dumbfounded. She was the daughter of one of the richest men in the state of New York? No fucking way. How could they have missed something like that? Why didn't it show up? He didn't want to admit it but the truth was pretty clear. If it were true— and she seemed adamant that it was—it was too ugly. It was the sort of thing that simmers under the surface, but no one ever lets it bubble through because the truth was too shameful to admit. And it reeked of prejudice. He knew why they had missed it, why they didn't even bother to check.

She was the daughter of a black woman whose husband had left her with a child. That happened all the time. No one ever questioned it. Hell, he hadn't even blinked when he saw it. Often, there was no husband at all, just an unknown sperm-donor somewhere from a brief encounter. No one checked on the dad this time because, well, because they didn't think it would change her story, the dad was not important. They assumed he didn't want to be important in this child's life.

Sophie said the words he had already said to himself: "Shame on you. Shame on all of you." As he looked back at her, his heart sank to his ankles. He could see her father's eyes staring back at him with disgust and he couldn't bear to acknowledge how painful it was. Not because they were her father's eyes. Because he had let *her* down.

"Sophie." He wasn't sure what to say as the tension in his voice came through. Nate held up his hand to stop Trev. Had he recognized the emotional turmoil this induced?

"Ms. Henderson," Nate began, "we'll be glad to check out your story. But don't you think it's a little extreme though to claim one of the richest men in the country as your father? Are you sure you want to do that? What if he doesn't back you up on it?" The skepticism hung in his voice.

"You wanted the truth. I gave it to you. It doesn't really matter whether he backs it up or not verbally, but he will. Not to mention my birth records, those bank records, the trust fund that the EFT transactions came from. They all have the name of his company and he himself plastered all over them—*if* you bother to dig deep enough to find out."

Trev hung his head and muttered, "I didn't know. *We* didn't know." He reached his hand toward her, wanting to reassure himself that she'd forgive him, then stopped. No contact. She didn't miss the gesture.

She seemed weary as if the tenseness of the emotional war she'd gone through had drained her. "You didn't bother to check. You just assumed the worst. You assumed I didn't have a father, or that he was someone unknown and irrelevant, right?" Her glance followed the motion as he retracted the hand that had started to reach for hers. The hand that had been pressed against her back only hours before.

"Yes. I guess that's true," he finally admitted.

"And because of that, you stretched even farther and assumed I was a thief?" The tears were puddling again and Sophie lifted her chin in defiance. He observed her summoning the last thread of strength available before she spoke. "Call my dad, and get me out of here, whoever the hell you are."

Trev pushed himself back from the table and stood as if she'd slapped him. He fisted his hands and plunged them into his pockets as he looked down at the papers in front of her. One of the hands nervously moved from his pocket and up to rub the back of his neck. There was really nothing he could think of to say. Nothing that would take away the fact that he'd treated her in a way he'd promised himself years ago he'd never do to anyone. His own family was a blended family. He knew better than a lot of people what that was like, and how people reacted. The stupidity of it was that they were trained to not make assumptions—not jump to conclusions. And yet, they'd done so without intending it.

Nate's voice summoned him from the back wall. "Trev?" There was still one transaction that didn't fit with what she told them—one remaining part that continued to point to her involvement.

Trevan's eyes moved slowly to Nate. He felt Sophie's weariness, too. He listened as Nate spoke his last concern in Spanish. He wasn't satisfied with her answers. Sure, she'd explained away most of it, but Nate wasn't going to let Trev's emotional involvement overlook any details. Trevan's shoulders slumped as Nate prodded him to ask about the last transaction.

"*Intiende Español,*" she said flatly after hearing Nate's words to Trevan. Trevan wanted to smile. She understood Spanish. Spoke it fluently.

"*Lo siento.*" Agent Hernandez's quick apology blurted out. "I'm sorry, I didn't realize you were bilingual. It wasn't in your file. Can you explain the last transaction, Ms. Henderson? Can you tell us about that one?" He pointed to the bottom of the report in front of her.

She looked down. The final transaction on the list was printed as if it had been pasted into the report from another document. The date, time, amount, account, bank code—everything was listed clearly as they were on the others. "No, I can't."

"Can't? Or won't?" He raised a brow.

"Can't. I have no reason to withhold information. But I'm sure if you actually investigated it rather than jumping to conclusions as you did on the others, you'd figure it out." She'd lost all interest in helping them now. "You seem pretty intent on finding my guilt. Perhaps you should look at it from a different perspective. You know, maybe consider the possibility that I'm *not* the guilty party?"

"That's a lot of money," Nate pushed.

Trevan frowned. He returned to the table and sat, pulling the report to him and reviewing the last item just to make sure what he originally saw was true. "Nate, let me ask you something. I've told you all along that she didn't do this, haven't I? That she didn't fit the profile?"

"Yeah, but even you make mistakes once in a while, Trev," Nate responded.

Sophie's eyes shot up. "Profile? You profiled me? What exactly do I fit? What did you find—how did you classify me? Do I have *easy target* stamped on my back?" Her voice hissed.

He looked at the report again, ignoring her questions as he found his answer—at least where she was concerned. He pushed the paper back at Nate and said without hesitation, "This one wasn't her, either."

Nate wasn't about to give up. "Of course it was—who else would it be?"

"I don't know, but it's not Sophie. Let's step out again for a second." Trev went through the door and waited on the other side, not a word to Sophie, not even a glance.

Nate followed; he started talking as soon as the door clicked shut. "Look, Trev, I know you don't want it to pan out like this. I'd like to think she wasn't involved, too, but the money went into *her* account. What else could have happened?"

"Yes, the money went into her account but I'm telling you she didn't put it there. It wasn't her. I know it."

"How do you know?"

"I just know. Let me ask her a few more questions and you'll see."

"Okay, but are you sure you're thinking straight and not letting your hormones get in the way?"

"If you were anyone else, I'd deck you right now. I'll pretend you didn't say that. Just listen and look at the report again." Trev scowled at him and yanked the door open, leaving Nate to either go back in the room or stand alone in the hall.

Sophie had started folding the pages of the report slowly into paper airplanes as she waited. Trevor thought the act was her way of telling them to take a flying leap off a tall building. When they returned to the room and sat together opposite her, she launched the first airplane into the air, watching it float up then sway down a little to the side, then down again until it landed on the floor on the side of the room.

"Ms. Henderson," Trevan started soberly. He knew she would figure it out, if she hadn't already done so. The only thing he couldn't be sure of was what would happen next. Would she still be angry about everything? "Can you explain the process of sending funds like this electronically to my partner here?"

"Why bother—you know you already have it down. You don't need me to explain it." She kept her eyes on the floating airplane as she spoke.

"Not to me, but Nate here needs a little help." He nodded at his partner. He sat silently, patiently waiting for her to answer.

She shrugged with indifference, not bothering to look his way. "Once the fund transfer file is created and ready to send, the sender connects to the bank via an FTP or encrypted connection. Once the connection is established, they have to enter a code within a few seconds . . . " Her voice trailed off as she looked at the report, then her eyes shot up to meet his. She jumped to pick up the paper airplane from the floor. Nate started to rise up and grab her, but Trevan planted an arm firmly on his forearm. A frown and shake of the head encouraged Nate to lower back into his seat.

Sophie slowly unfolded the paper and smoothed it on the floor with her hands as she sat on her knees. She turned and focused her gaze on his eyes as his mouth started to dip up at the corners. Trevan grinned and nodded to confirm what she saw on the report. The data was there—it told the truth.

As Sophie stared at Trevan, a huge sense of relief washed over her face.

"What?" Nate still didn't get it. "So, if you don't enter the code in a few seconds, then what?"

Sophie pulled herself back to the present, tore her eyes from Trev, and turned toward Nate. She rose and returned to the table, placing the wrinkled paper in front of him. "The connection is terminated and the fund transfer doesn't succeed."

"So, someone has to physically be present to enter the code, right?" Nathan asked. *Ah, finally, the light bulb went on.* Nathan looked at the report and registered the time stamp on the transaction. *1:14 a.m.*

Trevan's next words were rushed. His enthusiasm uncamouflaged. "Sophie was nowhere near a computer at 1:14 a.m. that day, Nate.

She could not possibly have entered the code," he stated confidently.

"And you know this for sure?"

Trevan waited for her to respond if she wished to do so. She could have blurted it out, let them know why he could vouch so confidently for that timeframe, but she chose not to. She just watched him, cautiously. Why? He assumed she didn't want anyone to know. Was she concerned for him, or just embarrassed? Did she think he'd deny it?

"Yes, I know this for sure. I was with her at that time."

Sophie's eyes narrowed as she studied Trevan's face.

"You were watching her?" *God, Nate, come on. Does it have to be spelled out?*

"Yes, I suppose you could say that." A mischievous glint flashed across his eyes as he remembered his mouth and hands exploring every inch of her. He returned Sophie's gaze. She looked away. Did she want him to be silent about this? Did she wish she'd never been there? He couldn't withhold it because doing so put her back in the suspect's seat.

"From where?"

"My house."

"Christ, Trev. What are you saying?" Nathan didn't need confirmation. If he couldn't see it in the expression on Trevan's face or the way that she avoided looking at him, he was an idiot. Trevan shifted his gaze to Nate without answering. His hand was tapping on the table. His voice slowly and softly responded. "I'm telling you there's no possible way she did that fund transfer. Check my security cameras if you don't believe me."

"Security cameras. *You have security cameras there?*" Her eyes blazed as she spat out the words.

"Only on the outside of the house, front, back, and sides." He watched her face as embarrassment flooded her cheeks now that she knew the full impact of what he'd just said—that someone might have seen them—that someone would definitely see them now. Yes, his whole office was going to see her bare breasts, not just an old fart on the hill with a telescope. But he was pretty sure the old fart had seen it, too. The embarrassment gave way to further anger in no time.

"Damn!" she spat and dropped her head into her hands, clenching her fingers tightly against her scalp.

"Yeah, that's what I said, too." He had tried to keep it off the cameras but she hadn't helped him any. He gave her a reassuring smile, hoping the fact that it proved she was there was more important than her modesty right now, but no such luck. She was pissed. The daggers in her eyes had just turned to spears.

Sophie sat silently. He hoped there was a way to salvage something here. She hated him, he knew that. She probably thought the entire relationship was part of the investigation, and who would blame her for thinking that? His entire entrance into her life had been fabricated for the sole purpose of finding a criminal. The criminal just *wasn't her.* Still, he had to help her. The document didn't prove exactly who *did* the fund transfer, but the timestamp and Trevan's confirmation were sufficient to show that she *didn't do it.*

Trev spoke calmly to Nate, "The camera recordings are streamed to a secured site on an FTP server." He wrote a number on Nate's papers and shoved it toward him. "Here's the IP address to get to it and the password information to view the recordings. Have Cheryl or one of the guys pull them. It will prove what I'm saying, but if anyone mentions one word about anything else on those recordings, I swear I'll make them wish they'd never seen it. Extract the part you need, nothing more."

"No problem." He knew Nate didn't understand why he was getting all upset. There was no way in hell he was going to have pictures of Sophie half-dressed pinned to someone's cubicle wall. He and Nate exchanged glances for a second. Then they both stood up.

"Can I go now?" Sophie asked. Her words were layered with anger but she hesitated to stand up—probably for fear that she'd just get pushed back into her seat once more. "Are you done with me?" Her tone seemed to imply that she wished to be rid of them. In truth, he didn't see how she could not feel abused by the chain of events.

Trevan touched her arm. "Almost. Give us just a few more minutes." She snatched her arm from his grasp and looked away. She focused on her hands, which she pulled in and clasped together on the table in front of her. He winced.

Nate had observed all this, probably making a mental note of what an emotional fuck-up he was. Trevan motioned with a slight movement of his head for Nate to step out so they could talk.

The two men exited.

"I'm not even going to ask exactly what happened, or what the hell that was all about," Nate started as soon as the door shut.

"Then stop talking. I don't want to hear it." Trevan didn't need anyone telling him whether it was okay or not. He wouldn't listen, anyway. "She didn't do the transfer and if what she's telling us about her dad is accurate—and I'd bet my life it is—then we've wasted our time watching her. But the bigger question is: who did do it? I think we may have found that yesterday, but we need Cheryl's help to be sure. We've wasted most of the day on this."

"Whoever did it knows we're watching her. That's why they chose her." Nate leaned against the wall. "Or, they want her out of the way *and* they know we're watching her."

"Good point," Trev admitted. " Either way, she still might not be safe."

"Judging by what happened to Bob, I'd say there's no doubt about it. Let's go talk to the rest of the team and see how they want to handle this."

Chapter Nineteen

Sophie waited in the room by herself while they validated her story. Trevan spoke with her dad personally, but then instructed Nate to confirm the call. Nice enough guy, he thought. It sounded like her mother had as much to do with his absence as he did. Whatever their issues were, Sophie was telling the truth. He knew it the minute she said it, and he hated himself for not digging further into the details on her dad. He'd left it up to Nate and under normal circumstances that would have been fine. But for the last few weeks, Nate's head had been on his own dad. Trevan should have checked it out himself. Not once, until the bank records came in, did he think she was involved. Knowing she had this trust fund she'd refused to use just because she wanted to make it on her own made him even more amazed by her strength. And more angry at himself for not believing her completely. He was slipping. No, he was distracted.

He had to meet her dad sometime. Seemed like dad had drawn the short end of the parent stick. Still, she didn't have anyone else and she needed to mend that fence now while there was still time to get to know him. Whether she liked it or not, he was her family . . . and that mattered.

He watched her pacing the room for a little while, afraid to go in and talk to her. She had looked at the glass and cussed him out. Everyone else watched, a little surprised, and then laughed. It made him mad that they thought it so funny. She hated him now and she seriously wouldn't like having to spend the next couple of weeks with him while they finished the data analysis and hopefully made the arrests. If it lasted longer than that, she'd probably kill him or he'd get reassigned. He wasn't sure which would be worse at this point.

An hour later, he was still sitting in the other room, watching her through the glass. He would have been amused if he didn't really care what happened next. She was sitting with her back to the window—to him—facing the other wall. Nothing could be mistaken about the intention in that. He knew she was crying because she put her hand to her face a couple of times like she was wiping her eyes. Everyone else had grown bored and left, thankfully. He didn't need more witnesses as he talked with her. Still, even as mad as she was, he wanted her to let him touch her. He couldn't help it.

He stepped in the door, closing it quietly, and waited for her to face him. When she didn't, he sat at the table. He rested one hand on the table and the other in his lap, watching the back of her head. The curls were pretty much a disaster from the stress of the day but they still framed her head nicely.

"So, Trevan Prater of Prater Ranch," Sophie said matter of factly, her back still to him.

"Yes."

"Do you always go to this extreme to close a case?" Her voice cracked a little at the end. He wondered if she was still crying, but she wouldn't turn around and look at him.

"No. Come on, Soph, surely you know what was real and what wasn't?"

"Do I?" she hissed. "How would I know that? Nothing you've said, nothing you've *done* is true."

"Yes, some of it was. Actually, a lot of it was." Her words cut into him like razor blades.

"You said you were a good guy. You swore it." She hiccuped now and he knew for sure she was crying. He couldn't stand it anymore. The chair scraped loudly on the floor as he pushed it back and moved around the table to face her.

"I was a good guy. I still am." He knelt in front of her. Her face was red and blotchy. Mascara colored tears ran down her cheeks. He sucked at this part; he couldn't handle crying. "Look at me." He willed her to raise her eyes to his.

When she refused, he put his hands on her arms and shook her gently. "Henry, look at me."

"No." Her bottom lip was quivering. "Why would you play me like that? Do you really have to go that far to solve a case?" Her voice came in short gasps. She'd cried so much she couldn't really string a sentence together. "Because if that's what you do as one of the good guys, then maybe you're not as great a guy as you think you are. What a shitty way to make a living."

"I wasn't playing you. I never was. I had to get you away from here to make sure that we had time to figure it out, and whoever was trying to hurt you wouldn't be able to. I needed to keep you safe."

"Well, you really went the extra mile on that. You must be one of the best agents they have. I bet all the criminals want to have you chasing after them, screwing them." She was being sarcastic now, and bitter.

"Soph, you're angry. I deserve it, but I didn't use you to solve this case. I understand you feel that way, but—"

"Stop it! Stop psychoanalyzing me. You don't understand me at all." She fumed.

"You're right."

She glared at him. "You are the most disgusting man I have ever met. No one I've ever known would have stooped so low to get a project done." She clenched her eyes shut to stifle the tears. "I was so stupid. I thought it was real for a few minutes there. You should be really proud of yourself. You're really a great actor."

"I wasn't acting; it was *real*." He put his hand under her chin and stroked her throat. He was exhausted with all the emotional turmoil in this room. "Everything between you and me was real. It *is* real. You can pretend it isn't if you want to, but I can't. I know what I felt. What I feel now. And this is no act."

"Yeah, yeah, yeah. Tell that to someone who cares." She jerked her head back from his hand.

He stared into her face. "I thought I was," he said quietly, admitting defeat.

"Can I leave now, *Agent Prater?*"

"No, I'm sorry, but you can't." He backed away to the other side of the table and sat again.

"Why not?"

"Because until we have this guy, or guys, in custody, I'm still stuck to you like glue."

"Well, you're pretty good at that, but no thanks."

"You don't get a choice in this, Sophie. This is a federal investigation. If we think one of our star witnesses is in danger, they are put under twenty-four-hour protection."

"So now I'm a *witness*, not a suspect?"

"That's right."

"Wow, that's a relief," she said sarcastically. "Do you also sleep with witnesses or is that only reserved for suspects you're trying to expose?"

Trevan clenched his jaw. "I'm a little more selective than that, whether you believe it or not. I'll be back in a few minutes, then we'll go."

"Where are you going to lock me up now?"

"We're going back to the ranch, until all the analysis is finished and it's safe for you to come back." He rose and walked out of the room, leaving her alone.

*

By mid-afternoon on Monday, Sophie and Trevan were once again hurtling east on Interstate 10 toward Fredericksburg. They'd stopped at her apartment, collected more clothes and her mail, and then got back on the road. Sophie sat still and silent in the passenger seat. The look on her face plainly told him to keep his mouth shut, so he had some nineties rock music blaring on his Sirius radio.

The music was interrupted by a load *brrring* and she looked at him out of the corner of her eye. Trevan hit the answer button on his hands-free phone. "Hey, Mom."

"Hello Trev, how's your day going?"

"Not too bad for a Monday. Everything going okay for you guys?"

"Sure. Sure. Hey, we dropped by the old ranch house this morning and saw you'd been there."

Trev looked sideways at Sophie and rolled his eyes. She wasn't going to like this, either. "Mom, you know you watched the house and you saw me there. I saw Dad on the back porch Saturday."

Sophie's eyes darted to his face and he knew she was just getting more frustrated as he spoke. How was he supposed to tell her his dad was the old man with the telescope? He held up his hand to stop an imminent explosion.

"Now, why would we watch the house?" the voice on the phone questioned sweetly.

"Because you knew I was there and you were checking up on me, weren't you?"

The voice on the other side capitulated. "Okay, okay. Yes, we wanted to make sure you were okay." There was a small pause, then: "Who's the girl?"

Trev laughed. They had gone from pretending they didn't know to getting in his business in about two seconds.

"Her name is Sophie and she's sitting right here, Mom." He sent a warm look at Sophie, only to get a scowl in return.

"Oh, uh. Hi, Sophie, nice to talk to you," she said pleasantly.

"Nice to talk with you, too, Mrs. Prater." He was glad she didn't continue the silent treatment on the phone.

"So, are you two still in town or headed back to Houston?"

"We're in between right now," Trevan admitted, "but we'll back at the ranch in a few hours. We'll turn off the interstate in about fifteen minutes. We had to take care of some work stuff this morning."

"Good. Then come by for dinner at seven. Your dad's barbecuing and we want to meet your girlfriend."

Trevan started to protest when Sophie shot him another deadly scowl but the phone on the other side went dead before he could say anything. He hated the way they did that when they thought he'd refuse. They made the demand, then gave him no chance to respond.

"Your parents? Your *parents* live on the hill?" She raised an eyebrow at him, her voice getting a little too loud.

"Yeah, I took the old ranch house when they built their new place up there. Their place is a lot nicer and has a fantastic view. Unfortunately, that view includes my backyard." He looked at her with a sheepish half grin. "Sorry, I couldn't tell you."

"Jeez, could this possibly get any worse? Are there going to be naked pictures of me posted on the Internet next?"

Trev laughed out loud at that. "No, only half-naked ones. Just kidding. That won't happen—not that I know of. But, that hero-worshipping thing you were trying to help with? Well, I think it worked." He saw her try to hide a smile as she looked out the window. He thought for the first time since they'd interrogated her that maybe things would work out okay.

The silence stretched between them for five minutes but it felt a lot longer. "Sophie, have you ever ridden a horse?"

"Not since I was ten and that was just a pony tied to one of those leads. Why do you ask?" She looked at him, curious.

"We usually take the horses between the two houses. There's a real nice trail up the hill." He waited for her to make some sort of wisecrack about cowboys and horses but she didn't.

"I don't think I'm ready for that."

"No problem." He was glad. "You'll ride with me."

"I didn't see any horses when we were there."

"You weren't looking."

"But I don't really want to."

"You'll go," he stated flatly.

*

At six-thirty that evening, Trevor lifted Sophie onto his horse, Blackie, then pulled himself up behind her. Blackie was the biggest of their horses, a sturdy pulling horse, and would have no problem hauling the two of them up the hill. Sophie had argued with him about going. She had no desire to meet his parents. He insisted and she refused again. In the end, he gave her a choice, walk or ride. There was no staying behind.

"You call him Blackie?" she asked nervously as she held onto the saddle horn. Trevan's arms rested gently around her, holding the reins.

"Yep. We also have a solid white horse called Whitey and we used to have a solid brown mare . . . guess what her name was?" He teased.

"Let me guess, Brownie?"

"Yeah, real original, huh? She died three years ago."

"So if you have a paint horse, are you going to call it Spot?"

"As a matter of fact, that's exactly what we did." He grinned in her hair and she chuckled.

They walked the horse down the hill away from the house and he felt the warmth of her back leaning against him, her hips moving gently with the equine's gait.

"Henry?" He tightened his arms around her as they started up the steep trail toward his parents' place.

"What, Trev?"

"Do you hate me?"

"Yeah, pretty much."

"Anything I can do to change that?"

"Probably not."

"Okay then." They rode in silence the remainder of the way up the trail. He watched her face as she looked back over her shoulder at the view. He could see she appreciated it almost as much as he did. Most people did. It was beautiful. The Texas Hill Country was one of the best kept secrets that he knew of. It was close to the big city attractions but had a slower, more comfortable pace. As they cleared the trees at the top of the trail, Sophie spoke.

"Are you going to tell them why I'm here?"

"What do you mean?"

"From the conversation earlier, I got the impression they

thought we were, I don't know, involved."

"Does it matter?"

"Yes, of course it does. That's lying."

"Is it?" He paused. *So that's it, then.* "If it matters so much to you, tell them yourself."

His mother rushed toward them. He admired how she'd kept her hair long all these years. Her olive skin remained in good condition, despite the addition of numerous smile lines around her eyes and mouth. His favorite thing about his mom, though, was the way she could make anyone feel at home. Dad always said she'd never met a stranger, and it was true. When someone met Lisa Prater, she made them feel like she'd known them all their life. Both of his parents were highly intelligent and successful in their careers, but more importantly they were just good people.

"Oh, I'm sooo glad you're here." she exclaimed as Trevan dismounted from Blackie. He lifted Sophie down next to him before tying the horse up to a post in the yard.

"Yeah, me too, Mom." His voice choked as she squeezed him tightly around the neck. He wrapped an arm around her in return. "This is Sophie." He laid his hand affectionately on Sophie's arm. She didn't pull away. From his mother's vice-grip hold, he motioned with his head. "Lisa Prater."

The door of the house flew open and his dad's bulky dark frame hurried toward them. "She looks just as good with her clothes on," he shouted in Spanish.

"Dad!" Trevan blurted. His temperature rose a notch or two and he shifted his eyes to gauge her reaction. "Watch your mouth. She speaks fluent Spanish." Sophie stiffened and shot Trevan an angry scowl.

"Oh, sorry." He looked at his feet as he held out his hand to introduce himself. "Hi. Robert Prater."

"Sophie Henderson. Good to meet you, sir. And sorry about that display." Sophie didn't look him in the eye.

"*You* don't need to be sorry." Trevan couldn't help showing his frustration. "He should mind his own business and stop being such a damn Peeping Tom."

"Well then." Trevan's mom changed the subject. "Now that we know everybody, no pun intended, let's go inside."

Trevor noticed the buckskin horse leaning over the fence with its left foot lifted and resting on the right front hoof. "How's old Goldie's foot doing, Dad?"

Sophie followed his gaze to the tan colored horse with golden haunches and giggled.

Ah, there she is. He smiled with satisfaction.

His dad cast a funny glance at Sophie before he answered. "She's still favoring it a lot. Vet's coming on Wednesday."

Trevan was glad he'd been able to elicit a positive response from Sophie. He knew the horse was going to be fine. He'd looked at the hoof a couple weeks earlier and could tell it was on its way to mending. If Goldie were a person, she'd certainly be a hypochondriac. They often laughed about how the smallest scratch or bump would cause her to limp for days. That's why they rarely rode her anymore. She preferred to take it easy. Very easy. And since she was getting older, his dad didn't seem to mind. She had been a work horse on a much larger ranch when she came to them. She had already done her time and deserved a rest. Trevan always thought her smarter than the other horses, but maybe more experienced would be the better descriptor. She'd figured out how to get out of the strenuous work.

Inside, Sophie sat at the kitchen bar talking to his mom and he listened for a while before he realized he was kind of a third wheel. He grabbed a beer from the fridge and went out to stand by his dad in front of the grill. He could see in the kitchen easily from where he stood.

"She's pretty, son."

"Yeah," Trevan admitted.

"More than pretty, really."

"Yeah." Trev didn't say more. It wasn't necessary.

"How long have you known her?"

"Not long." Trevan didn't want to go into the details. It was none of their business.

"How long are you planning on knowing her?" This was his way of asking intentions.

"As long as she'll let me," he answered with a shrug, "probably longer than she'd like me to."

A loud burst of laughter came from the kitchen and he watched Sophie shoot a glance at him. His mom had tears in her eyes from whatever they were talking about. He assumed he was the butt of their joke. His mom loved to tell stories about him just to embarrass him. Normally, she'd wait till he was there to fully enjoy the humiliation.

A warm shiver ran through his shoulders as he watched them. It was good to see Sophie relaxing after all she'd dealt with today. It was also good to see Mom had taken such a liking to her.

An hour and a half later, Trevan lifted Sophie onto Blackie and once again slid up behind her on the horse. The sun was going down behind the trees. They'd need to hurry to get back down the hill before it was pitch dark. The horse could get them there regardless, but he didn't want to take a chance meeting up with a stray coyote, skunk, or bobcat. The hills had a lot of wildlife that came out mostly at night. His parents had hugged both of them before they left and told them to come back when they had time. He didn't tell them how long they were staying and he was glad they didn't ask. He also didn't tell them that Sophie probably wouldn't be with him next time. The trail down was a little more comfortable than going up because Sophie had to lean back against him to balance and he was glad for that, even though she didn't talk until they were almost to the house.

"Your parents are nice," she said quietly.

"Yeah, I guess."

"They're pretty proud of you."

"Where'd you get that from?"

"Just the way they talk about you, and to you." He heard her sigh and leaned down to see her face in the shadows. She had an odd expression. One he hadn't seen before.

"You okay?"

"Yeah. I guess I just miss my mom a little. I'd forgotten how nice it was to talk to her."

A twinge of sympathy hit him and he squeezed her gently, hugging her between his arms. Her hair was coming out of the knot on her neck and blowing against his face, tickling him. Two days ago, he would have smoothed it back and kissed her. Probably not a good idea right now. It pissed him off that he wanted to.

"Still hate me?" he asked, for no particular reason.

She hesitated a little then answered, "Yeah, pretty much."

He waited a second, then spoke softly in her ear. "You hesitated." When they reached the house, he lifted her off Blackie. "I'm gonna brush the horse down and put him the barn. Go on in. I'll be back in a while." He turned the horse and left.

When he returned, he started the wood in the fire pit, got four beers out of the fridge and walked down to the pool. He stripped and dove in, swimming the full length of the pool underwater before coming up. It was almost pitch dark now so no need to worry about witnesses. He swam to the other end quickly, his hands and arms gliding through the water. Two minutes later, he plopped with a towel around his waist in one of the chairs around the fire pit. His second beer was almost gone when Sophie opened the door of the girls' room and came outside. He downed the remaining beer and twisted the cap on the third.

"Henry, do you know a guy named Bob Greenwood that worked at your company?"

Her eyes registered the name. "Yes. He died a few months ago in a car accident. Very sad."

"Yep, that's him." Trevan took another long drink from the bottle in his hand and lifted it to look through it at the flames. He chose his next words carefully. "I'm going to tell you something confidential. If you repeat this to anyone, I'll deny it and I'll probably still get fired anyway but you need to understand why you're here, with me."

He brought the drink to his lips again briefly, then said, "Bob came to us twice the month before he died reporting possible fraudulent activity. The last time he called, we interviewed him. He had found basically the same thing you did. Only he asked around at work about it. He thought someone was following him. We thought he was a little paranoid but agreed to protect him while we did the investigation. He had a freak car accident the morning that he was supposed to meet with us to go into protective custody."

Trevan finished the third beer in silence, letting his words sink in. "That's when I started following you. When we started following you. Hate me or not, I'm not letting you out of my sight until we catch whoever's doing this. There's big money at stake and whoever's involved—they don't seem to care who gets hurt." He picked up the last bottle and popped off the cap, holding it as he turned to Sophie. He watched the flames reflected in her eyes. "Do you understand what I'm saying?"

She crossed arms in a hugging motion and rubbed the upper portion of each. "I understand. This is your job and you intend to make sure it gets done right, whatever it takes."

"Damn right." He tipped the bottle at her.

She looked into the darkness past the fire for a few seconds, then her eyes shifted down to her feet. "Did you really have to take it so far though?"

Trevan gulped another mouthful of beer. She acted like he intended everything to happen the way it did. As if he planned it out. He looked at her, amused she thought him that egocentric. In truth, he had never been attracted to anyone he watched. Ever. Until now. Once you see all their crazy habits and personal idiosyncrasies, it normally turns a person off, not to mention he usually watched men. He had to be honest with himself though. He'd been attracted to her—or at least curious—from day one. She was classier than anyone he'd ever known before—including his ex. She was also smart and funny, but even with that, she oozed sex appeal without trying. Nate had been right from the beginning. He was way out of his league, and it pissed him off that he had not kept it as clean as he should have. He should have been more prepared for Sophie Henderson.

He answered, "Did you have to be so *fucking beautiful?*" The anger in his voice was evident in the crisp tones of his words. He looked past the flames into the darkness of the hills on the other side of the creek. The wind gusted across his bare chest causing him to shiver, so he rose, holding the towel at his waist as he headed toward the Jacuzzi.

"I could say the same thing to you, Trev."

His back muscles stiffened as he looked at her briefly. Jesus, she liked to screw with his head. He walked quickly away. Why the hell did she say *that?*

*

Somewhere around two a.m., something woke him from his alcohol-enhanced slumber on the couch. He pulled up and looked around. Just before he settled on the sofa, he vaguely remembered watching her go back into his sister's room while he was locking up and setting the alarm.

Trevan heard a ding from Sophie's phone. She'd left it on the counter when she went to sleep. He rubbed his eyes and glanced at the screen, then smiled at the text messages.

Callie: *Hey sicko.. u gting any better? Ready to trade in Trev for a real doctor?*

Another ding.

Callie: *I'll take him if u don't want him. Seriously, I need to talk to u. When r you coming back to work?*

Third ding.

Callie: *Call me, dammit*

He glanced at his watch. *Christ, the woman is a little clingy.* He considered answering back with a short blast but decided not to. Instead, he went to the room and opened the door to look in on Sophie. He stood in the doorway, his arm braced against the frame, admiring the way her hair fell over his sister's pillow and tumbled across her shoulder. He muttered under his breath, then slipped down the hall to his room and got under the sheets.

An hour later, he was still awake lying on his back. No way in hell he was getting any sleep. He'd almost decided to get up and shower when the door opened quietly. Sophie's silhouette stood there, hesitating.

She couldn't sleep either, apparently. Knowing she was having as much trouble brought a mild sense of satisfaction. Trevan flipped back the covers leaving the space next to him open, the relief inside him was hidden but he was keenly aware of it. He lifted his arm and put his forearm over his eyes and waited. The rest was up to her. His chest burned when the bed moved from her weight and she eased close to him. He was in his briefs; the light breeze from the ceiling fan above the bed cooled his exposed skin. She slid against him, laying her hand where the warmth in his chest was burning and the coolness from the fan died. He remained still until her steady breathing signaled she had nodded off. He moved the arm from his eyes to her shoulder to get more comfortable.

She hated him. She pissed him off. But, he guessed, it would be easier to sleep when she was in the same room and he didn't have to check on her every couple of hours. Surely sleep would come.

Except for the fact that every curve of her warm skin was now wrapped around him like a boa constrictor. Sleep? Not a chance.

Chapter Twenty

Sophie rolled over in the bed the next morning and rubbed the sleep from her eyes. He was up already and, judging by the smells coming from the other room, cooking breakfast. She stretched her arms over her head, pointing her toes and relishing the last few seconds of rest. Coffee. She smelled the pungent aroma. Her stomach grumbled in anticipation. She rose and walked barefoot into the kitchen without even taking the time to wash her face or tame the wild curls. "Something smells really good in here." She plopped herself on a kitchen chair and watched as he pushed a cup of coffee in front of her, along with a plate of toast, eggs, and bacon. "You like to cook breakfast, don't you?" she stated, recognizing that this was starting to become a pattern.

"Not really, but I like to *eat* breakfast. So, in order to eat breakfast, I have to cook it."

"Good point. I like to eat breakfast, too. Guess it worked in my favor to sleep later than you."

"Yeah. Funny how that worked out. If I were a suspicious man, I'd think you planned it that way."

"I'd never admit it if I had, as long as I get breakfast like this every day till I go home. My arteries will probably clog up and I'll gain twenty pounds but who cares?"

Trevan frowned playfully. "I get the distinct impression I'm being manipulated. First you take over my bed, now you have me slaving in a kitchen. Somehow that's not what I thought I'd be doing when I took this job. It all sounded a lot more glamorous back then."

"Glamorous?" He opened the door and she stepped right through it. "As in, you thought you'd be traveling the world, driving fast cars, chasing bad guys, and sleeping with pretty women? Seems to me you can probably check all that off your list—especially the last one. You have that down solid, if that's really your goal."

Trev's brow shot up. "A little bitchy this morning, Henry?"

"No, just stating the facts as I know them."

"Yeah, well, maybe your facts don't jive with mine." He took a bite of eggs, grabbed a piece of bacon, and heaved the rest into the trash. "I'm going running. I'll be back in an hour. Don't leave the house. I'm setting the alarm when I leave." He walked back to his room, returning shortly in running shoes and clothes. "You know, you really piss me off. You automatically see the worst in all of this. You're so fucking naïve about taking precautions for your own safety but when it comes to men and sex, you think every guy's automatically out to take advantage of you. You're so damn scared something might go wrong, you can't just accept what's good about it."

"What exactly would that be, Trev?" She settled her eyes on his.

"If I have to tell you, then obviously I'm the only one that recognized it in the first place," he growled at her. "Forget it. What's the point, anyway?" His shoes crunched on the gravel as his steps picked up speed outside and move away from the house.

*

When Trevan returned from his run, she was sitting in the living room with a blue envelope and a piece of paper in front of her on the coffee table. She was motionless, her face completely blank. It was an expression he had only seen once before—as they left her apartment after the break in.

"What's the matter with you?" His voice was still gruff with anger. The run had helped but he hadn't completely shaken off the frustration.

Sophie pointed at the paper and envelope in front of her. It stated in large, bold type "MIND YOUR OWN BUSINESS AND STOP MESSING WITH THE ACCOUNTING SYSTEM REPORTS OR YOU'LL REGRET IT."

"Fuck!" Trevan spouted.

"Geez, you say that a lot," she snapped.

"Yeah, well, sometimes it fits." He shrugged. "Don't touch that or the envelope any more than you already have. I'll have someone pick it up and see if they can find anything that identifies who sent it. It doesn't really matter though. I'm pretty sure we will know within the next few days who's behind the money grab. I told you this was serious. Believe me now?"

"I already believed you. You didn't believe in me."

He ignored the jab but he knew what she was getting at. He just didn't want to talk about it anymore. "From now on, wherever you go, I go, too. And if I run, you run. Got it?"

"Yes, sir. But that came to my apartment so I don't think they really know where I'm at and I doubt they're likely to show up here."

"Doesn't matter, we're not taking a chance. And I'm not fighting with you about it, okay?"

By Thursday, they had fallen into a routine of sorts. They rose early and ran the country roads on and around the property for an hour. Trev stayed in pace with Sophie the entire time, but he wore his firearm in plain view. She noticed but said nothing. When they came back, Sophie showered while Trevan made breakfast. Trevan showered, then was on the phone and computer until just before noon. Sophie made them lunch which they ate in the courtyard. In the afternoon, Trevan was back on the computer and Sophie tried to catch up on her projects at work remotely. She was getting farther and farther behind though. It was becoming difficult to get anything done without access to her staff and presence in the office. He sensed her growing disappointment and frustration with the effect this had on her career.

They took the guns down to the makeshift practice range every other evening just after dinner and practiced shooting, then came back before it got dark.

Thursday, when Sophie checked her work messages, she had a panic voicemail from her assistant, Ana. "Sophie, I know you're sick and don't want to be bothered, but something's going on here. You need to get back. The auditors are in your office and they're searching everything. They're practically tearing your office apart. What's going on? What did you do?" She felt her face pale as she heard the words. She repeated the message twice before she dialed in on her cell.

She hit the speaker and placed the phone on the counter between them, forcing cheerfulness when it was answered. "Hey there, Ana. Wow, I feel like such a stranger."

"Oh thank God you called. It's crazy here. Do you know about this? Is that why you're out?"

"Know about what?" she asked, pretending ignorance.

"There's a three-man audit team in your office. They're going through every drawer and every file cabinet. What's going on?"

Sophie wished she could talk openly and remove herself from suspicion but she knew it would cause problems. "I haven't got a clue. Did they say what they're doing? What they're looking for?"

"No, not a word, but they asked Jeff to reset all your passwords so that they could read your data and emails." Sophie's heart sank. Her days of working remotely were probably over now. Her days of working at all, most likely. *They must know and think I'm involved, just like Trev and Nate did.*

"Really? Why would they want to read my emails?"

"Obviously they're looking for something. What's this all about?" Strange how someone could work for you for years and still not believe you. She could hear the suspicion in Ana's voice. Ana's panic most likely stemmed from wanting to get away from the drama. She was distancing herself from Sophie so that whatever

Sophie supposedly had done wouldn't taint her employment. Sophie cringed at the betrayal.

"I told you. I haven't got a clue what it's about. I've been out sick for several days. Whatever it is, I don't have anything to hide, so let them have whatever they want. Let them tear the whole office apart if it helps."

"Okay." She stretched the word out as long as her Texas drawl could handle.

Sophie hung up the phone. She bit back the acrid tears that stung her eyes. Too much had happened and it was getting harder and harder not to just fall apart. She stared at the wall in disbelief, trying to understand what steps would best save her job. Unfortunately, nothing came to mind.

*

She was sitting in a trance on the sofa when Trevan walked in.

"I need to go back to Houston tomorrow," Trev advised her after talking with his office. "They're pretty much done with the data part of the investigation. We are meeting to discuss how we're going to finish this up."

"Okay, so what do I do—stay here?"

"Not a chance. You go, too."

"So, it's over now and I can go back to work and back to my life?" *If there's one to go back to.*

"Not yet, a few more days probably." He rubbed the back of his neck. "You've handled this a lot better than most people would."

"I didn't really have much of a choice, did I? You and your agency thought I was involved, so I had to go along with it until you figured it all out and saw it differently."

"For what it's worth, I wasn't the one who thought you were involved. I never did, except for a few minutes when Nate showed me your bank statements. You straightened me out pretty quickly on that. I think you're pretty good at taking care of yourself, Soph. Your mom would be proud."

"Thanks." She seemed focused on his chest. "I'm not going to sleep worth a crap when I go back home." It surprised him she'd say that. There she went, screwing around with his head again. *Dammit.*

"Once they're all in jail, you shouldn't have too much trouble sleeping anymore."

"That's not what I meant." She walked out of the kitchen barefoot, and headed back to the girls' room.

Chapter Twenty-One

Trevan cut her off in the hallway before she passed his door. "Don't say something like that and just walk away. I don't have a clue what you're trying to get across. Let's finish this discussion." His feet were touching hers and he had one arm raised with his hand braced against the wall to keep her from passing. "What exactly *did* you mean?"

"I don't know . . . I guess it's just been nice not being so alone all the time." He couldn't believe his ears. She was being honest, without the anger, distrust, and sarcasm. "I realize it was all an act to you and you do this all the time, but I don't."

Okay, well, almost without it. Her eyes were wet.

"Do *what* all the time?" His voice escalated as he etched the words out through gritted teeth.

"You know, seduce your 'subjects' or whatever this was."

He laughed out loud. "Are you serious? How many times are we going to talk about this? Sophie, come on." He sobered up. "You met my parents, for Christ sake. My mom told you all my embarrassing history. "

"Yeah, but that was only after I knew who you were."

"So let me get this straight." He thought for a minute before finishing. "I kissed you a hundred times and had sex with you so you would want to tell me your crimes? Or so I could find out who the real criminal was? Not just because I wanted to?"

"Well, something like that. I guess."

"And you think I believe I'm really good enough at all this to do that with just about anyone, including yourself? That they would fall for it?"

"I don't know what you think, but . . . "

"Stop trying to analyze me and everything that happened. Take a look at yourself in a mirror, girl, and maybe just try to have a little faith in me."

"What do you mean? I'm not analyzing anything."

"Yeah, you are. You're trying to read something into what's happening here rather than just letting it happen. Try this on for size. Maybe I can't be around you for five minutes without wanting to kiss you—and yes, have sex with you—I'm sorry, but I *am* a guy and I *do* want you. That's what we think about. Maybe it has nothing to do with my job or anything else. Maybe it's just you. That's not a bad thing, is it? Maybe these last few nights where I had to keep telling myself you didn't want it, too, even though you were right there next to me, have been murder. So, you tell me what the hell is going on, because I don't get it." Trevan didn't wait for a response. He lifted his arm to let her pass and walked outside to get some wood for the firepit.

Even though he kept her within eyesight, he made a point to keep distance between them the rest of the day. He wanted to help ease himself into losing her, which he knew he'd have to do. While she had slept in his bed every night, snuggled up against him, he'd kept his hands around her waist or shoulders and nowhere else. He was pretty proud of himself for keeping his composure up to this point. Especially when she'd slide into bed in those little shirts and shorts that left so much skin touching him. He couldn't count how many times he'd woken up when she rubbed against him in her sleep. Just a few more nights and then she'd go home to her apartment and her friends, and he wouldn't have to keep reminding himself to keep his hands off her ass.

As the sun took its last dip behind the trees, he started the fire again. Once the flames were doing pretty well, he took off the T-shirt and gun holster and walked down to the pool, laying them on one of the chairs. He dropped the jeans, too, and slid into the water to cool himself off. These swims had helped him a lot the last few nights, mainly just to stay away from her. He swam underwater to the other side, then rose and took a breath before starting back. His hands again swept quietly through the water as he moved back toward the shallow end. He came up on the other side just before the steps with his eyes closed. As he wiped his face and eyes of water, his skin came into contact with warmth—flesh. His eyes shot open. Every muscle in his body tensed but he kept his expression calm.

"Henry, what are you doing?" She was naked against him.

"I thought I'd join you if that's okay."

"No, it's not okay. There are a lot of eyes watching us." It was a lie. He'd disabled the cameras by the firepit, facing the pool, and left only the ones facing away from the house.

"Then why are you swimming like that?" She surveyed his lower body with a raised eyebrow. "No one's watching us. It's pitch dark. Even if they were, no one could possibly see a thing. Besides, I believe it's too late for modesty. It seems like everyone you know has seen me."

"Not quite this much of you—and I tried to stop you."

"Yeah, well, I didn't really know what I was dealing with then, did I?"

"No, I guess not." He let a chuckle go, remembering her embarrassment at his dad's comment. Then he sobered up. "Do you still hate me?"

"I thought about that and well, you're kind of a hard guy to hate." She eased her wet hands up his chest and trailed them along his chin, tracing the thin line of his beard.

"Really? You seemed pretty intent on that," he mumbled softly, sliding his hands down her shoulders to rest on the small of her back. He knew he should back away.

"Well, you lied to me."

"Dammit, Soph. Why do you keep saying this crap? I didn't want it to be like that. And I couldn't tell you who I was and ruin a federal investigation. You know that. Besides, you were as much a part of it as I was."

"And what exactly do you call this?" She looked down at him in the darkness. "You strip and swim in this pool every night and I'm supposed to just ignore it?"

He grinned. "I didn't know you were watching. If I did . . . well, that would have been good to know."

"You're also a pretty hard guy to stay away from. It seems the only thing I'm intent on is . . . " She put her hand on his chest and walked her fingers through the small hairs.

He cut her off before she could finish. He'd held back for days and now she was up against him like this. He wasn't a saint. He didn't want to be. His mouth pressed against hers as his fingers dug into the softness of her back. A soft, hungry moan escaped her throat and that was all he could stand. The restraint was gone. The way her hands were tearing over him, he didn't think she wanted restraint now, anyway. Her hands moved up and down the muscles in his chest as if oiled. The water made her hands slippery, and she slickened them along his hips, then waist, and then tightly squeezed the flesh on his ass. He laughed softly as his body responded to her touch and he buried his face in the bend of her neck then kissed his way up to her mouth again.

"God, I love the way you feel," she murmured against his mouth as his teeth trailed back down along her neck. He loved hearing that. His entire body buzzed with desire. He turned her toward the steps of the pool, not taking his arms away but gliding them along and around her waist as she rotated.

"Soph, stop talking, please." He lifted her toward the steps. "As much as I'm enjoying this. Let's go inside."

"Why? Are you embarrassed?"

"No, hell no, but my sex life is no one else's business. That's between you and me . . . only." He held her against his chest and leaned down to brush his lips across her shoulder. "They pretty much own me, everything about me, except my family and my love life. I don't intend to share that. I have to have something for myself—to myself—don't I?"

Trevan lifted his hands and moved them down her shoulders, then grazed along the sides of her hips as he continued to nudge her toward the house. Sophie sucked in air and held her breath as his hands, slick with water, skimmed along the bottom of her breasts before reaching her hips. Every muscle in his body tightened against her back as he propelled her forward. *Does she have any idea how the water shimmers as it drizzles down her body in the moonlight? It's unbelievable.*

"I'm good with that." She reached for the towel she'd left on the chair and wrapped it around her before she sped into the house in front of him. "Race you inside." She threw Trev's towel at him on the way and he lunged after her, picking up his firearm and clothes, a quick chuckle escaping as he watched her move.

"You win," he conceded as he closed the door. He didn't care about racing. They were going to do this real slow this time. Slow so she'd remember every second. So she couldn't get it out of her mind. So she thought about it every minute like he did.

Chapter Twenty-Two

"We have an arrest warrant for your guy now. We're going over there this afternoon around four to pick him up." Trevan said as he entered the kitchen in a white undershirt and navy slacks.

"That's great news. What about the others? Do you know who he's working with yet?"

"Yeah, actually it was kind of interesting how they found it. They had registered the foundation under the board member's husband's name. She goes by her maiden name, not her married name. So our guys didn't see the connection at first. We subpoenaed the bank records for the Brotherhood of Hope. There were EFT payments to another corporation but no individuals. We had to get another subpoena for that corporation. While our guys waited for that to come through, they saw one small check to the husband for an expense report related to a trip to the Dominican Republic. Once they started digging under his name, hers popped up and we had the connection. The rest was easy after that. The other corporation that the trust sends the EFT to, it splits the money to four people. Your friend there . . . "

"He's not my friend, just an employee."

"Okay, and the CEO, the board member . . . you probably remember her. We saw them at lunch when I first met you. The last person is an auditor that's been covering up what they do. Apparently he was focusing his audits such that it not only covered what they did, but also targeted anyone that got in their way."

"Will you get them this afternoon, too?"

"We're sending guys over to pick them up right now. It should all happen about the same time if they're where we expect them to be. They should be at work." He stepped close to her and put his hand on her arm, rubbing her gently with his thumb. "It'll all be over by tomorrow morning at the latest if all goes well."

"What a nightmare. I'll be so glad when I can go home and not worry about who's on the other side of the door."

"You want to listen in on the arrest? I can't take you along but if you want to, you can wait at the office and listen in. You won't be able to listen to all of it as there are legal ramifications to that, but you might find it interesting."

"Nah, that's okay."

"Come on, Soph, I'd feel better if you did. You can hang out with Nate till we get back." He wasn't really comfortable leaving her anywhere else until everyone was in custody. "Besides, you'll get to hear the whole thing."

"You won't let me out of this, will you?" He heard the smile in her voice and knew she understood him . . . even though he was pushing her, it was only to keep her safe.

"Not really, babe." He kissed her forehead. That word, it just slipped naturally off his lips as if he'd said it a thousand times. Babe.

"Okay, then I guess I'll listen in."

"Great, get your shoes on . . . we need to get going." He turned his back to her as he eased his arm into the safety vest he had to put on for the arrest.

"Whoa!" She looked a little startled. "Why do you have to wear that? Is this going to be dangerous?"

"Probably not, but we never take chances. Sometimes people do crazy things when faced with something like this." He shrugged his shirt over the vest and started fastening the buttons. "Don't worry, everything's going to be fine . . . and you'll be there to hear most of it. Now, get your shoes on, okay?" Trevor tucked his shirt into his pants. He'd never been this nervous going into an arrest before and the anticipation was making him jittery. If he were honest, he would admit it wasn't the arrest he was worried about.

*

At three-fifty, Trevan spoke into his microphone as he approached the sidewalk to Bennet Lassier's front door with his team. "Nate, is Sophie listening?" Nate had agreed to let him use the equipment for this, but only for a few minutes before they got started.

"Yeah man, she's here."

Trevan held his hand up for the team to wait. "Give me a minute," he mouthed to them as he stepped a few feet away from the walk. Thankfully, only Sophie and Nate would hear the next few minutes of conversation. He dreaded what Nate would say if it didn't go well.

"Henry, I have to tell you this before I go in there because everything's going to change afterward." He hesitated, took a deep breath, and kept talking, "There's a file on the table there near the speaker with your name on it. Do you see it?"

"She sees it, Trev," Nate responded.

"That's everything I know about you, everything I *knew* before you saved me from the lightning storm that night." He swallowed. "Although, technically you really didn't save me because I was never in danger . . . but that's a different story. About you, here's what I know now . . . " He closed his eyes and clenched his fists. "Henry, I'm so fucking in love with you. I wish I wasn't. It really pisses me off, but . . . well, that's it. I want you to open the second folder. Inside it is what I want you to know about me. Us. Look at us. No one can look at those pictures and tell me we don't fit."

"Trev."

"What Nate?" Trev sighed, he should have had him put a microphone on Sophie.

"Don't drop the f-bomb man, you're ruining it, and stop calling her Henry. You sound gay." Trevan imagined Nate was trying to charm Sophie with his wit. It was irritating. By now, Sophie had opened the second folder. Inside the folder was a stack of pictures. Pictures of the two of them walking down the street, eating lunch, standing outside her office talking. Pictures that someone else had taken while watching them. They looked like any couple. He was smiling at her, watching her. The look on his face was happy and adoring. He knew once she opened the folder, she'd know what he meant. There wasn't any detail, no write ups on either of them. But it was clear to see.

"Shut up, man. Stay out of this."

"Can't. I'm stuck with you if this doesn't work out, and you pretty much suck at relationships. Oops, guess I shouldn't tell her that."

"Yeah, well you're no prize yourself, asshole. Shut the fuck up and let me talk. Is she still listening?"

"Yes."

"Soph, I'm going in now. But after this, you're free to go home. To your apartment. I'm coming by to check on you as soon as we're finished. Whatever happens from now on is completely up to you."

Trevan Prater smiled as he strode up the walkway to the door, flanked by his teammates. When the door opened, they heard his voice say, "Bennet Lassier, my name is Special Agent Trevan Prater. I'm with the Federal Bureau of Investigation and I have a warrant for your arrest."

As he spoke, a look of acceptance passed over Lenny's face. Trev got the distinct impression that Lenny had expected this and was almost relieved. That was an unexpected reaction and Trevan and his team hesitated at the door. "Do you understand what I'm saying?" Trevan prodded.

"Yes." Lenny said softly. Sounds came from behind him inside the house. A television rambling or something.

"Do you understand what this is about?" His lack of resistance was spooky. A sad expression came over the man.

"Yes. I understand you're here because of the money." Lenny stepped back from the door and motioned the group into his home, maintaining his composure.

"That's right."

"Everything you need to know can be found in my lockbox at the bank." Lenny's voice was calm, sadly calm as they cuffed him, read him his rights, and transported him away. The fact that he gave up so easily stunned everyone. They expected him to run, or at least fight. In the end, he appeared as if he was tired. Worn out by all the efforts. Resigned to accept his participation.

*

Nate muted his microphone and turned the sound down on the speakers. He grinned at Sophie. Then he walked over to where she stood and hugged her. "Welcome to the team, Miss Henderson. That's my best friend there . . . and he's probably the best guy I know. I guess I'd better mention that if you break his heart, I'll have to hunt you down and maybe even hurt you." He said it in a teasing way but she felt the seriousness in his voice.

"He's definitely that. The best guy I know, too," Sophie answered as he released her. "So, he already knew everything about me before I even met him, huh?"

"Not really. He just knew what was on paper. You could have been a total bitch for all we knew."

She started flipping through the file on the top of the stack, looking through notes and pictures they'd taken of her. Nothing really startling in it, but she was a little uncomfortable that her life was there for people to read. She glanced through the pages, then stopped and stared at a picture. A picture of her stalker.

"So, the stalker guy was one of yours, too?" she asked.

"What?" Nate seemed confused.

"Nothing. Just kidding. No wonder he was so intense." She shrugged it off. "I have to get going. I want to make an appropriate celebration dinner. Just curious, what's Trevan's favorite food?"

"If it's edible, he likes it . . . I don't think he has any preferences."

"That was helpful." She shrugged and rushed toward the door. "By the way—" she rotated her body halfway toward him and shot him one of those toothy smiles that seemed to floor Trevan "—you're kind of a jerk."

"So, I'm told. " He paused, as if debating something. Then he said, "He nearly married once, you know. He probably wouldn't tell you that because it was such a mess and he, well, it should have never happened. He wouldn't want to admit he'd made a mistake. Especially one that stupid."

"So, you think marriage is stupid?"

"That's not what I meant. She was the wrong girl and it was the wrong time."

"You're kidding me, right?" Her face drained of color

"No. He met her while he was on vacation and jumped in deep, right off the bat. I think he did it because he wanted what his parents have. And likely because he'd just come back from a pretty tough job and was exhausted and maybe a little lonely. His parents are the exception. They still have the real thing and you can see it when you're around them. I think he wanted that so bad that he just leapt at the first girl that seemed likely. He didn't even take the time to see what she was really made of." He stopped for a second and listened to the voices on the other side. "She was way immature and couldn't handle him traveling so much. Our jobs aren't really conducive to relationships, because we're gone a lot and sometimes it can be for weeks or more at a time."

"I've figured that out. It doesn't matter. I'm pretty used to being alone. I've lived that way for the last few years."

"Maybe so, but you need to know that for him to say what he just said after all that's happened, it's a pretty big step. If you don't care about him and don't think you can handle it, now's the time to get out. Before you screw him up really good."

"Are you telling me to stay away?"

"*No!* Hell no. I wouldn't do that to Trev. That's not what I mean at all. Just, you need to know. He's not always an open book and probably never will be."

"Okay. You made your point. Now I need to get some groceries if we're going to celebrate." She flipped her hair away from her face with one hand and headed for the door. "You're still a jerk, you know, but I can see why you're his friend. See you around, Nathan."

"Will I?"

"You can bet on it."

"Good."

*

Trevan dialed Nate's cell phone.

"Hey, Trev, how'd everything go?" Nate said upon answering.

"Fine. Fine. No problems. It was strange, almost like he was glad we caught him." Trev dismissed the arrest pretty easily. "Is Sophie still there? Can I talk to her?"

"No, man. She left hours ago. Said she needed to make sure you had a 'proper celebration.' I haven't seen her since around four-thirty."

"She's not here." Trevor was puzzled. "I'm at her apartment and it doesn't look like she's even been here. Her mailbox is still full."

"Hmmm . . . don't know. Maybe she's still at the store getting groceries. You know how women shop . . . or maybe she decided to ditch you now that she's met me." Nate chuckled, then said, "Hey, just curious. Who's the 'stalker dude'? She called her friend's boyfriend the stalker dude and wanted to know if he was one of us."

In an instant, terror seized Trevan.

"Trev?"

"Where does she live, Nate? Sophie's friend, Callie, where does she live?"

"Why?"

"Just give me the fucking address and get someone over there *now*! Sophie's in trouble."

Trevor was already in his car by the time Nate rattled off the address.

"Thanks, man. Start a trace on Sophie's cell. I need to know exactly where she is. If we don't get there in time, who knows what he'll do to her. And get me a name on that guy, whoever the fuck he is."

"What does he have to do with this?"

"I don't know, but he tried to kidnap her in a bar parking lot a few months ago."

Chapter Twenty-Three

Sophie called Callie on the way home. She was so ready to get her life back . . . talk to her best friend and sleep in her own bed—hopefully not alone. Callie was going to scream when she told her everything that had happened with work and with Trev. The last that any of her friends knew, she was kissing him in the parking lot. They would really be surprised at how quickly it had progressed.

"Hey girl! Long time, no talk to." She smiled into the phone. "Mind if I stop by for a chat?"

Sophie had never been to Callie's apartment. In fact, she hadn't even realized they lived so close to each other until now. As she knocked on the door, she considered how odd it was that her closest friend's life was somewhat unknown to her. She felt bad for not delving further to learn more personal information about Callie outside of work. Callie hadn't really shared much and she'd been so wrapped up in her own life, she didn't ask.

"I'll get it," a male voice on the other side of the door said loudly as Sophie's knocking resonated through the apartment.

She must have knocked on the wrong door. She started to walk away and call again to make sure she had the address right. At that moment, the door swung open and a man leaned forward with one arm on the door.

Sophie's mouth dropped as she saw the face. Even after several weeks, the face was easily recognizable and she panicked when she looked into the cold, empty eyes staring at her. She drew a deep breath and turned on her heel to run. He reached for her but caught only the material of her shirt. She yanked it from his grasp and bolted toward the stairs. Why did Callie have to live on the third floor? No time to wait for the elevator.

She lunged through the stairwell door and took the first set of stairs as fast as she could. Her steps pounded like dribbling basketballs down them. She heard his steps coming right behind her. As she approached the landing of the second floor, she reached for the trashcan in the corner and flung it across the stairs behind her. She heard a large groan as he fell over it. A quick glance over her shoulder saw him flailing to pick himself off the floor. Blood was dripping from his cheek where he'd caught the corner of the arm rail. It gained her a precious few seconds and she increased the gap between them.

Sophie ran down the second set of stairs and again sent the trashcan sprawling across behind her. Unfortunately, he was ready this time. He vaulted over the container and landed on the steps below. His landing was off balance and his feet slipped away from him. He pulled himself up with the railing and started after her again. Ahead of her, getting closer as she rushed toward it, was the door to the outside world. She anticipated screaming her lungs out while she sailed through it. She reached for the handle and twisted. Just as she was breathing the freedom, opening her mouth to scream, his hand snaked out and grabbed her arm. He had jumped over the rail and landed on the floor in front of her. His grip was hard, bruisingly hard. He pulled her back up the stairs, away from the door, slamming it behind her.

"Where the hell do you think you're going?" he spit out between clenched teeth. She started to scream again but he yanked her arm up behind her back. "You make another sound and I swear I'll beat the shit out of you and throw you off the roof." He kicked her in the back for good measure. She yelped in pain.

Her legs stung as he dragged her up all three flights of stairs. She resisted all the way but it didn't help. At the top, he lifted her up by the arm. "Walk!" he ordered. He escorted her back to Callie's apartment. He flung the door open and they entered. His face was beet red and dripping with sweat.

"Who was it?" a voice called from within the apartment. That voice Sophie knew. It was Callie. She wanted to scream . . . how did this man know Callie? How did he get here, and how long had she known him?

"It's your friend."

"Oh, great! Bring her in. I haven't seen her in forever." Sophie's heart sank. Callie wasn't in danger apparently. It sounded like this man was pretty familiar with her. As a matter of fact, it sounded like the only person that might be in danger was Sophie herself. But why?

"Hey there, Soph! I've missed you." Callie acted as if nothing had happened . . . as if there was no reason for concern. "I've tried calling you. You haven't been at work or at home in forever. You sure make it hard to keep up with you!"

"I was sick."

"Sick? No, you weren't sick," she said confidently.

"Yes, I was. I stayed with a friend until now." Sophie looked from Callie to the man in front of her that she only knew by one name: stalker dude. She wasn't sure why he was here and what the two of them had going, but it couldn't be good. No possible good could come out of this situation. "In fact, my friend is waiting downstairs for me in his car."

"Oh, you mean your new boyfriend, Trevor?" Callie asked innocently. "That's strange, I thought I saw you drive up in your car alone." She crooked an eyebrow at Sophie. "Where did he park? I'll go ask him up."

"He dropped me at the door and was making a quick stop at the store, then waiting for me downstairs."

"Really? I just was so sure I saw your car and you were driving." Callie was not going to be misled no matter how hard Sophie tried.

"Callie, who's your friend here?" Sophie tried to change the subject.

"We've already met, haven't we, dear?" The stalker was watching her intently now. Callie's face glazed over as she glanced first at Sophie, then at him.

"You two know each other?" Callie's brows arched in curiosity.

"Not really." Sophie tried to measure the situation up. "The only name I know for this guy is *stalker dude,*" she quipped, watching Callie's reaction.

"Ahhh." A knowing look crossed her friend's face. "That explains a lot. So, tell me, Kevin, since you seem to be orchestrating this drama, what exactly is going on?"

"You know exactly what's going on, sweetie . . . your friend here is our bank account. And it's time to make a withdrawal." Stalker sneered and jerked his grip on Sophie's arm to emphasize his words.

"What the . . . " Sophie's head snapped to look at him sideways. "I don't know what you're talking about but I think you've got the wrong girl."

"No. Right girl. Right dad. Right trust fund, which has millions of dollars sitting wasted in it. And you're going to 'share the wealth,' so to speak today. You're going to take us down to the bank and make a nice, hefty withdrawal along with a relatively nice sized fund transfer."

"I don't think so." Her voice snapped.

"Yes. I think you will." He started pulling her toward the door. "You know you could have made this a lot easier if you'd just shown a little interest in me in the beginning."

Callie's eyes grew larger and she looked around the room as if looking for a weapon, something to stop him with. Her eyes rested on her laptop. "Hey, Kevin. Why don't you just have her do the fund transfer from here? Surely they have some sort of website to do that kind of thing . . . don't they, Soph? My computer's right here." She gestured at the laptop, open and running on the kitchen counter.

Stalker's eyes registered the plan and agreed. "Good idea, Cal. Let's get that done before we head down to the bank to get the cash." He pushed Sophie toward the chair in front of the laptop and forced her down to the keyboard. "Get busy, girlfriend," he ordered.

"No."

Without hesitation, he doubled his hand into a fist aimed at Sophie's right eye. "Stop! Don't hit her face! If you're intending to take her to the bank, you don't want them to see her with a giant welt on her face, you idiot."

Sophie's eyes shot up and focused on Callie. "Cal? You . . . you're in on this? What's going on?"

"Your dad's a good guy, Soph. He didn't deserve what you and your mom did to him, deserting him like that."

"What? How do you know my dad? *What the hell is going on?*"

"I worked for him in New York, did an internship there. You didn't deserve what he gave you, setting aside a percentage of every business deal for you. You don't deserve it now. You've never shown him an ounce of thought or respect. That money should be used—not just sit in a bank because you're such a spiteful kid you can't appreciate what he's done for you. If you don't want it, let someone else put it to use."

Sophie's mouth dropped open as she stared at this person talking. The person that had been her friend through her mom's death. The person she'd confided in and worked alongside. A complete stranger.

"You don't know anything about my dad, or my mom." Panic and anger boiled deep inside her gut. She was on her own. Her friend was no friend at all.

"I don't really give a shit, Soph. You have a landslide sitting in a bank. Money that most people would give their right arm for and it was just given to you. For no reason, other than the man had delusions that you'd someday come back and be his daughter and appreciate his generosity. You don't want it. We do. Now, get moving on that money transfer or I'll personally blacken your eye myself."

Sophie's mouth stiffened and her chin drew up defiantly as she mouthed the word, "No." As soon as it came out, a blinding pain went through her left side and she fell to the floor. When her body hit the tile, Stalker's shoed foot started jabbing repeatedly into her rib cage. He pulled back and heaved it with as much force as he could gather on each strike. She couldn't get a breath between the kicks, the pain just kept coming and coming.

"That's enough." Callie's hand went out to pull him off.

"So, what's it gonna be, rich bitch?" Stalker's hands pulled her up from the floor and dumped her back in front of the computer.

"Fuck. You," she said as she reached a heel up and jabbed it into his shin from behind. Trevan would have been proud. She rolled the other leg over and kicked as high as she could, aiming for his face. Her leg caught only air as he ducked, then sent a fist into her back.

"Okay." His teeth gnashed. "We do this the hard way." He looked at Callie and snapped out orders. "Get something to tie her up with and some tape in case we need to tape her mouth. I'm going to her apartment to get her checkbook, then go to the bank. You stay here and watch her." He yanked Sophie's arms behind her back and waited for Callie to restrain her in the chair.

"It won't work. They have my signature on file. They won't accept a forged check for that amount of money." *This guy's really an idiot,* Sophie thought.

"Callie's got your signature down pat . . . don't you, hon?" He grinned. "Why, she can sign *Sophie Henderson* better than you can. That's what happens when you assign one of your staff to help authorize bills and invoices."

"That's right. Get moving. We wouldn't want her boyfriend to start missing her and come looking. If he really exists."

*

"Trev. I'm sorry. I should have kept her here until you got back. I just thought it was over." Nate was on his cell. Trev heard the faint ding of the elevator in the background. Nate was on his way out of the office, headed to meet him or beat him to Callie's.

"It was over. This is something else. I'm not sure what, but something else." Trev was darting his car in and out of traffic. He'd switched on the lights and had the siren running. No time to be quiet. "I thought he was just a perv who tried to grab her and missed. She didn't even have a name for me to check on him. If she had, I would have checked him against sex offenders. That's what I thought . . ."

His mind wandered to what could happen to her and he tightened his lips and gritted his teeth. *No, don't think about it,* he told himself. After everything she'd already dealt with, there was no way he could let that happen. He had to find her. In reality, though, it had to be more than just a sex offender, right? He tried to grab her, then he purposely got close to Callie, which meant there was a plan in place. Something more than just a random thing. Something detailed out in advance. But what?

"Nate, Callie moved here from New York, right?" Trev asked.

"Yeah, that's what the file says."

"Call Cheryl. Find out more about what happened in New York and why she came back. Also, do we know how and where she met this guy?"

"No, we don't have that but we'll get it, Trev." Nate's voice was calm. There was a short silence on the phone. "We'll get her, man," he reassured. "We're on our way. We'll get Sophie. She's going to be okay." Trevan appreciated his words but knew they were working against the clock now. She had been gone for a while. He could only hope she was just visiting with her friend and all was well and she'd lost track of time. Unfortunately, it just didn't feel right.

Maybe she just didn't want to see him. No, he couldn't think like that. She wasn't the type to avoid someone. If that were the case, she'd tell him outright. There were too many scenarios to consider and his thoughts ping-ponged randomly from one extreme to another. He shook his head, then concentrated on what he knew and could control.

"See you there," Trevan said and clicked the end button on his cell. He immediately tried calling Sophie again. Voicemail. He shot her a text and waited.

*

Sophie's sides were burning and her breathing was stilted from the kicks in the ribs. The duct tape over her mouth made it even harder to get oxygen by forcing her to breathe through her nose. She watched Callie move nervously around the kitchen, glancing through the curtain periodically looking for stalker boy's return. Sophie chided herself—if she ever got out of this alive, she'd be a lot more picky about her friends. And a lot less trusting of everyone. Her mom had tried to shelter her from this, unsuccessfully. Unfortunately, she had no desire to live in a bubble without friends, without people to care about. Besides, if she'd been more careful, she would never have met Trevan. Okay, that was probably not true because he sought her out. But maybe she would have figured it out sooner if she'd been less trusting, and maybe she wouldn't have been so susceptible to all his grouchy, angry, funny, sexy charm. If that was what it was called. It wasn't doing her any good right now, though. He was nowhere to be found and didn't even know she was here. So much for keeping her safe. She was on her own right now and always had been.

"Why is it, Sophie," Callie started talking to her without even looking her way, "that you have everything handed to you so easily and you do nothing with it? You don't even appreciate it." The bitterness dripped from her voice.

What the hell is she talking about? Sophie wondered. I've worked since I was fifteen and earned everything I have, except the trust fund, which he only gave me so he could feel better about not being there all those years. She's crazy. Maybe Dad is a nice guy, who knows. I never really had the chance to find out. If I survive this, maybe I'll work on that. Maybe.

Bam. Bam. Bam. Someone was beating on the door in the other room. Callie gave her a frown, placing her finger over her lips to signal Sophie to be quiet. "Just a minute!" she shouted.

"Callie, open the door." Trevan's voice. *Thank God.*

"Coming," she called.

Callie opened the door and slipped outside. "Well, hello there, Trevor. How are you?"

"I'm fine. Is Sophie here?" He tried to look past her but Callie closed the door.

"No. I haven't seen her. What's up?"

"Where's your boyfriend?" His voice boomed.

"He left a couple of hours ago. I haven't seen him since."

Sophie could hear him from the other room, could feel him. She knew he was out there but this damn tape made it impossible to call him. She tried to scream, just a muffled murmur. She had to get him to notice. Somehow. She rocked the chair back and forth, back and forth. One more time back and forth and she felt it teeter backward. Yes! She crashed to the floor, hitting the shelves behind her, and knocking everything down on top of her. Ouch. She grunted. Surely he heard that!

"What the hell was that?" She heard his growl. She tried again to scream his name. Instead, she kicked and scuffled, hearing the jangle and scrape of broken glass around her. "Sophie?" His voice. Thank God for his voice. She wanted to run to him. She watched the opening as the gun preceded him. His face was scrunched in fury. Callie said something behind him and he flashed a look over his shoulder briefly, then screamed, "Get the fuck back!" as he swung the gun around for a moment to punctuate his words.

As he came around the corner into the kitchen, he looked around. His glazed look softened as his eyes landed on a pile of broken glass over a pile of dark curls and a body taped to a chair—and big, brown, macadamia nut shaped eyes looking at him. She saw a huge burst of relief flow across his face. He checked the remaining rooms. No one else was in the apartment. Callie had heeded his warning and stayed outside as Trev moved back into the kitchen and knelt down to help Sophie. As he ripped the tape from Sophie's mouth, the stalker eased quietly close behind him. Sophie's expression changed to fear. She motioned behind him but it was too late.

"Don't move!" a male voice surprised him. "Put the gun down and don't move, or I'll shoot her."

Chapter Twenty-Four

The boyfriend. Trevan looked into Sophie's eyes and placed his gun in front of her on the floor. He smiled softly and slowly raised his hands up for the man behind him to see. *No . . . sorry, you're not going to shoot her. No way.* He hoped she knew what he was thinking and knew what to do. She should. They'd practiced enough. If she had to, he expected her to use the gun. Hopefully, she wouldn't have to. He nodded and once more looked into her eyes at the reflection of the man behind him, holding a gun to Callie's head.

"Turn around so I can see you."

Trevan slowly turned around. "Destin James, I'm Trevan Prater. I'm a federal agent. You really don't want to do this." He was glad to at least have the guy's name from his staff before he'd arrived. He didn't know a lot more but it helped to act as if the guy was an open book. It gave him a sense of command in a completely out of control situation.

"Shut up." Destin's eyes darted around as he pointed the gun at Trevan, then back at Callie.

"If you stop now, you're in pretty good shape," Trev said softly. "Let's end this right now, Destin. Let's just stop it, and everyone's okay. Don't do anything stupid. It'll only make things worse. I don't know what all this is about but we can work it out."

"What part of 'shut up' did you not understand?" Destin shoved the gun in his face and cocked it sideways. He was off balance, and that was the only opportunity Trevan would get. He lunged forward, pushing the gun up out of his face and ramming his body against both Destin and Callie. The gun went off, a loud boom amongst their scuffle, then one more slam and Trevan broke it free and it fell to the ground. He kicked it away and rammed again to knock Destin down. Trevan's fist slammed into Destin's ribs. Once. Twice.

Callie crawled away from them trying to get free from Trevan's fists and Destin's boots. She scrambled toward the abandoned firearm Trev had kicked aside. Out of the corner of his eye, Trev glanced sideways at her movements but concentrated on Destin. He had rolled Destin over on his stomach and was yanking his hands out from under him. He had the full weight of his body anchoring the guy down so movement was limited.

Sophie felt a series of sharp tugs and looked down to see a knife cutting tape away from her legs. Callie worked roughly, not concerned about nicking her legs. She rushed to get her free. She had the gun in her hand. The anger glazed in her eyes like a volcano ready to erupt. Her concentration flashed back and forth between Trevan and Sophie. When the tape was hacked away, Callie yanked Sophie from the floor and started dragging her away. Out of the kitchen toward the door. She jammed the gun to Sophie's temple. Sophie watched the distance to Trevan increase.

"Don't do it," Trevan yelled. "Callie, you're one step away from being in prison for life. Is that what you want?"

"Shut up."

Trevan still had to cuff Destin and couldn't move. His weapon was on the floor. He slipped the cuffs on Destin's hands, shoving his knee in his back as he lifted himself to get his gun. His eyes were locked on Callie and he didn't glance away as he backed toward his gun on the floor where he'd left it with Sophie.

"Don't move, Trevor. I have no qualms about using this gun." As if to punctuate her remarks, Callie waved the gun against Sophie's head and yanked her arms back as they moved more quickly toward the door.

"Okay, okay." He held his hands toward them. "I'm not moving, but Callie, you're not getting out of here. My entire department is outside."

"Really? Then why did I only hear one siren?" she challenged.

He knew they were on the way and should be onsite in seconds.

As Callie and Sophie backed out of his view, he reached behind for his firearm but didn't feel it. He patted around on the floor. It wasn't there. He looked. Nothing. He had to stop Callie, but had no way to do so. *Don't let her leave, he thought. If she leaves the building, Sophie's chances are gone.*

Trevan lunged toward them, just as a shot rang out. Callie had aimed the gun toward the kitchen entrance, expecting him to follow. A sharp sting pierced his chest He looked down. Damn, she'd got him. Callie used the opportunity to shove Sophie out the door and drag her to the elevator.

Trevan's vest was on. He didn't worry about the small hole in his shirt. He kept following them, walking slowly so he didn't aggravate Callie into firing again. He focused only on the two girls. There was panic in Sophie's eyes. But there was also Trevan's handgun tucked into her waistband, out of view from Callie. The sound of sirens was muffled by Callie's voice as she screamed orders. "Stay back!" The elevator opened and the two of them entered it. "You know I'll use this. You know I will. Stay out of this and keep your people back."

"I can't. I won't. You're not getting out of here with her, Callie. Give it up. You're not getting out."

"Yes, I am. And if I don't, she won't, either."

She meant it. There was nothing sane left in her expression. She'd kill Sophie if she had to. The elevator doors closed and Trevan was standing alone in the landing. He looked around, panicked, and saw the stairwell. He rammed through the door and flung himself down the stairs. He hit speed dial for Nate.

When Nate picked up, he didn't bother with pleasantries. "Callie has Sophie in the elevator with a gun to her head. She's already shot at me so don't take a chance. She will use the gun."

Trevan bolted down the stairs. He felt jabbing pain in his

shoulder as he moved, but kept going. He leaped over the trashcans and slammed out the door, racing toward the elevator in the entry. Two shots rang out from inside the elevator. *Oh, God, no!*

The doors opened. Callie stood over Sophie, sprawled on the floor holding Trevan's weapon up with two, tape-covered hands. Sophie looked up at Trevan, just as one more shot rang out from the gun in her taped hands.

Nate had arrived. Callie slumped to the floor in the elevator. Sophie scrambled on her back to get away from her. Trev lunged into the elevator and removed the handgun from Callie's hands. No need. She was dead.

Trev and Sophie both shifted their eyes to the front door of the building, where Nate stood with firearm drawn. "How'd you get here so fast, man?" Nate asked. "I was probably five blocks closer." He scrunched up his face as he glanced at Trev then down at Trev's shoulder. "Oh, man."

"Good Karma, I guess . . . and driving like a bat out of hell. The guy is upstairs in her apartment. Can you take care of him?"

"Is he dead, too?"

"No. Very much alive. He needs to be taken in."

Trevan sat down on the floor and dragged Sophie in against him. "You okay?" he said, his voice a little gruff with emotion. She dropped the handgun and collapsed against him.

"I wondered when you'd get here."

"Sorry I'm late."

Sophie put her arms around him and he winced slightly at her touch, startling her. She reared back and looked at him. "You're bleeding." She touched the spot on his shoulder, a dark wet stain that oozed thick blood.

"Yeah, she missed the damn vest." He looked down, frowning. "It's a straight through, should heal okay. You did good there, Henry." He motioned his head to the elevator. He paused to catch his breath. "But you scared the shit out of me. Anything else I need to know about? You know, maybe another psycho-stalker, angry ex, or something?"

"Not that I know of, but things are changing every day." She gave him a wry wink and smiled, even though her hands trembled.

Trevan felt a little giddy. No, that wasn't it, not giddy. Crap! The hole in his shirt was surrounded with an ever-increasing blood stain. He slid down backward on the floor and closed his eyes. "Need to . . . rest . . . a . . . minute," he whispered.

Chapter Twenty-Five

Four weeks later, Sophie pulled across the cattle guard to Trevan's ranch house in her blue Dodge, her tires crunched down the gravel trail until she reached the front of the house. She didn't see his car but there was a Jeep and a Toyota SUV parked in the front of the house. She'd taken a big chance coming here. She worried that she'd made a mistake. Several times during the drive over, fleeting thoughts that she should turn around came into the foggy plan to surprise him, but she quelled them and continued. She had to at least try. As she tapped on the door, she listened for sounds inside. Silence. She decided to walk around the back and check outside.

The yard was greening up from the rain, making it even more beautiful than she remembered. As she walked out to the end of the courtyard to look at the pool, she couldn't help but feel a little rush of appreciation. He had added on to the pool. On the opposite side of the pool, a lattice wall flanked the far side and circled halfway around the area where the pool chairs sat. It came up about ten feet and a slatted wood and lattice trellis covered the top. The end result shaded the shallow end of the water and blocked the view to the hills from that side, but left the deep end with a spectacular view. Guess he decided he needed a little more privacy. Just as the grin broke free from Sophie's worried mouth, she heard voices and turned toward the sound.

Her eyes landed on Trevan, tall and lanky, sitting atop Blackie and coming toward her. His faded T-shirt stretched across the muscled arms. He talked to a shapely, dark haired girl. Sophie watched him playfully squirt water on her and she noticed that under the white T-shirt, the woman wore the swimsuit Sophie had used when she was here. *Oh my god. He's brought someone else here and they're out riding.* She whirled around and rushed toward the house, grabbing her bag from the chair by the firepit and digging in it for her car keys. She couldn't look up. Had he seen her? She rushed around the side of the house trying to get to her car and leave. *How stupid! I should not have come. This was a crazy idea. What was I thinking!*

*

As he and Blackie cleared the trees and started back to his house, Trevan admired the way the hills greened up with the small amount of rain they received the week before. A short-term lushness, he knew, as this area normally got pretty dry by mid May and then stayed that way all summer.

"Trev, can I have a drink of your water?" Tiffany asked as she came up next to him on her horse. He glanced sideways at her. She looked pretty good for a new mom, tired but happy.

He originally wanted to live here because it was remote and he could get away from all the craziness at work. When his parents talked about selling the place, it was an easy decision to take it off their hands. It worked out pretty well as far as keeping up with his family. When he traveled, they used it for a vacation place. When he was home, they visited a lot. He hadn't seen Tiffany in almost a year and it was nice . . . but truthfully, it made him feel a little like a third wheel with her husband and kid. How can just a few short months completely change a person's perspective on life? He'd never felt envious before of big sis's life but in a weird way he wanted that now.

"Sure, no problem." Trev lifted the water bottle from the bag he had looped over the saddle horn and moved closer to Tiff so he could hand it to her. As soon as she reached out for it, he gave in to a sudden urge to squeeze the bottle and water spurted up into her face and down her shirt.

"Hey!" Tiff's fist lashed out and belted him on the thigh, startling his horse a little. "Thanks a lot, jerk." She wiped the water from her eyes and reached for the bottle while Trevan snickered with satisfaction.

Tiffany took a slow drink as her horse moved lazily along. She glanced over the top of the water bottle as she drew in from it. "Looks like you've got company, brother." She gestured toward the house with the plastic in her hand.

Trev turned to look where she motioned and almost missed Sophie's rush across the patio. But when she emerged a few seconds later in a dead race to the front yard, he realized she intended to make a getaway to the Dodge. *Nope. Not this time.* He kneed Blackie into a gallop and got to the car just as she opened the door to slide in. He slid off the horse and rushed toward the car but she slammed the door. "Sophie, wait!" He yelled after her as she started the car, spun it around, and headed for the gate. Gravel spewing scared Blackie. He made a snort and took off for the barn.

"Dammit!" Trev jumped in the Jeep, started it up and drove it straight across the grass in an attempt to get to the gate before her. She followed the gravel path, which hugged the line of the hill, so if he just went straight up the hill, he'd beat her there. He bounced up the hill, hitting his head on the roll bar, and knocking through the gravel to slide to a stop in front of the Dodge about fifty feet before she reached the gate. He bolted out of the Jeep, striding toward her before the engine had even died.

"Sophie, get out of the car," Trevan said as he held his palm up to stop her. She just started backing up to go around the Jeep and he moved to block her by placing both hands on the hood of her car. "Stop!" he shouted. "Get out of the damn car!" His eyes focused on her as she shook her head and bit her lower lip.

"Trev, what's going on?" Tiffany came up next to them on the horse in a full gallop, watching him try to block the car with his body.

"This is Sophie, Tiff, and by the looks of her face, I don't think she knows who you are." His brows furrowed angrily over his eyes in frustration.

"Your Sophie?"

"Yes! No." He shook his head. His Sophie? "Hell, I don't know. Would you please put your horse between the gate and her car until I can get her out of the damn thing?"

"No problem, brother, why don't you just take the rope and tie her up while you're at it!" Tiffany laughed but nudged the horse in front of the gate.

Sophie's escape route was completely blocked by the horse, rider, and Jeep. She stopped the car and sat behind the wheel, shaking her head and pounding the steering wheel.

Trevan refused to give up. He slid around the car, keeping his hands on the hood, and yanked the door open before she could hit the lock button. He snaked a hand into the car and pulled on Sophie's arm to get her out of the car. "What's your hurry, woman!" He growled as he reached into the car and pulled the keys from the ignition and threw them into the trees.

"Hey!" Sophie protested.

"Good grief, brother, stop manhandling the poor girl!" Tiffany scolded. "That's no way to win her over."

Sophie glanced from one to the other with confusion.

"Yeah. That's right!" The exasperation in his voice was beyond blatant. "My sister, Tiffany Sorrenson." He made an introductory wave toward Tiff, who stepped forward and held out a hand in greeting.

"Nice to meet you, Sophie. I've heard a lot about you."

A long pause, uncomfortably long, grew between them as she looked from the girl to Trevan. Then Sophie cleared her throat, squared her shoulders, and held out her hand to shake Tiffany's briefly.

"Can you leave us alone now, sis?" Trev shot over his shoulder as he continued to face Sophie. He looked away briefly to see Tiffany get on the horse and trot toward the house and beyond to the barn. Slowly his eyes narrowed and returned to Sophie's face. He sucked in a deep breath. "Nice to see you, Henry. What brings you out here?"

"I came to see you. To see how you're doing," she stuttered.

"I was pretty good until the last five minutes." He reached up and rubbed his shoulder, wincing as he felt the sharp tinge of pain where the scar rubbed against his shirt.

"I tried to visit you in the hospital." Her eyes concentrated on the ground and she moved the toe of her shoe in a circular motion in the dirt. "They wouldn't let me in."

"Yeah, they get pretty protective when something like that happens. Immediate family only. Sorry."

"So, you have a scar?"

"Yes, but it's not too bad. I'm on eight weeks of R and R, while I rehab the shoulder. Two surgeries to repair the wound and some internal damage, nothing major."

"No problems with your arm?"

He flexed the hand and fingers but only lifted it partially from his side. "It'll take a while to get it back, but I'm told I'll have full use of it in a couple of months. We'll see." He studied Sophie's face. "What about you, you doing okay?"

Sophie averted her eyes toward the house and then the trees, studying the way the house fit into the countryside. "I went to see my dad."

"I know," he stated softly. "I came to see you as soon as they let me out of the hospital. You were gone. I called your office."

"I quit my job."

"Yeah, they told me you'd gone to New York." He felt the pain again when he learned that she'd decided to move there. "How are things with your dad?"

Sophie hesitated. She seemed to be picking her words carefully. "Good. Good. I needed to know why everyone . . . everyone who knows him loves him, except me. I couldn't understand why I couldn't get past it. I wanted to understand why he didn't care enough about me to stay. I guess I thought that I wasn't the daughter he wanted." She looked back down at her shoes. "I wasn't sure if it was because I wasn't capable of loving anyone or—"

"Afraid to give them a chance?" Trev finished for her. His good hand raised and he ran his fingers over his hair then dropped them to his side, slipping them into the pocket of his jeans.

"Maybe."

"So, did you figure it all out?"

"Pretty much. At least, I think I did. I guess it was easier to—"

"Leave someone that cared about you before they decided to leave you?" He quirked an eyebrow at her and narrowed his eyes again, shielding the emotion. "It doesn't take a rocket scientist to figure that out. Your dad left when you were a child. Your college boyfriend deserted you, your mom died. But in a way, that represented leaving, too, didn't it? So, you just decided to make sure it wouldn't happen again by being the first to leave."

"Yes, Dr. Phil. I guess you could put it that way." She put a hand to her hair to move a curl back out of her face.

"So, why are you here?"

"I don't know. It didn't make sense. Giving up on something because you're afraid to lose it. That's kind of forcing yourself to get what you feared in the first place."

"Figured that out, did ya?" He smirked, shifting his weight from one leg to the other.

"Yeah, with a little help from my father."

"So, how's New York life treating you?"

"I wouldn't know. I didn't stay. I was only there a week." She took a deep breath then winced at the pain in her ribs caused by the movement.

"God, Henry, I forgot to ask. Are the ribs healing up okay?"

"I wasn't sure if you knew or not. Two broken, lots of bruising." She patted the air outside the tender spot.

"Nate told me. He called regularly with updates."

"Yeah, he stopped in once in a while when I was in the hospital." She watched his face.

"So you're not staying in New York?"

"No, why would I do that? Everything I want is here."

"Not your family."

"New York is cold all the time and dreary. I couldn't live there if I wanted to." She shrugged. "Dad gave me an ultimatum though."

"Really?"

"Yeah, he told me if I intended to live here I had to get a bodyguard or he would do it for me. So, these past few days I've been interviewing all sorts of candidates. Most of them huge, muscle-bound dudes that could probably lift a truck." She watched as his eyes flashed and his jaw tightened but he said nothing, just watched her face and listened. "They weren't real big on the hours or the pay."

"That bad, huh?"

"Well, it's mostly nights and weekends. Sometimes it would require accompanying me to social outings if I go anywhere." She paused for a minute, aware that he edged a little closer to her. "Or just hanging around if I don't."

"So, what didn't they like? Where's the bad part?"

"There's travel, too. To New York once in a while on family visits." Sophie stared at her feet, pausing to take another rib ticking breath. "It's been difficult to find a good candidate. Know anyone that might be interested?" She stepped toward him.

"I can think of one guy." He shoved his hand deeper in his pocket as he closed the gap between them. "But there's one problem. Sort of a big one."

Sophie's hand brushed softly up his chest, her fingers stroking against his collarbone. "What would that be?"

"He doesn't live in Houston. He lives here." He tossed his head in a gesture toward the ranch house. "And the commute would be too long." He looked down at her through veiled lashes, enjoying the movement of her hand.

Sophie stepped back and reluctantly withdrew her fingers. "I see."

"But I hear there are jobs available in Austin in your field," he said. "And it's close enough."

"Austin, hmmm." She hadn't thought about moving to Austin.

"You could make the drive easily," he suggested.

"From here?" She raised an eyebrow. Was he asking her to move here? With him?

"Yeah." He looked away as if tensing for the answer.

"Okay, well, in that case, there's more." She smiled slyly.

"Let's hear it."

"He'd need to sleep in the same room that I do. Since the break-in at my apartment, I don't sleep well by myself. Maybe even cook breakfast once or twice a week?"

Trevan snaked his good arm out and slid it around her hip, pulling her tight. "Yes, you're pretty demanding, but I think it could work. Where do I sign up?"

"Right here." She caressed the side of his face, sending a shudder down his length. "You want to help me find my keys so I can move my car?"

"No. We'll worry about that in a couple of days when the tendency to run wears off." He grinned, half serious.

"I brought a swimsuit with me this time, just in case." She smiled back.

"Really? That's good." Trevan took her hand and started to pull her toward the house. "Where is it?"

"In my bag in the seat of the car." She motioned toward the vehicle behind them.

"Great. Hang on just a minute while I take care of that." He jogged back to the car, opened the door and punched the lock button then slammed it shut before returning to her side. "Oops. I guess it'll have to wait a couple of days, too. You'll just have to do without."

Sophie laughed. "Sneaky. What about your sister?" She glanced sideways at him, eyebrow crooked.

"She's leaving with her family in a few minutes." He walked toward the house with her hand in his, squeezing her fingers. She loved him. He knew she did. She was afraid to say so but she did.

"You know, you can say it, Soph."

"What?"

"I pretty much told you everything before I got shot. There was nothing more to say. The rest was up to you. That's why I didn't try calling again after you went to New York. I figured if it wasn't enough, then you didn't want it—me. It wasn't going to work." He focused his eyes forward, holding her hand, but not looking at her.

She tugged lightly on his hand. "You would give up that easy?"

"You really think that was easy for me? You're not the only one that's afraid to be left." He pulled the keys to the Jeep out of his pocket and put them in her hand. "So, here's the deal. I'm not going anywhere. When you're ready for me to leave, you can give these back. Or you can go dig your keys out of those trees and leave yourself."

Sophie looked at the keys. A lump formed in the back of her throat and she blinked her eyes a couple of times. She tossed the keys in the general direction that he'd sent hers earlier and tightened her fingers around his.

"I love you too, Trev."

They walked a few paces and he turned and took both of her hands in his as he faced Sophie. He glanced warmly back at the two vehicles sitting haphazardly across the drive. "I have a question for you . . . "

"I'm listening." She traced her fingers up his arms and clasped them behind his neck before pressing her lips against his in a slow, wet, kiss.

Not wanting to pull away, Trevan spoke softly against her lips as she continued to kiss him. "It's about this bodyguard gig. What happens when I travel for work? Should I find someone to stay with you?"

"Not necessary." She smiled slyly as she pulled back enough to see his eyes. "I'm fine by myself."

"But you said your dad—"

"My dad told me to get a bodyguard," she said. "And I told him to mind his own business. I can take care of myself."

Trevan smiled. For the most part that was true. Letting out a small groan, he leaned in to taste her mouth again. "I think I have just been conned."

"Feel free to grab your keys if you want to," Sophie gestured toward the trees.

"I think I'll take my chances." He murmured into her ear and turned her back toward the house.

"Yeah, me too."

About the Author:

Shelley K. Wall grew up on a farm outside of Kansas City, Missouri. She's a graduate of Oklahoma State University with a bit of post-graduate work at University of Wyoming-Casper. She worked for many years in information technologies, as a network engineer, a project manager, operations director, and IT department head. She holds several technology certifications in various security, server, and network related avenues. After writing numerous project plans, IT directives, budgets, personnel evaluations, and strategic plans, she decided fiction sounded more interesting.

Shelley started writing in junior high as a member of the school journalism club. She wrote her first romance in high school English and subsequently pitched it in the trash once she had her "A." She went on to take additional courses in college, but later veered in the direction of technology instead (not many women technology engineers in the world at that time and it sounded fun and a path to great fortune).

She now lives in Houston, Texas with her family.

In the mood for more Crimson Romance? Check out *Shot Through the Heart* by D'Ann Lindun at *CrimsonRomance.com*.